More

A You & Me Novel

Lisa Shelby

For A.
One of the strongest people I know. If only there were more humans in the world like you.

Also, for my amazing husband.
I will ALWAYS love you MORE.

MORE: A YOU & ME NOVEL

By Lisa Shelby

Playlist

Unsteady by X Ambassadors
Hypnotize by The Notorious B.I.G.
Color by Finish Ticket
Dreams by Beck
Something to Believe In by Young the Giant
Shiver by Coldplay
Deep by Marion Hill
Heads Will Roll by Yeah Yeah Yeahs
Treat You Better by Shawn Mendes
Starving by Hailee Steinfeld (feat. Zedd)
Waves by Mr. Probz
Sweet Thing by Mary J. Blige
Family Portrait by P!nk
Throw Down Your Guns by Wild Belle
King of the World by Weezer
My House by Flo Rida
Big Pimpin' by Jay Z (feat. UGK)
Get Out by Casey Abrams
Something New by Zendaya

Make It Rain by Ed Sheeran
Guillotine by Jon Bellion (feat. Travis Mendes)
Work by Rihanna (feat. Drake)
Can't Stop the Feeling by Justin Timberlake
California Love by 2Pac (feat. Dr. Dre)
Forever Like That by Ben Rector

Listen to this playlist on Spotify
http://spoti.fi/2jv8de7

Trigger Warnings

This book contains scenes depicting an auto accident, domestic abuse, and sexual abuse.

Prologue

I can hear the sirens in the distance.

I can't believe I made the call.

But I had no other choice.

Dad collapsed right in front of me and had what looked like a heart attack. There was always an unspoken promise in our house that what happened behind closed doors stayed behind closed doors. Tonight was different. I knew I had to get help before it was too late or dad may not make it.

After years of praying that something would happen to him so that the nightmare that was my mother's life would end... I just couldn't let him die. The moment came and I couldn't just stand by and watch him die.

Waiting on the front steps of our modest two story home in the suburbs of Portland, I can see the red and blue lights in the distance and I can hear the sirens. It's a balmy night, but I can feel myself shaking. My nerves are on edge and I really don't know what I'm going to say when they get here.

I feel so much older than my eighteen years, but keeping family secrets will do that to a kid. Nobody knows what happens in our happy-from-the-outside-looking-in home. My best friends, who I know I can trust with my life, have no clue. I know calling for help could potentially let our family secret out, but what was I supposed to do?

There's no more time to think about it. They're here. The police car pulls into the driveway and I can see the ambulance is coming up the street as well. The officer on the passenger side of the police cruiser gets out first. He's a middle-aged man with gray hair and a potbelly. He rounds the car and heads my way.

"Are you the person who called for assistance, ma'am?"

"I am. Thank you for getting here so quickly. He's in here," I say as I turn to lead him through the front door and to my father.

I'm stopped in my tracks when I hear a deep, familiar voice come from behind me.

"Alex, is that you?"

No! This cannot be happening. Of all of the officers that could show up tonight, why him?

I continue walking, purposely not turning around. I'm not ready to face him. I've never been ready to face him.

Why is this happening?

Is this really happening?

"Alex," he shouts again.

As I cross the threshold, I hear, "Excuse us, ma'am."

The paramedics have arrived and are pushing their way through the door. I push myself into the doorjamb and make myself as small as possible to let them by. They rush to my father's side while my mother cries over the top of him. It's all happening so fast, and I'm so overwhelmed that it feels like my head is full of cotton. My father has collapsed, our family's secret is being revealed, and all of it while the boy I have pined over since I was twelve years old is here to witness the whole thing.

"Alex," he says as he grabs my shoulder and slowly turns me around to face him. "Are you okay? What's going on?"

"I'm fine, Mick. My dad needs help, though. He just started slurring his words and then collapsed in front of us," I reply back. I'm trying to use my long hair as a shield to cover the right side of my face so he doesn't notice my eye starting to swell shut.

"Okay, let me get in there and see what I can find out for you, and we'll see that he gets treated well."

To my momentary relief, he leaves me standing in the entryway while he makes his way into the family room to check on my dad. I slowly walk behind him and am just entering the room when I see him take in the complete picture of what's happened here tonight. It's not too different from any other random Tuesday night. The only difference tonight is that it wasn't just my mom that was in my dad's line of fire, and for the first time 911 was called.

They've moved mom aside so that the paramedics can work on my dad, and Mick is standing with the other officer who is questioning her. My sweet, petite mom, who currently has a split lip, bruised cheek, a ripped blouse and an eye that is about to swell shut. Dad is usually better at strategically placing his marks on her. My 'always in control' father seemed somewhat out-of-control tonight before he fell to the ground.

Mick turns, and as soon as his eyes land on mine, I can see them darken. He moves through the room, and in my shocked state, it feels like he's moving in slow-motion as he walks right toward me.

"Alex, talk to me," he says once he's standing in front of me.

He's mere inches from me. It's a place I have always dreamed of him being, but in this moment... in this moment, I wish he wasn't here.

"Alex, what happened here tonight? Talk to me. It's just me."

Keeping my gaze towards the floor, I answer him the only way I know how. "Thank you, Mick. We're fine. We just want to make sure my dad is going to be okay."

Not letting me get away with my lack of eye contact, he uses his forefinger to lift my chin and, in the same motion, moves my hair out of my face to push it behind my ear. That's when he sees it. My eye clearly looks as bad as it feels, if his reaction is any indication.

"Shit," he whispers. "Alex, did your dad do this to you?"

I've dreamed of this moment my entire life. The moment Mickey Jacobs would gently touch my face and look me in the eye while tucking my hair behind my ear. But in my dreams, he wasn't seething with anger. No, in my dreams, he was looking at me with love and desire.

"Alex, answer me," he yell-whispers in my ear.

I'm given a moment's reprieve as the medics lift my dad onto a gurney and start to wheel him out of the house. One of the medics stays behind and asks my mom if she would like to ride in the back of the ambulance with him, and of course she does. On her way past me she touches my arm and simply says, "It's okay Alexandra... no more secrets, my darling girl. It's your time to live your life and let me take care of all of this." She makes this last statement while making a twirling motion with her finger. She leans forward, kisses me on the cheek, and follows the medics out the front door. To an outsider, she looks like a distraught, abused woman, but I can see the relief settle in. I actually see a new light in her eyes. A light I don't recall ever seeing before.

I'm not sure why, but I feel like everything is about to change for the two of us. All I've ever wanted was for Mom to be safe and happy. As horrible as it sounds, I feel the weight of my mother's pain and our family's secret lightly lift off of my shoulders as I watch them put my father into the back of the ambulance.

The other officer approaches me with a small notepad in one hand and a pen in the other. "Miss Stotts, I'm Officer Truman. If you don't mind, we'd like to ask you a few questions about what happened here tonight? Your mother explained the fight that took place between her and your father and that you were caught in the middle of it all. Could you tell me what happened from your perspective? We can also give you a lift to the hospital if you need one."

"Thank you for the offer, but I can drive myself," I reply, ignoring his first question.

"If you're sure, Miss Stotts, but do let us know if you change your mind. So, tell us what happened tonight."

I look at Mick, who hasn't left my side, and he gives me a small smile that doesn't reach his eyes. He rubs my arm and gives me a nod of his head that encourages me to go ahead and share my story.

My story.

Nobody was ever supposed to know my story.

"Um, well... my mom was in the kitchen cleaning up and

my dad was trying to watch TV but couldn't hear it because she accidentally let a cupboard shut a little too loudly. Dad got out of his chair and started yelling at her. He hit her across the face and she stumbled back against the refrigerator, and then he started to choke her. I ran up behind him to try to pull him off of her, and he turned around and hit me. I fell to the floor and he was back to hitting mom. He was hitting her in the stomach, but then he hit her in the face and she fell to the floor too. All of the sudden, he was trying to yell at the both of us, but his words started to slur, and he was stumbling. Before I knew it, he was on the ground and looked like he was having some sort of seizure or something."

I stop my rambling and Officer Truman asks, "Was this the first time something like this has happened?"

"No."

"How many times before has this happened, Alex?" This time it's Mick that asks the question.

"He doesn't usually hit me, but he hits Mom often."

"For how long, Alex?"

I'm too embarrassed to answer. I've never wanted anybody to know that my entire childhood has been full of fear and heartbreak. Watching your mother be mentally and physically abused most of your life isn't exactly something other people understand or relate to. Yes, he hits me too... but not often. Usually only when things get too rough and I step in to try to help Mom.

"Alex," Mick asks again, but gently.

I just look at him and shake my head back and forth as the tears stream steadily down my face.

Shame.

I am so ashamed.

Not a moment later, I feel Mick's powerful arms holding me at the same instant I feel my knees go weak. If his arms weren't around me, I would be in a puddle on the floor.

"I got you, sweet thing. Shh... I'm here, Alex. You're gonna be okay."

Mickey freaking Jacobs is holding me in his arms and just called me "sweet thing". If only it wasn't for all the wrong reasons. He feels bad for me and he's comforting me out of pity. Pity is something that I always feared seeing in the eyes of those I care about if they knew what happened in the Stotts household. I've managed to make it almost 19 years without being the recipient of their pity, and I'd really like to keep it that way.

I pull myself away from the one pair of arms I have always dreamed of being in and look up into his deep brown eyes. "Mick, please don't pity me and please don't tell Cam and Emily."

There are only two secrets that I have kept from my two best friends, Cami and Emily. The first, the truth about what happens behind the closed doors of my home. The second, the fact that I have been in love with Emily's brother, Mick, since the first time my twelve-year-old eyes met his fourteen-year-old eyes.

"I won't say anything, Alex, but you know you can trust them. Cami and Em love you like a sister, and they would be there for you if you let them. They certainly wouldn't pity you. They would do whatever they could to help you. You know that, right?"

"I do know that, Mick. But I'm not ready."

"Well, if you don't want to talk to them, you can always

talk to me. You're practically family, and if you ever need anything at all, just call."

And there it is. I was "practically family". He thinks of me as a sister, yet I will forever be in love with him.

Such is life...

My life anyway...

Chapter 1

Mick

"**H**ey, Riley!" I yell over the noise of the crowd.

Kells is packed tonight and its nights like these that I thank my lucky stars. When your best friend is the bartender and Assistant Manager at one of your favorite bars, you count yourself lucky. Kells isn't a nightclub, but an old Irish pub that is a classic here in Portland and always packed on weekend nights.

"Whatcha need, Mick?" Riley yells from behind the bar.

Leaning over the bar to make sure he can hear me, I yell back. "Emmers and the girls are going to be here tonight. Make sure all their drinks and whatever else they want go on my tab."

While slowly, yet perfectly, putting the finishing touches on a *black and tan,* he replies. "Will do, Mick. It's good to have Emily back! I can't wait to see that baby sister of yours, and Ireland, too. I can't even imagine how big she is now. I'll make sure everybody knows you got the girls covered." He turns his attention to the middle-aged man in front of him and slides him his drink. "Here you go, O'Keeffe."

Tonight is gonna be a great night. All my friends are here and my baby sister should be here any minute. She's been living in California for the last eight years, and I am so relieved to have her and my niece back home. Home. Right where they belong. Emily has been through a lot and I'm glad she's finally listening to reason and letting me help. I know she thinks that living with me will be a nightmare, and she's hesitant about the whole idea. But what she doesn't know is that I'm starting to grow tired of my lifestyle of partying and sleeping around. Having them at my place is just what I need to start this whole process of growing up. I don't plan on ever getting tied down or doing the whole marriage thing, but I know I spend too many of my nights sneaking out of dark bedrooms in strange houses.

I just moved a few weeks ago and am now a proud home-owner. That feels like the first step, and having the girls at my place will be the second. I hope I'm not kidding myself, but we'll see what happens. Tonight, my mom is watching Ireland so that Emily could come out and meet all of my buddies from work. Many of them she already knows from growing up with a dad who worked for the department, but there is a new generation of officers she doesn't. Cops are a tight group. Like a family, really. She needs to meet them all sooner than later and tonight is the night.

I can't help but anxiously watch the front door. I'd be lying if I said it was just because I was waiting for Emily to get here. The truth is, I know that Alex will be with her and it's been too long.

There is just something about Alexandra Stotts.

Always has been.

The first time I ever met her, she was nothing but a gangly, little twelve-year-old. But there was still something about her that drew my arrogant fourteen-year-old self to her. Back then, I was too cool to have liked one of my sister's annoying little friends, but I always knew she was something special.

Now, my twenty-eight-year-old self is standing here waiting for her to walk through the door so I can watch her from a distance. From a distance... just like I always have... well, except for that one night seven years ago.

2008

90's night at Lola's Room, one floor down from the Crystal Ballroom, is not my usual idea of a fun Saturday night. But the chick that Riley is dating wanted to come, so here we are. I'm a sucker for 90's R&B and Hip Hop, so I couldn't really argue when Riley pointed out there would be 90's tunes, a bar, and a dance floor full of chicks. Works for me and here we are.

I'm standing off to the side, checking out the scene that I can instantly tell isn't really my thing. The dance floor does provide some entertainment, and there are some decent-looking women here, but nobody is really grabbing my attention. The crowd is a bit older than I'm used to. I'm only twenty-one and getting to go out is a great time, no matter what at this point, but I think I'm going to head out as soon as I can get Riley's attention.

Riley and She Whose Name I Can Never Remember, are

currently slow dancing to an old Jodeci song and I just don't have it in me to interrupt what they have going on. Riley really seems to be into this girl, and I know I should get to know her, but Riley and I never keep any chick around for too long, so I haven't really made an effort. She doesn't seem to be my biggest fan either, so... why bother?

The song finally ends and *NSYNC's Bye, Bye, Bye starts and that is about all I can take. I have to get out of here. I spent the actual 90's with *NSYNC blaring out of my sister's room day in and day out. I need to find Riley and say bye - bye - bye to him pronto!

I put my not quite empty beer bottle on the bar and turn to make my way through the crowded dance floor to say goodbye to my best friend. The problem is, I can't move. Frozen to the spot I'm standing in. This just can't be. She's only nineteen. How the hell did she get in here? Things here at Lola's just got a lot more interesting. I tuck myself as far back from the crowd of dancing bodies as I can and settle in to enjoy the show.

This is what I have always done. Watched.

Alex is one of my sister's best friends and therefore off limits. It doesn't mean I haven't lusted for her for years now. There is no denying she is, without a doubt, the most beautiful girl I have ever seen. She doesn't look like every other girl in Portland and tonight, just like every time I see her, she stands out from the crowd. The fact that she's just under six feet tall helps in that department, but it's so much more than that. Her dad may be whiter than my Irish ass, but her mom's family is from India. With her height along with her light brown skin, long dark hair and dark brown eyes, she looks like she should be wearing a pair of bedazzled wings and be walking down the runway for a freaking Victoria's Secret runway show.

Watching her out there on the dance floor, singing along to her favorite band, with that rare smile on her face, is something to behold. She's always been so quiet and shy when I've been around her. I would hear the girls in Emily's room giggling hysterically or singing and dancing, but as soon as I would enter the room, Alex would always clam up and seemed to be in a constant state of embarrassment. As the girls got older, and a little less giggly, she opened up a bit and would actually talk to me, but she always seemed shy. This is a new side to her that I've never seen. I like it.

I know I could ruin her evening and make her leave since she's clearly not of age, but I'm enjoying the show too much right now. God, she looks good in her tight jeans and that crop top that shows just a sliver of skin. I feel like a perv standing in the background watching her, but this isn't anything new. I have always watched Alexandra Stotts. She's the one girl I have always wanted but never had, and I'm a guy who tends to get what I want.

When one of my favorites starts playing, and I see her swinging her hips in a slow motion that matches the beat of the classic Biggie Smalls tune, I find my feet are walking me out onto the dance floor and up behind the hottest ass in a pair of jeans I have ever seen.

I reach her, and just as I do, her friend's eyes widen. I put my finger to my lips and beg her not to say anything with a slow shake of my head. Her friend does me a solid and stops her reaction just in time. Before I know it, I'm directly behind Alex, and my hands naturally go to her hips and I sway in time with the music. I feel her stiffen and try to turn around, but my hands hold her in place. That's a good sign. I'm glad she doesn't just let random guys come up and touch her.

13

Putting my mouth next to her ear, I take in the intoxicating smell of her hair before I say, "Alexandra Stotts, funny seeing you here. How old are you again?" I hear her gasp my name as she tries to turn around, but once again I stop her. "Dance with me, Alex, and your secret will be safe with me."

She turns her head so she can look at me and the moment our eyes meet, we're both transfixed. Damn! There has always been something there, but being this close and having my hands on her has me feeling much more than I ever expected. She tries to say something in protest, but I silence her when I say, "Just dance with me, Alex."

With my order given, she starts to sway to the rhythm again. Within a matter of seconds, her ass is gently rubbing on me in a way that I am more than certain gives her an idea of what she's doing to me. To my surprise, her arms come up, and she puts her hands behind my neck and exposes even more of her skin as her shirt lifts. My hands instinctively move to touch her. I leave one hand splayed across her lean stomach and the other I slowly slide up her side and then her arm. I use this move to turn her around so that she's facing me. We don't miss a beat. Eyes locked on each other.

Fuck, she is more than I ever thought she would be. Who knew that the beautiful Alexandra Stotts could move like this? Who knew she could exude sex appeal like she is in this moment? It's almost like she's wanted me all these years, just as much as I've wanted her. I'm so lost in her eyes, her touch and at the moment, that I don't even realize that there's a new song playing. We haven't changed our rhythm, though. She straddles my leg; my arm is around her waist, keeping her tight to my body, and we continue to move together like we've done it a million times before.

It's getting a little warm out here on the dance floor, and as if she's reading my mind, she pulls her hair up in her hands and cools her neck. Shit, even her neck is sexy as fuck. She drops her hair once again and lets it all fall over one of her shoulders, leaving the other exposed. Not thinking, just acting on instinct, I lean down and kiss her neck and it's quite possibly the softest skin my lips have ever touched. The moment I touch her, I feel her hands that were on my hips grip my shirt as she takes in a deep breath of air. Looks like she is just as affected as I am.

All too soon, though, she breaks the spell when she yells over the baseline that I feel pounding in my chest. "Mick, what are you doing?" I lift my head from my new favorite spot and can't help but grab her by the back of the neck and rub my thumb over the spot that my lips were just kissing. As soon as our eyes meet, I can see the worry shining back from hers.

"Sorry, Alex, but I have always wanted to do that. I just couldn't help myself," I reply honestly into her ear.

Sounding shocked and confused, she asks. "What do you mean, Mick? You've always wanted to do what?"

Shit, why did I have to open my mouth? I don't know if it's because I've known her for so long, or if I feel close to her after that night at the hospital, but I don't seem able to lie to her when I say, "I've always wanted to touch you, Alex. You've always been that forbidden fruit that I knew I wasn't allowed to taste. I couldn't resist you tonight."

"You've always wanted to touch me?" She looks beyond confused and is looking at me like I have three heads. Okay, she may be sexy as shit, but she is cute as hell, too.

"Come on, let's go talk."

I don't let her reply. I just take her by the hand and lead

her off the dance floor. Like there is somebody up above looking out for me tonight. There is a tiny booth open to the left of the dance floor, and I gently push her into the wooden seat and slide in right next to her. It's a tiny booth and a tight fit, but it's too loud to talk from across the table. So, here I am pressed up next to her, still holding her hand.

"Mick, are you drunk?"

I can't help the smile that spreads across my face. "Nope, I've only had one beer. I was just about to leave when I saw you on the dance floor."

"You were?"

"I was."

She wrinkled her forehead in confusion, and she's biting her bottom lip. God, her lips are a thing of beauty. I can't take my eyes off of them and before I know it, my lips follow my line of sight and kiss her. I can feel her pull back at first, but I lean toward her to follow her retreating mouth and finally, I fully capture her. Once our lips are locked on each other, she's no longer resisting me as she wraps her arms around my neck and both hands grab the back of my head. I would give anything to take her right here on this table, but unfortunately, I think the establishment might frown upon that.

"Let's get out of here, Alex. Please?"

A simple nod of her head is answer enough for me. I grab her by the hand, and she pulls me toward her friend, who is leaning against one of the big posts that runs through the middle of the room. It appears she's been watching our PDA, and she seems quite entertained. As Alex approaches her, to let her know she's leaving, her friend is shooing her away before she can get a word out. Now that right there is what I call a wingman. I like this friend.

I spot Riley at the bar just as he spots me. I give him a flick of the head that signals that I'm leaving, and I see the moment he realizes who I'm leaving with. His eyes widen and I can see the shock on his face, but I don't want to think about what he or anybody else has to say.

Still holding her hand, I lead us in the direction of the exit and in a blur we're downstairs, and standing out on the corner of Burnside waiting to cross the street to get to my truck. I should have known it was going to be a good night when I scored this rock star parking. I guess Riley will have to call a taxi. He's a big boy, he'll figure it out.

She hasn't said a word. When we get to my truck, I go to open the door for her and can't help but push her up against it to take another taste of that sweet mouth of hers before helping her inside. I walk around the back of the truck and take a moment to adjust myself before I climb in and join her in the cab.

Those few moments alone in the truck seem to have given her time to think. When I look over at her, she's wringing her hands and her knee is bouncing with nerves.

"Mick, I don't know what's going on, but we can't do this. Your sister is my best friend and she would never forgive me."

"Emily doesn't have to know, Alex. She's all the way down in California and I know I'm not gonna call and tell her."

She doesn't reply. She just shakes her head and reaches for the door. I lean over and grab her hand and now I'm practically in her lap as I hold my weight with my hand that's on the door. I'm so close that I can't waste the moment and I take her mouth in a fierce kiss. She kisses me back, but not quite as fiercely. Something feels different now that we aren't in the dark bar.

"What is it, Alex? This can't just be because of my sister."

Quietly... almost on a whisper I hear her say, "But you're Mickey Jacobs. I don't want to be one of the many girls that sleeps with Mickey Jacobs. I'm not like that, Mick."

And there it is. She basically just called me out and tagged me a man-whore. I can't say that she's wrong. I don't do repeats, for the most part, and I don't do relationships. I still manage to have plenty of sex, though. Whenever and wherever, sex is something that seems to always be at my disposal.

With a serious look on my face but humor in my voice, I ask, "You calling me a slut, Alex?"

"No. Well, I mean maybe. I'm just not like that, Mick, and it's not worth ruining my friendship with Emily just so all my childhood fantasies can be full-filled."

And just like that, I am harder than I have ever been. Her confession feeds my ego, but also fortifies my plans for the rest of the night.

I tuck her hair behind her ear and then get in nice and close when I say into the same ear, "Did I just hear you say that I was your childhood fantasy, Alex?"

"Shit."

"Don't worry, sweet thing, the feeling is mutual," I say as I kiss her soft neck.

"What in the world is going on, Mick? What do you mean, the feeling is mutual? Since when?"

"Oh Alex, you have no idea," I whisper into her ear as my free hand slowly glides up her side and to her perfect breast. "There has been something about you since the first time I saw you. Watching you grow into the beautiful woman you are here tonight has been something to witness. If you didn't practically live at my house all summer long and if you weren't my *sister's friend, I would have been all over you years ago. Don't you see? Tonight is our chance. Sounds like we both want to see how good this could be." I'm back to what just may be my favorite spot on earth... Alexandra Stotts' neck.*

I gently kiss and nibble on the side of her neck when she says, "Emily can never know, Mick."

"I can keep a secret, Alex. Trust me?"

"Hey Pretty Boy!" I hear Emily yell from a few feet behind me. I turn from Jonathan and Devon just as Emily jumps into my arms and gives me a big hug. I see Cami behind her, but no Alex.

"I thought Alex was coming with you guys. She scared to hang with me and the boys tonight?" I say, trying to mask my disappointment.

"She's here, but Kevin already grabbed her."

And just like that, all the excitement I had to see her vanishes. I forgot about the boyfriend. Watching her from afar with some douche attached to her isn't as much fun as my usual stalking.

I leave my arm around Emily's shoulder and introduce her to a couple of people. Just as I introduce her to my co-worker, Jonathan Kelly and his friend Devon McCoy, I hear Emmett call my name. By the look on his face, it's important.

"Sorry, Emmers, be right back."

I make my way towards Emmett and, on my way across the bar, I finally see her. Just as I suspected, she's standing with some douche in a suit—and if I am seeing things correctly, he has on cufflinks. Who the fuck wears cufflinks to Kells? He looks like about as much fun as a heart attack. I mean, I guess he's a good-looking guy. He's close to my height, which means he's got to be around 6'3". He's got dark hair and looks fit, but he doesn't look strong. Maybe I'm just telling myself that because I don't want Alex to be attracted to this tool. Right now, she's just standing there staring at the ground while he talks to a bunch of other suits and completely ignores her.

I finally reach Emmett, without taking my eyes off of her, and he tells me that the apparent emergency is that he just heard from some girls we met last week at Brew Fest and that they were on their way. Seeing Alex across the bar makes my excitement at the prospects that are on their way a little less than it normally would be. I really need to shake this off, but it's a little hard to get excited over some random chick when the best night of my life is standing in the same room.

I know I need to keep my distance, but seeing the way Alex is standing there being ignored is unacceptable. Any man that could have her by his side and disregard her like he is right now, well... that is no man at all. As I get closer, she raises her head and her eyes instantly latch on to mine. One side of her mouth turns up in a little half smile, but it disappears just as quickly as it had appeared.

I approach the group of four men and Alex, and I can see her ever so slightly shake her head as if she's telling me not to approach. Well, because I'm me, that just makes me want to go and say my hellos that much more.

I can see Kevin notice me as I walk up to Alex and pull her into my side and give her a brief peck to the temple, just like I would to Emily or Cami. Nobody knows about our night and therefore it isn't out of place to say hello this way. If only they knew that every time I touch her, I feel like I'm on fucking fire.

"How's it going, Alex?" I can feel her stiffen under my arm. She's almost shaking.

"Good, Mick," she says as she tries to scoot away from me.

Taking my arm off of her, I reach in front of her and offer my hand to Kevin. "Hey, what's up, man? Mick Jacobs."

He begrudgingly takes my hand and says, "Kevin Lannister... and how do you know Alexandra?"

He lets go of my hand, and grabs her by the arm to pull her closer to him. I can tell it hurts, but she goes along with him.

"I've known *Alex* since she was a twelve-year-old singing along to *NSYNC in my sister's bedroom." I make an obvious look at his hand on her arm and when he notices, he loosens his grip but doesn't let go. "She's like family to me. How did you two meet?" I ask, staring down at him and looking him dead in the eye.

"I work for the hotel, as well. I'm in HR back at headquarters, in Maryland. We met when I was out for a market visit."

A glance at his hand and I can see that he's squeezing her so hard again that his knuckles are turning white. There's no way she would be with a guy like this, right? Maybe I'm seeing things, but I need to address this. Now.

"Hey Alex, I need to talk to you about Em's welcome home party. I need your help with a few things. Can I steal you for a minute?" I had no idea how I was going to get a second alone with her, but I pulled that little gem out of my ass rather nicely, if I do say so myself.

She looks at Kevin as if asking for permission and then once he gives a nod of his head, he finally lets go of her arm. Her arm that now has perfect finger impressions on it.

What. A. Fucking. Dick.

This has to end.

She steps towards me, and I let her pass in front of me. With my hand on the small of her back, I lead her outside to 2nd Ave. Once we're outside, I take a left and move her so that we aren't in front of the bar windows. No need for her to have Kevin's stare burning a hole through her while we talk.

"What do you want, Mick? There isn't really a party to plan, is there?"

"You always were a smart one, Alex. No, there's no party." I can't help but pace in short steps in each direction. I just can't believe I'm about to have this conversation with her.

She seems anxious, like she wants to be anywhere but alone with me out here on the street. "What do you want to talk to me about, then?"

I finally stop my pacing and turn to her. "What are you doing with that douchebag in there, Alex?"

"Who I date is none of your business, Mick," she practically seethes back at me. I must say, I wasn't expecting that kind of anger from her.

"Why are you pissed at me? He's the one grabbing you so hard you have the marks on your arm to prove it."

Silence.

She's got her arms crossed in front of her, almost hugging herself. She's staring at the ground and won't look at me. I bend my knees so that I am level with her and gently take each side of her face in my hands and say, "Why are you with a guy that treats you like that, Alex? You deserve so much better."

"He's fine, Mick. It's not like I'm gonna marry him. He doesn't even live here," she says while dropping her eyes back to the ground. She lifts her hands to mine on her face and tries to remove them. I shake my head and lift her gaze again. She's not getting away with this that easily.

"Sweetheart, a guy like that has a girl like you, and he's never gonna let you go. I don't like the way he man-handles you. You need to break the cycle, Alex. You've been through enough with your dad, you don't need to take any shit from anybody. You are worth more than that and I don't ever want to see you like I did that night at your house."

"Mick," she whispers.

"Shh... don't worry. Your secret will always be safe with me, even though I think you should tell Cami and Emily. But it's not my secret to tell. That asshat inside is a different story, though. I will not let him hurt you, Alex. Me not tearing him limb from limb just now, from what little bit I saw in there, is a miracle in itself."

"Mick, please don't cause a scene. Those guys are my co-workers and I really don't need the drama."

"Alex, if they have eyes, they saw what I saw and you are already giving them plenty of ammo for the rumor mill."

She pulls away from me and now she's the one pacing. "Shit! I don't even know why I'm with him. The first time we went out, I didn't think it was a big deal because he lives in Maryland. The next thing I know, he's working on some project with the HR team here and now he's here all the time! I know that you're right, Mick. It's just that I really love my job. I need my job. I don't know that he would do anything to get me fired, but he is a bit intense and he works in HR."

"You don't need your job bad enough to put up with that."

"Yes, I do Mick."

"Well, maybe start looking elsewhere then. Any company would be lucky to have you."

"Mick, I really lucked out and got a position that I shouldn't have so early in my career. I need the money."

"Get a roommate!"

"I don't need a roommate, Mick!"

Are we yelling at each other right now?

"Then what is it?" I ask, but try to lower my voice and calm the situation down a bit.

"It's none of your business, Mick," she replies with her back to me.

I walk up behind her but make sure to put my hands in my pockets. No need to cross any lines tonight. "You know you can tell me anything, Alex."

"It's my dad, Mick. I have to help pay for his care in the assisted living facility that he's in."

This takes me back a bit. I knew he had never recovered from the stroke that he had that night years ago, but I didn't realize his care rests on Alex's shoulders.

"Why you? He doesn't deserve it, Alex."

"He might not, but my mom does."

What do I say to that? She turns around and is standing in front of me with the most beautiful, yet saddest eyes I have ever seen.

"She can barely afford the little one-bedroom apartment she moved into. She works, but she doesn't make enough to support herself and the costs of my dad's care. Even after all the misery he put her through, she's still loyal to him. She never divorced him and still visits him several times a week."

"Okay, I get it. You need your job. You don't need him, though. Your mom wouldn't want you falling into the same life that she led for all those years. I can't tell you what to do with your life, but Alex... if I see so much as a scratch on you, he's a dead man."

With that, I lean forward and place a light kiss on her forehead. I place a hand on her low back to lead her in, but she doesn't move.

"What is it?"

"Mick, why do you care so much?"

"I think you know why, Alex."

"No, I really don't. I haven't seen you in ages and when I do see you, there is always some girl hanging on you. We never even talk. So why, Mick?"

"I told you once before, Alex. There is something about you. I will always be here if you need me. Always. In fact, give me your phone." I take her phone from out of her back pocket—I couldn't help but look at her ass when she had her back to me—and enter my digits. I wonder how long it will take for her to find it under the name I gave myself?

"Thanks, Mick."

"Of course, Alex."

Chapter 2

Alex

I can't believe I did it. I finally grew a pair and broke up with Kevin last night.

Luckily, last week was the final week he was going to be in Portland working on his project. The timing couldn't have been better. As we drove to the airport, I put it out there that long-distance relationships were too hard. I made it clear that I was going to be too busy with my family to make time to travel to see him and that maybe we should just end things while they were still good, before we drifted away from each other.

He surprised me by agreeing, and he didn't seem angry at all. I dropped him off at the airport; he gave me a hug and we said our goodbyes.

Sitting here at my desk this morning, I feel like I have a weight lifted off of my shoulders.

Just as she does every Monday, Olivia, our other event manager, walks in and places a coffee and a croissant on my desk.

"Thanks, Olivia. You know you don't have to do this

every week..." I take my first sip of the sweet, caffeinated goodness. "But I love that you do. Mmmm... so good."

Olivia and I met in group therapy years ago when we were still teenagers. After my dad's stroke—and our family secret was out to all of those involved that night—I finally decided that I needed help. After a year or so my therapist recommended I try group therapy. That lead me to Olivia and we've been friends ever since. When a job came open here at the hotel, I didn't hesitate to put in a good word for her. It's been great and I couldn't be happier to work with her every day.

"I know I don't, but it's our thing. Besides, you always get the first drink at happy hour, so we're even. Now, tell me, how was your weekend with Kevin? Sad to see him go?"

Keeping my eyes on my computer screen, I confess nonchalantly. "Uh, we broke up yesterday."

"Oh, Alex, I am so sorry. Are you okay?" She asks with genuine concern.

"I'm fine, Olivia. He wasn't *the one* or anything. Besides, his project is over and it would be even more of a long-distance relationship than it is already. No need to drag it out," I say with a shrug of my shoulder. It's the truth. I'm fine. More than fine.

"Well, okay. If you say so. He was pretty cute, though."

"He wasn't that cute, Olivia. Enough about me. How was your weekend?"

"It was good. Tom and I drove to the beach and the weather was perfect..."

I am such a horrible friend. As soon as she starts talking, my mind wanders back to my conversation with Mick outside of Kells. It took hearing him say the words to remind me that

I didn't want to become a cliché. I needed to break the cycle of the women in my family being in abusive relationships. Kevin may not have hit me... yet, but I knew it was coming. It was in his DNA and his fist would have connected with my face eventually. It's best to get out while I can and while he's on the other side of the country.

That conversation also reminded me that I needed to get to a meeting. I'm feeling free, independent, and brave, but I know enough to know that my relationship with Kevin was a setback. I need to find time for a meeting.

"... And we were talking about the fact that maybe it's time to move in together. We're always together anyway; we might as well save the money. What do you think?" Thank goodness I actually heard her last sentence and question because I didn't hear anything else she said.

"Well, do you love him? You don't want it to be a room-mate situation, do you? It's always risky to live with a guy if he's not *the one*. I'm not telling you what to do, but just remember, it's not a normal roommate situation."

Who am I to give advice? It's not like I have some great love life. I'm a twenty-six-year-old event manager who just got out of a not so healthy relationship with a co-worker. Throw that on top of that the fact that I have been in love, yes love, with my best friend's brother since I was twelve and my place in the list of people Olivia should go to for advice plummets.

"You're right, Alex. I do need to really think about it."

"No, Olivia. Don't listen to me. I don't know what I'm talking about. It's not like I've ever lived with a guy or even gotten close to that point in any of my relationships. Just do what feels right and safe for you. Just remember what we say in group... follow your heart, but bring your brain with you."

"Oh, stop it, Alex. You know I value your opinion *and* I know you'll find the right guy. Look at you. You're super-model beautiful, and the nicest person I know. I don't know who out there could even be close to good enough for you. You're gonna need some kind of Superman to knock you off your feet. He's out there, though. I know he is."

"Thank you, you're sweet, but you sure do exaggerate. I hope you're right and Superman is out there somewhere. I wouldn't mind a little bit of the reigning man of steel in my life. Mr. Cavill can take me flying over the city anytime he likes," I say with a giggle, and effectively end the conversation about my love life. In the blink of an eye Olivia is off talking about Cavill vs Affleck and who's hotter.

She has no idea that my Superman doesn't wear a cape, but he does wear a badge. I've already had the best night of my life with him and nothing else will ever compare. My blond hair and brown-eyed superhero ruined me for all men when I was a mere nineteen years old.

* * *

Mick

I slowly open my eyes and realize that yet again, I have no dame clue where I am. Not that this is anything new, but waking up in random bedrooms is getting old. I'm twenty-eight years old, for fuck's sake.

Wishing I could blame being drunk on my current situation, I look over at the body lying half covered by a sheet and take inventory. Sure, she's hot, but she's also so damn fake. She's blond, but it's clearly not her natural color. She has big tits, but those are far from real—God, I hate the way fake tits feel. Her eyelashes are way too long and are clearly not hers. She's unnaturally tan—almost orange. I am generally an equal opportunity kind of guy, but she's just really not my type. What the hell was I thinking?

Flashes of last night come back to me and it's then that I remember exactly what I was thinking. She was at the bar with a bunch of other fake looking blonds, but *she* was tenacious. Not taking no for an answer. She stuck to me like glue and I finally asked her to dance. After a little bump and grind, we had a little make-out session back in the hallway by the bathrooms.

Classy.

It took little persuading to get her back to her place and naked in her bed.

But sadly, I cannot remember her name. Come to think of it, I'm not even sure that I asked her what her name was.

I am such a dick.

How is this the life I had always dreamed of? I thought a lifetime of not settling down and getting laid whenever I wanted it would be the ultimate way to live. Who knew that I could be so wrong? I've always told myself that I don't do relationships, and that men aren't meant to be monogamous, but is that just my dad talking?

My dad always said that in nature animals aren't monogamous, and that we are really just animals too. He says that relationships committed to one person, and one person only, aren't realistic and that he hoped I didn't follow in his foot-steps. That I didn't make the same mistakes that he did. He had convinced me that marriage and being tied down with a family weren't the way to go, but the older I get, the more I'm not so sure I agree with him.

After watching my dad hurt my mom for years, I have always vowed to myself that I would never make somebody feel the way he made her feel. I'm sure I've broken a few hearts along the way, but I am always up front and honest and I have never cheated. It's not possible to cheat if you're never committed to somebody. The problem is the more tail I get, the lonelier I feel.

I know that I take too many risks in life. I always say that because I don't have the responsibilities that my married friends have, that I'm living for them as much as I am myself. I do stupid shit like skydiving, rock climbing and the occasional cliff diving—when I'm on the right kind of vacation. Not to mention I don't have the safest job in the world. The truth is, those brief moments of adrenaline replace the empty feeling deep inside me. After those moments, for just a small bit of time, I feel more like myself.

The only other time I've felt like that was one night seven years ago. What I wouldn't give to feel that way again. The only problem is she's the only person to ever make me feel like that. I think that's why I keep chasing that rush. I can't have Alex, so I try to find that feeling anywhere else I can.

We may have had the best night of sex that I've ever had, but it was everything else that made that night so memorable. After the hottest, yet sweetest roll in the hay that I have ever experienced—who knew sex could be both things at the same time—we talked. We sat and talked until the sun came up. I have never sat around and chatted it up with a girl after sex. I will never forget the way she threw her hair up into a pony-tail while wearing my green PSU Vikings t-shirt. It was the hottest thing I have ever seen. Not only was she hot, but she was funny and surprisingly a smart ass. We raided the kitchen, ate whatever we could get our hands on, and laughed all night long.

The next morning when she got out of my truck, she made me promise not to tell anybody. She said that she knew not to expect anything, and that she was thankful for the great evening. It was the first time I hadn't gone into the night having to tell the girl that she shouldn't have expectations of seeing me again after the night was done. The thing is... when Alex said she knew not to expect anything from me... it felt like a punch to the gut. It was the one time in my life I had wanted somebody to expect more from me. If only I hadn't been so stupid. And so twenty-one. If only I could have a do-over.

I've replayed that night over and over in my mind thou-sands of times. We had sex one last time that morning and it felt almost solemn to me. I knew this was it and I wasn't going to get more. I cherished every moment of it. Then, with my body reeling with turmoil over never having her again, I drove her home.

As we sat in my truck outside the house she still shared with her mom, we agreed we would still be friends. We were both glad we got to have *our* night. A night it was clear we had both fantasized about. Friends it was and friends it has been ever since.

She doesn't need to know that after the incident with her father, I have driven by her house at night when I'm on duty.

Almost every night I can. She doesn't need to know that after she moved out and lived with roommates, I continued to do drive-bys of her new apartment. Shit, I still do drive-bys of her townhouse. She has no clue I have always watched her from afar when we're in the same place. We're just friends. That's all she wants us to be, but it doesn't mean I'm not going to be there if she needs me. That's what friends are for.

Enough laying here in this strange bed while I fantasize about Alex. Alex, who deserves better than that. I need to get the hell out of here before No Name wakes up.

Quietly, I pull my naked ass out of this mystery woman's bed. I gather my things off of her floor—as a courtesy; I toss the used condom in the bedside table trash can that I clearly missed last night—and get dressed as fast as I can. I don't put my shoes on until I'm out the front door. No need to take the chance of waking her up. I don't leave a note, a goodbye or a fuck you very much. Nope, instead I live up to my reputation and just walk out the door.

Something's got to change.

I am too old for this shit!

Chapter 3

Alex

September

"No regrets. Live today like it's your last and along the way kick some ass!" Emily, Cami and I chant our best friend's motto and then clink our glasses together and in unison say, "Cheers!"

"I'm so glad to have you two back home! It was nice to visit you in California, but this is where you both belong."

"Agreed," Emily says. "It's so good to be back. You're right, Portland is home. I'm glad we came back before Ireland got any older. This is definitely where I want to raise my baby girl."

"I still can't believe that Jonathan has been here all this time and knows Mick *and* your mom. What a small world! I mean seriously, what are the chances?" Cami breathes out while staring out at the river as if she's in a dreamlike state.

It is somewhat hard to believe. That Jonathan has been here in Emily's hometown all this time. It's like some sort of second chance romance novel taking place right in front of us. I can tell that Emily has mixed emotions about the whole situation. As much as Cami and I love to see the possibilities that are there for the two of them and are anxious to watch it all unfold in front of us, I don't think Emily is ready yet.

"Can we *not* talk about Jonathan today? Please?" Emily begs. "So, how are the plans for the wedding going, Alex? Tricia hasn't turned into Bridezilla or anything, has she?"

As it turns out, it really is a small world. The girls, as well as Mick, will all be at a wedding I'm helping to coordinate. One of Mick's co-workers and good friends, Wesley and his fiancé, Tricia's wedding reception, is taking place in my hotel. Mick will be in the wedding while Emily and Cami will be in attendance as guests. This will be the first event that I've planned for work that my friends will get to take part in. Now that I'm working my way up in the company, I'm hoping to move on to more large-scale high-profile events. I really do love my job and getting to share it with the girls is pretty cool.

"Not at all. She's one of the most chill brides I've ever worked with. Wesley and Tricia have both been super easy during the entire process. I hope we can give them the day that they're both dreaming of. I think it's gonna be pretty amazing though. Tricia has great taste."

It's so nice to spend this Saturday with the girls. I couldn't be happier that they're both back. I have plenty of friends, but these two girls are special. The three of us connected from the first time we met and there was no looking back. You would think that with there being three of us that there would be an odd man out, but that has never been the case.

Emily and Cami were already best friends when I came along in the sixth grade, but they made room for me and never made me feel like I was the third wheel. I know that Emily and Cami are closer. I mean they've known each other longer, went to college together and have lived together for the last eight years. Of course, they're closer, but it's never gotten in the way.

This morning we met downtown for manis, pedis and mimosas. Now we're eating outside at *The Harborside* along the Willamette River, overlooking the marina. My favorite lobster bisque is in front of me. The sun is shining and my two best friends are sharing the day with me. That's all this girl needs right now.

Eventually, the conversation moves from Emily's job at the school, her daughter Ireland, Cami's adventures in Real Estate and my job and recent photography gigs to our love lives.

"Come on ladies, don't leave me hangin'. You know I have to live vicariously through you two. Spill it," Emily insists.

"I haven't dated anybody since I ended things with Kevin, so I don't have anything to contribute to this conversation. It's all you, Cam."

"Oh, you guys, where do I start? The guys here are so different from California. There's an adjustment period and I'm trying to figure it out. To go from surfer chic Southern California to the ultimate hipster land here in Portland is quite the change. I think I can get used to the whole beard thing, though. Beards are kinda hot. Who knew?"

With that, Cami's on a roll telling us about her many adventures in dating. She never ceases to let us down when telling her stories about all the boys that she meets. Cami is a big old flirt and has more personality than most, but she isn't really as carefree as she pretends to be. She can flirt a good game, but Cami rarely actually sleeps with anybody. She likes to have fun, but deep down, she just isn't that kind of girl and has more self-respect than to sleep around. That's one of the things I love most about her.

Emily and Cami both have been through a lot and yet their self-respect would never let them just settle for any guy that came along. Why can't I be more like them? Why was the last guy I was with just like my dad? Why would I be with somebody that didn't respect me and treated me more like property than anything else? I really need to pull my head out of my ass and follow the lead of these two amazing women sitting in front of me.

The ringing of my phone interrupts my perfect day. MOM appears on the screen and I know I have to take it.

"Sorry guys, it's my mom. I'll be right back."

"Hey Mom, what's up?" I say as I walk over to the sidewalk and away from the table for privacy.

"Alexandra, I need you to come over right away," my mom says in her usual panic. Everything is urgent with her since my dad went into his new facility. I think the change has been harder on her than it has been on him.

"Mom, what's wrong? I'm with the girls at lunch. Is there a problem?"

"It's your father. He wasn't himself today. He seemed irritated when I was visiting him. I don't think he likes the new facility, Alexandra."

"Mom, he's always irritated, and it's only been a couple of weeks. We have to give it some time. Besides, they kicked him out of the last place, so we're lucky to have found such a nice place that's close, that we can afford, and that would take him and his cantankerous moods. Give it time, Mom."

"I know you're right, but I just hate to see him so unhappy."

I don't know how she can feel the way she does after decades of abuse, but she still talks about him like he walks on water. I will never understand it.

The night of my dad's stroke, when she walked by me and said 'no more secrets', I really wanted to believe her. As horrible as it sounds, I think she thought he may not make it through the night and she thought her nightmare would be over. But he made it. He can't hurt her anymore, but she knew she had to stay with him. It's all about perception and how would it look if she were to leave him when things were bad.

"Mom, I can go with you to check on him tomorrow, but right now I'm with Emily and Cami. I really need to get back to my lunch," I say as I sit back down at the table and give a weak smile to the girls.

"Okay, sweetie. Say hello to the girls, and I'll see you tomorrow."

"Sounds good Mom, love you," I say, but she's already hung up. We don't do the whole *I love you thing* in my family, but I have always ended calls that way when people are around thinking it would mask the way things really were. I know I can trust these girls with my life, but for some reason, I've never told them anything about what was really going on in my childhood home. Nope, Mickey Jacobs is the only person in my life who knows that truth. He has never brought it up, and he has never pitied me. He has dealt with the information just like I hoped he would.

"So, what did I miss?"

"I was just telling Cami how great Mick has been. I

mean, he's always been a great brother, but letting his little sister and her four-year-old kid move into his brand-new bachelor pad without batting an eye is beyond your typical big brother stuff. He hasn't once made us feel like an inconvenience and he's so good with Ireland. I really can't believe how lucky I am to have him there for us," Emily says, now taking her turn to stare out at the river in contemplation.

Bringing her attention back to the table, I say, "He loves you, Em, you know that. He'd do anything for you."

"I know, Alex. I just feel so bad. He finally buys his own place and he has to share it with us. He should be entertaining his bevy of beauties, not watching *Frozen* on a constant loop. I mean, it's not just some simple little ranch house. It's four bedrooms, plus the top floor of the house is a huge loft that leads to a primary bedroom and bathroom. It's huge. Most of the rooms and the walls are empty, but it's huge. Here he has a new house where he should be the king of the castle and we're downstairs cock-blocking him. I just feel bad."

"Chica, you know he wouldn't have you there if he didn't want you there. Mickey Jacobs doesn't do anything that Mickey Jacobs doesn't want to do," Cami says with a wink.

"I know, thanks guys."

It's all true. Mickey really is a great guy. Too bad he's a great guy that never plans on committing to one girl, because he would make a great husband and father one day.

If only he could commit.

I guess a girl can dream.

Mick

I don't want to wake up, so I struggle to keep my eyes closed.

I know what happens when I open my eyes.

She fades away.

In my dreams, I can feel her. It's like she's really there with me.

My dreams are so much better than my reality.

Every night since our talk outside of Kells, she comes to me.

I dream of smiling eyes that look at me like I've hung the moon.

I dream of us lounging in bed and talking for hours.

I dream of her hair falling like a curtain around us.

I can hear her shy giggle as her lips touch mine.

I dream of us alone on the dance floor.

Feeling her body against mine and her eyes filled with shock and lust.

I dream of that night years ago.

That night that I have replayed a thousand times over.

I dream of standing at the edge of a cliff but not jumping.

Holding her and watching the sunset is enough.

I dream of protecting her.

I dream of making her happy.

I dream of being happy.

I dream of her.

I dream of only her.

Chapter 4

Mick

Riley is rarely off on a Saturday night, but somehow he scored tonight off. We decided it had been too long since we'd had an old-school house party, and tonight we plan to remedy that situation. I love that Riley works at my favorite pub in Portland, but his hours are really tough when it comes to getting to hang out. After the shit week I've had at work, this is gonna be just what I need.

I came over early to help him prep for the party. We set up the keg and tap it, you know, quality control and all that. We're guys, so setting up the keg is really all there was to do since all the booze and mixers are already out on the kitchen counter. For now, we just lounge on the back porch, beers in hand with the sound of Frank, my English Bulldog, snoring at my feet. Frank is just as comfortable here as I am. Riley's place is like our second home. If we aren't at home, then we're at Riley's.

Riley Johansson and I have been friends since the first grade. He's like the brother I never had and a second son to my mom. His parents are the best and they treat me like one of their own, too. I usually spend half of Thanksgiving Day and Christmas Day with the Johansson's. They truly are family to me and they have been a stabilizing force in my life. Daniel and Karen were there for me every step of the way when Dad left, and I can't imagine my life without them.

Riley is the only person who knows about my night with Alex. He's always known there was something about her for me. I think he noticed it before I did, back when we were kids. He always said he knew she felt the same way, but I never believed him... until that night. He was at Lola's Room and he saw us on the dance floor. He was happy for me, but he's close to Alex too, and I know he worried I would hurt her.

"So, I haven't talked to you all week. Whose bed did you wake up in last weekend, and please tell me you gloved up?"

"Dude, I don't even know. I had never seen her before and I didn't even really like her. Fuck was she persistent, though. She just wouldn't leave me alone. I woke up the next morning and realized I hadn't even been interested enough to ask her name. I felt like such a dick when I was creeping out of her place the next morning. Man, I am getting too old for this shit. And of course, I gloved up. You know I don't take chances."

"Mick, you're the one that insists on never settling down. This is what you have always wanted. What is it you always say? There's no pussy like new pussy. That's it, isn't it?" He says with a smart-ass smirk on his face.

"Fuck you, Riley."

"Well, isn't that what you always say? Or was it for every hot chick there's some man out there that's tired of her shit? You've bestowed so many pieces of wisdom to me over the years I just can't keep them straight. I mean, they don't call you a legend for nothing."

"Whatever, man. I know you love throwing my own words back at me, but I can admit that maybe I was wrong. Even new pussy gets old."

"Hold on just a second. Do my ears deceive me? Did Mickey Jacobs just say he was wrong?" He gets up and walks over to where I sit and takes the cup from my hand and takes a swig. "Nope, just beer. You sure you weren't drinkin' any hard stuff before you got here?"

Snatching my beer back with one hand and holding my middle finger up with the other, he just laughs and sits back down.

"Seriously dude, you okay? You don't seem like yourself tonight."

"I'm fine. Just a shit week at work."

"Okay, well, if you need to do the whole chick thing and talk about your feelings and all that shit, I'm your guy. You know that, right?"

"I do know that, Ry, but you can keep your tampons to yourself tonight. I'm fine."

A few moments of silence pass, but I can tell there's something on his mind.

"She's gonna be here tonight, Mick," he says like I know who he's talking about.

"Who?"

"Alex."

Standing up and taking my now empty cup with him, he heads back inside. He leaves me alone with my thoughts. He knows exactly what he did by leaving me with that little nugget. Luckily, he's not gone long and I don't have to stay lost in my thoughts about Alex.

Handing me my now full cup of beer, he says, "You know, Mick, you two aren't kids anymore."

"What's your point, Ry?"

Just then there's a knock on the door and Riley gets up to answer it. As he passes by, he pats me on the shoulder and says, "I think you know what the point is, Mick. You're a smart guy and I'm pretty sure you'll figure it out eventually."

From there on out, the night is a constant flow of friends, old and new. The problem is, I've moved on from beer and on to some very strong rum and Cokes. I'm not a big drinker, so this is not the wisest move on my part.

The more I drink, the more this past week keeps creeping back into my mind. I was hoping this party and some drinks would be just what I needed to put it out of my mind, but it just won't go away.

At the moment, I'm being cornered by Courtney Sandberg. As per usual, she's trying to work her magic on me. Not sure how she hasn't figured it out yet, but I am just not into her. We may have hit it once several years ago, but that shit is never going to happen again. Besides, I don't hear a word she says because all of my attention is on the beautiful woman in the blue shirt standing across the room.

I don't know what's wrong with me, but I suddenly feel completely depressed and alone. I can't fucking stand here watching her from a distance, yet again. I have to get out of here. I make some lame excuse to Courtney about needing to make a phone call and head outside. Luckily, there isn't anybody out here. With the keg in the garage, the backyard is empty. Most people seem to be staying in the garage near the beer or in the house.

I take a seat on the deck stairs that lead to the yard and try to steady my emotions. I feel like such a girl right now. Full of inner turmoil. This is not like me. I rarely let work or women get to me, but tonight I can't seem to gain control of the way I feel about either.

I hear the back slider open and close and then hear a familiar voice. "Hey Mick, do you mind if I join you?"

As much as I tell myself that I don't want her out here when I'm feeling like this, I can't say no to her. "Sure, Alex. Take a seat."

She sits down next to me and asks, "Whatcha doin' out here by yourself?"

"Just trying to get away from all the noise for a bit," I say, telling her half the truth. I'm also trying to get out of the same room as her. I'm starting to feel like a creepy stalker.

The stairs aren't that wide, and her leg and arm press against mine. I feel calmer already. So much for getting away from her.

"I promise to be quiet, or I can go if you want to be alone?" She starts to get up, but I grab her hand and pull her back down next to me. Once she's sitting again, I don't let go of her hand. Not only do I not let go of her hand, but I link my fingers between hers and hold on for dear life.

I had no idea how much I needed somebody right now. How much I needed *her* right now. She doesn't say a word. She just lets me be. Without me saying a thing, she knows exactly what I need.

We sit hand in hand in silence for several minutes. Eventually I turn to look at her and she gives me a sweet smile, bumps her shoulder against mine and quietly says, "Hey."

"Hey," I manage to say back.

"You okay, Mick?"

"Just a rough week at work."

"You know if you need to talk, I'm here. I think it's safe to say I owe you one. Actually, two if I'm honest."

"Two?"

"Well, not only were you there for me that night when everything went down with my dad, but you helped knock some sense into me about Kevin and I broke up with him. So, I owe you, Mick."

"You broke up with that douchebag, really?" I can't help the fleeting hope that soars through my veins.

"Yep, it's not like I was in love with him or he was the one. I was just passing time."

Words have never sounded so good. She didn't love him! Thank God! I know it makes me a dick, but I don't want her to love anybody else. The thought of her getting married to somebody one day is enough to make me sick.

The silence is back. Five minutes must go by when she leans her head on my shoulder, gives my hand a squeeze and says, "Mick, talk to me."

"I don't want to lay my crap on you, Alex. You don't need to hear this kind of stuff."

"Mick, you always take care of everybody. Let somebody be there for you. Speaking of you taking care of everybody, I've been meaning to say thanks for taking such good care of Emily and Ireland. You've really gone above and beyond for them, and it means a lot to Emily. She's been through a lot and I'm glad that she has you to count on. So, thanks for taking care of our girl."

"Of course, I'd do anything for those two," I reply.

"I know you would, and Emily would do anything for you, too. Why don't you let somebody be there for you, Mick? If you don't want to talk to me, why not talk to Em or Ry?"

"Alex, Em's been through enough. I can't lay my shit on her. I go to Riley with everything and I feel like a pussy, not being able to handle the emotions of my job. I'm Mickey fuckin' Jacobs and shit isn't supposed to get to me."

She reaches in front of me with her free hand and grabs my face and turns it so I'm looking her eye to beautiful fucking eye. Just mere inches from her perfectly luscious lips. My God, she is extraordinary.

"Mick, you aren't made of steel. You're allowed to let things get to you from time to time, but you need to talk about it. You can't hold it all inside. Let me be that person who you unload some of your burdens on. I can be there for you, Mick." She bumps me with her shoulder again and says, "Come on. Give me a chance."

"Why?" I ask her. Searching her eyes for something, but I'm not sure what.

"Why what?"

"Why do you want me to share my burdens with you?" I ask her.

"Mick, I care about you. I always have. You were there when I needed you. Now let me be there for you. Tell me about your week."

I finally tear my eyes from hers and stare blankly out across the dark yard. To my own surprise, I start to talk.

"You know, Alex, I don't care that people don't like cops.

They call us names everywhere we go and people treat us like shit. I can handle that because I don't give a shit what people think of me. I can handle most calls and walk away knowing I did my job, and I sleep fine at night. There are times, though, where it sticks with me and I can't let it go."

I pause, and she lets go of my hand and anxiety fills me instantly. It's gone a moment later when she places that hand on my back and takes my hand again with her other hand. She slowly rubs my back and calms me. She's letting me take my time and that's what I need. I rarely talk to anybody about the emotional side of my line of work. How do you explain this part of the job to people? Most people don't hear about this part. Don't want to hear about it.

I finally take a deep breath and start again. "It's the kids, Alex. They're so innocent and don't do anything at all to deserve the hand they've been dealt. Seeing abused kids pisses me off like you wouldn't believe, and you dream about it at night. Taking a crying kid away from his abusive parents is hard, but I know in the end it's the right thing. I just hope and pray that they get cared for better elsewhere. I have to believe that good will come of it. There are times though, when there is nothing good and nothing I can do to help."

I've stopped again. She squeezes my hand and says, "It's okay, Mick. I'm here. You don't have to keep going, but I'm here and I'm not going anywhere. Just take your time."

Minutes go by before I speak again. I hate thinking about it.

"My week had been shitty with a DUII death and an abuse case, but on Wednesday night I was the first on scene to a SIDS death. I don't know how to explain it to you, but it's the worst feeling I have ever felt and I've felt it on several occasions. When you arrive to the house, the parents are hysterical. They've just found their precious child dead in their crib and they want you to save him. Alex, he was blue. They handed me their blue baby and begged me to bring him back. There was nothing I could do, but I couldn't *not* try. For the parent's sake, I did CPR on the baby. I gave little puffs of air into his mouth and did chest compressions with my fingers, just like I've been trained to do. Nothing happened. I knew he was gone, but I tried. Soon the paramedics were there and they took over for me and pronounced the baby dead. The mother was screaming and fell apart in my arms while her husband just stood there in stunned silence. I was a part of the worst day of their lives. They will always remember that I wasn't able to save their son."

Alex starts to speak, but I just keep going. I know what she's going to say.

"My brain knows that there wasn't anything I could do, but it doesn't make it any easier. I can still hear the mom screaming, and I can still smell the baby powder. I can't get the smell to go away. The last few nights when I try to go to sleep, I smell baby powder and I relive it over and over. I just want to sleep, Alex. I'm so tired."

She doesn't say a thing. To my surprise, she gets up, sits on my lap with her legs across mine, puts her arms around my neck and she holds me. She's cradling my head so that I am nestled in that spot between her neck and her chest. It's not at all sexual; it feels nurturing. She holds me and rubs my head and doesn't say a word. It's exactly what I need.

She's exactly what I need.

She soothes me.

Getting it out and not hearing her try to tell me it's all

going to be okay is exactly what I needed. Her holding me and the gentle rhythm of her hand gliding back and forth over my head is more than I could have asked for. I don't ever want to let her go, but I know I don't always get what I want.

"Thanks Alex," I lamely say as I lift my head from her neck; the only thing that I can smell now. The only place I want to be.

She leaves my lap, taking all her warmth and comfort with her, and sits back down beside me and bumps my shoulder yet again. "I'm not sure that I did much, but anytime, Mick."

"Thanks for not trying to make it all okay. Thanks for just letting me talk. For just being here."

"Mick, we've been friends a long time. I'm around if you ever need anything at all. If you need a friend, I'm your girl. In fact, let me text you so you have my number and you can call *me* day or night."

A few seconds later my phone pings, and I take it out of my back pocket to see a text that reads:

Call me anytime you Sexy Beast, you. Lol.

I can't help the laugh that comes barreling out of me. "I see you found my number," I say, standing up and feeling much better than when I came out here thirty minutes ago. It was great to get it out and end things with a laugh. "You think you can handle being just 'friends' with a Sexy Beast like me?" I say as I bring my hand down my body as though I am presenting it to her in all its glory.

"I'm not sure my heart could take much more than just friends, Mick. I'm sure willing to give it a shot, though."

And there it is. She knows me too well and that I can never give her what she needs; which is *more*. She deserves more than what a man-whore like me can give her. I've never really been just friends with a girl. Can I do it? Having Alex in my life is something I've always wanted. If being friends is what it has to be, then friends it is.

"Let's give it a shot. Thanks again for tonight, Alex."

"Anytime, Mick."

Chapter 5

Alex

October

It's been a couple of weeks since Riley's party, and since then, Mickey and I have been in constant contact.

It started that night when Mick made me promise to text him once I made it home safely. I texted him and he texted back and we haven't stopped texting since. We text each other good morning. Well, our mornings are at different times of the day, but we still text when we wake up. He sends me pictures of Frank throughout the day and we text each other when something interesting happens to either of us. We text each other good night. Every night.

For the most part, the texts have stayed in the friend-zone, but now and then he'll make a suggestive comment and when I call him on it, he always blames poor Frank. It's nice to have somebody who makes me laugh to talk to every day.

Who would have thought one of my most trusted confidants would be Mickey Jacobs?

He's so much more than the bad-ass party boy he likes to

portray to the rest of the world. He's actually a great guy. In fact, just yesterday, he told me I needed to have some fun.

He's right. Between work and my parents, I don't really incorporate a lot of fun into my routine. I have a standing happy hour with Olivia every week, and I have my occasional time with the Cami and Emily, but it's not as much as I would like. I know that I need to get out more, but my mom has this way of making me feel guilty, even if it's not on purpose.

I know a lot of it is the fact that she protected me from my father for years. She took many beatings over the course of my life that were intended for me. I remember each and every one of those beatings that I watched from the other room or listened to from my bedroom.

I owe her everything.

If that means being at her beck and call from time to time, so be it. I know she's lonely and lost with Dad and I both gone, but she insists that I have my own place and that I don't live with her. I do what I can to fill in those gaps for her, but I know it's not enough. She's lonely.

Mick has decided that tonight is the night I get out. I'm meeting him for happy hour at Portland City Grill. It's a staple in Portland and they have the best happy hour food around. It's also full of yuppies and suits and not Mick's usual type of hang out.

I try not to think about this as I freshen up at work before heading out. I know he's just a friend, but he's also the hottest friend I have ever had, and this whole being friends with Mick thing is still pretty new. Whether or not I want to admit it, I did take extra care in what I wore to work today and I'm feeling pretty good. I went with a black pencil skirt, white blouse with capped sleeves and black stilettos that make me at least six feet tall or just over. My hair is down, blown out and has a wave to it. I know he's just a friend, but he's still Mickey and I can't help but dress to impress.

On the thirtieth floor of the US Bank Tower, I get off of the elevator and, just as I do, my phone pings. It's Mick. He's already here and has snagged one of the coveted tables by the window.

Walking into the bar, my stomach is doing flips. My brain knows that we're just friends, but that girly heart of mine, that is clearly covered in lace and pink polka dots, still feels the flutter of my childhood crush. I let out a deep breath and make my way towards the windows that line the bar.

When I reach the table and see Mick waiting for me, the view takes my breath away. I wish I could say it was the view of Portland and Mt. Hood in the distance, but that's not the view stealing my breath. My view is stunning and it's because of the gorgeous man getting up from his seat to greet me.

Mick is always beautiful, but tonight he's dressed it up a bit. He's in a trim-fit black button-down shirt and dark jeans. I know this is the typical dressy casual attire all guys wear when going out to a nicer place, but I have never seen Mick dressed like this. He's a t-shirt and shorts kind of guy when he's not in his uniform, so this look is something new.

After my gawking is done, I realize we're both just standing here, like idiots, staring at each other. Slowly, a sexy grin takes over his face and he says, "Alexandra Stotts, you look amazing."

"You clean up real nice yourself, Mickey Jacobs."

"I have my moments," he says with a wink. "Bet you wish you had your camera to take a shot of this, I know, but you'll just have to burn it into your memory bank this time." I earn another wink and just shake my head at him.

He steps aside so I can take the overstuffed seat next to the window, but instead of sitting across from me, he sits in the chair to my left.

"You said that you loved the lemon drops here, so I went ahead and ordered one for you."

I'm relieved to hear the nervousness in his voice. Thank God, it's not just me.

"Thanks."

I take a drink of my lemon drop, Mick takes a drink of his beer and things get awkward. We seem to not have anything to say to one another when we aren't texting.

Minutes go by and he just stares at me but doesn't say anything. This can't really be happening, can it? This has to come to an end some way... somehow.

I know it's lame, but my own little internal game that I play comes to mind, and because I'm desperate, I go with it.

"Co-workers, but they're having an affair."

"Excuse me, but what the hell are you talking about, Alex?" He asks while looking at me like I've lost my mind.

"Those two... over there at the bar," I say as I point my head in their direction.

"How do you know that they're having an affair?"

"I don't. It's just a little game I like to play in my head. It was getting a little too awkward, so I'm letting you join in."

He smiles and says, "Oh, I like the way your mind works, little lady." He leans over so that he's closer to me and says, "So, those two? The woman in the red dress and the dude in the suit, right?"

"Yep. They're both married with kids. They're meeting

other co-workers here, but they got here before everybody else. He's the boss and they have a thing going and they think that nobody at work knows."

Just then, the man puts his hand on the small of the woman's back and slowly but surely, his hand goes lower and lower until it reaches her ass.

"Shit, Miss Stotts, you are damn good at this! I am impressed!"

Moments later, several other men in suits join them at the bar, and the man quickly removes his hand from the lady in red's ass. Now they're acting like strangers separated by co-workers and barely even glancing at one another.

"I have to admit, this doesn't normally happen. I usually just make stuff up in my head. It's just something to pass the time. I've kind of impressed myself tonight. Let's pick some-body else," I say, to keep the awkwardness at bay.

He doesn't realize that I started this little game years ago. Years ago, after I started going to group therapy. It was there that I realized it wasn't just me that always had a façade up. I learned that people from all walks of life are going through things you would never imagine. There are so many people out in the world that look like they have it all together, but inside... inside they are just barely hanging on. Before I knew it, I found myself watching people to see if I could see the cracks in their façade's and from that came my little internal game that I'm now playing with Mick.

He looks around, points to a woman leaning against the bar and says, "What's her story?"

I sit back and watch her for a moment or two. "Okay, you ready for this?"

"Ready. Give it to me, girl."

"Well, this is a nice place and all, but she's dressed up just a little too much. She's trying too hard to look sexy with the way she's standing and holding her drink." He just nods along with my rambling and seems just as into this little game as I am. "My first instinct was that she was a high-priced hooker, but... that's not it."

"It's not, is it?" He says with a small crooked smile as he turns in his chair, completely facing me and not even looking at the woman in question.

"Nope. I think this is date night with her husband of ten years. They're trying to spice things up and trying a little role-playing. They've taken their rings off and are going to pretend to be single and pick each other up in a bar. They'll act like they've never met before and before you know it she'll be going into the bathroom to remove her panties and then she'll come back to the bar and slip them in his pocket."

His eyes widen in shock for a brief moment before a glimmer of delight lights them up.

"Wow, I *really* like the way your mind works," he says with his elbow on the arm of his chair and his chin resting on his hand. He seems completely captivated by the little make-believe world I'm creating. "So, if it's date night, where is he?"

I give him a look that says, *you are such a novice,* and say, "Well, they couldn't show up together if they're going to play strangers who meet in a bar. She got here first and he'll get here shortly. Who knows, he may be somewhere here in the bar, watching her from afar and just waiting to make his move."

"You are very creative, Miss Stotts. Who knew you had such an active imagination? I must say, I think I like it."

"Well, glad I could impress you. My turn to pick somebody for you. Hmmm... let's see... I know. How about the red-headed bartender? What's his story?"

From there, we take turns assigning patrons and staff of the bar to one another and creating their fictional stories. We've each done four or five and we can't stop laughing as the stories get more and more outlandish.

I may have impressed him, but I have to admit I'm pretty impressed too. When I brought up this little game I was worried he might make fun of me, but it turns out he has a really open mind and just rolled right along with it. I'm having a great time and I think he is, too. That is until one in a long line of Mickey Jacobs one-night stands stops by to say hello.

He's turned towards me and doesn't see the petite, big-breasted blonde in tight jeans and come-fuck-me heels approaching, but I do.

"Hey, Mick!" she exclaims, completely ignoring the fact that he's sitting here talking to me.

He has the courtesy to make a pained face at the sound of her voice before he turns around and is eye level with her barely covered boobs.

"Hi," is all he says. There doesn't seem to be any recognition on his face.

"Mickey it's me, Ruby. I met you at that Halloween party last year. You were dressed as *hot shit,* and I was in the Catholic School Girl outfit. Don't you remember?"

"Oh, Ruby... of course I do. Sorry about that. How are you?"

"Great, Mick. I'm here with a couple friends and saw you

over here and just had to come say hi. You gonna be around later tonight?"

"Sorry, Rudy... I mean Ruby. I'm here with a friend tonight," he says as he reaches over and pats me on the knee.

Well, that was strange. I'm a friend and I got a knee pat. Interesting.

"Oh, okay," she says, giving me the once over. Her eyes are back on Mick and it appears she isn't giving up so easily. She makes this perfectly clear when she slips him her number on the napkin that she came over with. I wonder if she was a Boy Scout in a past life because she sure is prepared. "Well, here's my number in case you lost it. Call me sometime."

"Uh, okay, thanks," he says, taking the napkin from her. She walks away and then he turns back to me. "Well, that was embarrassing. Sorry about that. Now, where were we?"

"Mick, did you really not remember her name?" I say a little put off, but knowing Mick well enough to know that he does get around.

"I hate to say it, but I really didn't recognize her out of her school girl costume. I'm not proud, but my night with her meant nothing, and I always make it perfectly clear how it's going to be before things go too far."

Thinking back to our one night together, I say, "God, am I on the list of one-nighters that didn't mean anything?" Realizing I just said that out loud, I quickly say, "Don't answer that!"

Why did I have to bring that up?

We were having such a good time and I had to go there.

* * *

Mick

I am such a dick!

I can't believe I could make Alex, of all people, feel like *nothing*.

I always make my intentions clear so that nobody gets hurt... but I know better than that. I know that a lot of women say they're fine with one night, when they really aren't. I don't do repeats for that very reason and I am always up front. I've never really worried about those that say they can handle it, but really can't. That's their problem.

Alex is different, though. She always has been, and I do care if I've hurt her.

I know she told me not to answer her question, but I can't just leave it out there. "Alex, our night together wasn't *nothing*. In fact, that night was pretty great."

I can tell that I've taken her by surprise, but she tries her best to play it off. "Well, I'm glad to hear it, Mick. I have to admit I'm glad that we're just friends these days and I don't have to worry about it happening again. I would hate ending up on that list, after all."

Wow, that stung.

That didn't just sting... that hurt. I'm not sure why it hurts like it does, but I don't like this feeling. I've known all along that we were just friends. If it meant having her in my life, I was okay with that. The problem is, I know I want more from her. But I don't deserve more. I don't know how to give more, so I can't really ask her to give that to me.

She's acting like this was just a regular conversation and

has moved on already. After a bit of her talking—like she does when she gets going off on a tangent—I shake off the sting of her comment. We've been here for close to four hours and we've only had two drinks each. I think this is a first. When do I ever just sit and talk to a girl? In a bar. Especially when I'm not plotting how to get her in bed while not really paying attention to a thing she says.

Tonight, I find myself hanging on to every word that Alex says. Watching her amazing imagination go to work while playing her little game was quite eye opening. It was also quite the turn on. I'm not sure that I can do *just* friends with her. She's just too damn tempting.

Once we close the tab and I pay the bill—after a big argument that this wasn't a date and we should go dutch—we head to the elevators. We push the down button and wait in silence. The elevator arrives and once we're alone inside, things are awkward again, just like they were at the beginning of the night. Every fiber of my being wants to stand just a little closer and take her hand in mine, but I don't.

Thirty... long... quiet floors later, we finally hit the parking garage and I walk her to her car. I feel like a teenager on his first date and I don't know how to end things. I finally go in for a platonic hug and she hugs back. Once my arms are around her, I'm engulfed in her intoxicating smell. When our bodies connect... it's like we were made for each other, and it's apparent even with a simple hug Alex and I just fit.

I don't mean to, but I can't help it when I pull back from our hug, tangle my hands in her hair and gently whisper a kiss over her delicious lips. I feel her startle, but it only takes a beat before she leans into the kiss and grants my tongue access. Her hands that were still on my back from our hug, make their way up my back and down my arms until she holds onto my forearms. A soft moan escapes her throat, and I can't help but try to push myself closer to her, even though there is no space between us at this moment.

Things are getting more intense and all I can hear is the sound of our heavy breathing. Both of us are kissing the other back with everything we have. Suddenly, the sound of screeching tires makes her jump, and her hands that were holding on to my forearms for dear life tighten and pull my hands from her head. She denies me by moving her head away from mine and taking a step back. The words that follow break my heart, for me, for her... for both of us.

"Mick, I've been cheated on, treated poorly and, most recently, man-handled by the guys I've dated. I don't think I could take adding heartbreak to that list and I'm pretty certain that in the end, that's what would happen. I don't want that. Don't get me wrong, that was great, but I just can't, Mick. Can we just keep things the way they are?"

"Of course, Alex. Sorry about that. I guess I just got caught up. Friends," I say as I hold my hand out to her.

She takes my hand and her dark chocolate eyes look at me with a mix of emotions. I can see relief and sadness cross her features, and it kills me.

"Friends," she says, but I can hear uncertainty in her voice.

I wait while she gets in her car, starts the engine and then drives away with a wave. With the taste of her still on my lips I make my way through the parking garage.

The one thing I can't stop thinking about as I walk to my truck is that just like she did at Riley's party, she said she didn't want to add heartbreak to her list. Does that mean she's never been in love or cared about an ex enough to have her heart broken? Does it also mean that she has some of the same feelings that I do, and she really does want more but is afraid she'll get hurt?

I hope it's both. Selfishly, I don't want her to have ever loved anybody else, and I would feel so much better if I knew the feelings that I'm feeling weren't one sided.

She's right though... we can't ruin the good thing we have going with adding more to it. It's pretty great just the way it is, and I'm not sure I could go to bed at night without her good night text.

Chapter 6

Alex

It's late and I know I need to sleep, but I can't seem to close my eyes and shut my mind off. All I can think about is Mick and that damn kiss in the parking garage. I've never forgotten our night together, but having his kiss lingering on my lips brings it all back to the surface. The feel of his body pressed against me still burns my skin, and I swear I can still feel his hands in my hair and the taste of beer on his tongue.

I'm shaken from my lust-filled thoughts at the sound of a knock at the door.

Who the hell is knocking at my door this late at night?

Blaze jumps off the bed and meets me at the front door. I check the peephole and I'm not sure that I believe what I'm seeing. I look down at Blaze and he seems just as confused as I am. I look at myself to make sure that I'm decent. Luckily, I wore a black tank with my black and white plaid pajama bottoms. I may not have a bra on, but I'm decent.

I check the peep hole again and see that he's looking anxious and agitated. Something must be wrong and now I'm starting to buzz with anxiousness as well. I fumble with my locks but manage to unlock the door.

"Mick, what are you doing here?"

He stands in my doorway with his hands in his pockets, his chest heaving up and down but silent.

"Mick, what's the matter? What's happened?"

"You. That's what happened, Alex. I can't do this. I don't want to do this. I know that you *said* that you wanted to keep things the way they are, but I know you don't mean it. You want me just as badly as I want you, and you can't keep denying it. I know you, Alex. I can see your body react and hear your breath catch when I brush up against you. You know you want this just as badly as I do, and I'm here to prove that to you."

He rushes through the door and kicks it shut with his foot. I can feel the built-up tension radiate off his body as he stalks me like his prey. Before I know it, my back is against the wall and he's standing in front of me but not touching me. His chest is still heaving up and down and he almost seems angry.

"Alex, don't say no." His hand comes up to my face as he gently holds my cheek in his hand and lightly drags his thumb over my bottom lip. My breath hitches as I await his next move. I don't have to wait long as his hand moves to push my hair behind my ear. After my hair is in place, he leisurely takes his forefinger and barely skims the skin of my neck, down to my collarbone, over my heart and to my breast.

Just as his finger reaches my nipple, he surges forward and captures my mouth in a fierce kiss as his hand cups my breast. My hands do some roaming of their own as they search his strong back, shoulders, and biceps, and then back to his shoulders. He is all man and I cannot believe that he's here. Pressing me against my wall. Kissing me senseless.

He releases my lips and picks me up with his hands on my ass, forcing my legs to wrap around him.

"Alex, no more denying what we feel. Tonight is the night, baby. No more waiting. I've waited too long already."

Hearing him call me baby sends my body into overdrive and I couldn't want him more. I still can't seem to speak as he carries me down the hall and to my bedroom.

He tosses me onto the bed and I let out a squeal. He immediately starts kicking his shoes off while he pulls his shirt over his head. He is a masterpiece and I'm so glad that the only tattoo he has covering his perfect skin is the shamrock on his left deltoid. I can't help but sit up and move to the edge of the bed. I don't want to miss a thing and I just can't stop myself from blatantly checking him out as I watch every flex of his muscles as he continues to undress himself. When he finally stands before me in all his beautiful glory, it's clear that he's more than ready to take our relationship to the next level.

He takes me by the hand and stands me up from the edge of the bed. His hands reach for the hem of my tank and he slowly drags it over my head. The moment it hits the floor, his mouth is on my nipple. Sucking, kissing, biting and then flattening his tongue to lick away the sting of his bite.

Those same lips that were just wreaking havoc on my breasts are now on my lips as his fingers slide under my waistband and slowly push my pants down and over my hips. He stops his steady assault on my lips and pulls back to help me step out of my pajama bottoms.

"Damn, Alex. Look at you. You're fucking perfect. I need to make you see that we were meant to be together."

I'm still mute, but inside I agree with him. We were made to be together.

He lays me down on my pillows and sits on his knees in front of me. He grabs my legs and pulls me closer to him. He stares at me as I lay vulnerable in front of him. I couldn't hide from him right now if I wanted to. But I don't want to. I want him to see all of me.

He leans forward and kisses my nose, my forehead, my chin, each cheek and while his fingers work their magic on my core, he whispers in my ear. "I want you to feel as cherished as you are, Alex. Because I cherish you, and you are mine. I need to make you realize that... you... are... mine." On this last statement, his fingers enter me and I gasp in ecstasy.

"You ready for me, Alex? Ready to take this to the next level, sweet thing?" He removes his fingers and positions himself at my core. I can feel him start to enter me and I hold my breath, anticipating the feel of him finally deep inside me again.

Beep... beep... beep

What the hell?

My alarm screams to life, and with that, the sad realization that I'm alone in my bed and not about to climb to new heights with the man of my dreams comes crashing down around me like a wet blanket.

A cold, heavy, wet blanket.

This isn't the first dream I've had since our kiss in the parking garage, but it is the furthest we've gone in one of them.

It's official.

I hate hunting season.

Mick has been gone for five days and I feel a little lost.

I'm not sure how it happened, but Mickey Jacobs is not only my wet dream, but he has become my best friend.

I miss our conversations.

I miss his stupid jokes.

I miss the way he sounds when he calls me, *sweet thing* on the phone.

I miss *him*.

After our conversation in the parking lot, and our amazing night at Portland City Grill, things with Mickey have been easy. Natural. We text all day, and on his nights off we talk each night before I go to bed. We don't text or talk about anything exciting, but he's always there. We meet for coffee often and we've met for happy hour again. Turns out he likes my little game of creating fictional lives for total strangers. He's actually gotten really good at it. Better than me, if I'm honest.

Most importantly... he continues to make me laugh. Every day.

Mick has always been that guy in the room that gets all the attention. But when it's just the two of us, he's different. He doesn't have to try hard to make me laugh, he just does. There's no false pretense or putting on a show. The real Mick, the Mick that I talk to all day every day, is easy going, funny and sweet.

I know it's killing him to be gone while Emily has this crazy person leaving her notes at work. He loves all three of the women in his family with all of his heart, and it melts mine just to hear him talk about them. Little does he know that while he's been gone, the threats have only gotten worse. He also doesn't know that the love of Emily's life is currently staying in his house with his little sister. I would not want to be Emily when he comes back Saturday. She's going to have to tell him about the new threats and the latest between her and Jonathan. Mickey is going to lose his shit!

I know that I'll always wish that there was more between Mickey and I—my dream is proof positive of that—but it's not worth it. I would have loved to have crossed the line from friendship to more in that parking garage, but what we have right now is just what I need. I would rather have him in my life than not. Mick would be a horrible boyfriend, but he's a really great BFF.

I, however, am a horrible friend.

Emily and Cami have no idea that Mick and I have forged this new friendship. I've always used my friendship with Emily as the main obstacle to having more than one night with Mickey. The truth is, there is nobody kinder than Emily Jacobs. There is nobody who wants my happiness more than Emily. She wouldn't be mad at me if I got involved with her brother. She would, however, be concerned that my heart would be broken into a million little pieces. Emily, Cami and I have been joking about Mickey's love life for years. I would be a fool to get involved with him, and she knows it.

I know it sounds contradictory since I've been telling Emily to give Jonathan a chance and to take him out of the friend zone—and I am so glad that she listened to me. But things with Mickey are different. We've known each other forever, and he isn't like Jonathan. He doesn't do relationships. He can't be faithful and doesn't want to be. This is why my friend zone with Mick is different from the one Emily had Jonathan in. Much different.

To ensure that things stay in the friend zone, and to make sure that I keep my distance, I'm setting my co-worker Amber up with Mick at the wedding this weekend. She's a girl who's just looking for some fun, and, well, Mickey is perfect for her. I haven't told Mick yet, but Amber is more than excited to meet him. It's going to kill me to introduce them, but they are a perfect fit.

I must be some sort of masochist to do this to myself, but it needs to be done.

Chapter 7

Mick

I t's been a kick ass day.

The wedding went great and Wesley and Tricia couldn't be happier. Tricia is a beautiful bride and Wesley is a lucky man. I never thought that one of my friends getting attached to the old ball and chain would be a lucky thing, but lately my view has evolved.

It's not just because I'm happy to see my friends happy. I think having Alex as a constant in my life, and a part of every one of my days, is showing me how nice it can be to have that special person in your life. I had a great time hunting with the guys, but I couldn't wait to get back this morning. I missed talking to her every day and I couldn't help but wonder what she was doing with her time while I was gone. Getting to see her again has been another part of the day that has been kick ass. Well, it had been.

I knew I was going to see her tonight at the reception and I couldn't wait. To say it took me by surprise that as soon as I saw her she gave me a hug and then told me how excited she was to introduce me to her friend, Amber, would be an understatement. I know it shouldn't—because we aren't together—but it felt like she had just sucker punched me. I was excited to see her, and she was excited to set me up with somebody. I guess she didn't miss me as much as I missed her. And, well... that fucking sucks.

Nope, she didn't seem to miss me at all. She took me by the hand and walked me over to Amber, who was helping set up the buffet. The moment she laid her bloodthirsty eyes on me she seemed to follow me around like a freaking puppy. She was cute enough. Short, blonde hair and a banging body, but I couldn't have been less interested. And Alex, well, she was gone the moment she introduced us. She couldn't leave us alone fast enough. I don't think I could feel any shittier.

For the moment, I've managed to shake the Amber chick and am sharing a drink with my fellow groomsman when I look out on the dance floor. The moment my eyes land on my baby sister, I can feel myself turning red. Red with uncontrollable rage.

What. The. Fuck.

Why is my sister grinding all over Jonathan Kelly? Did I miss something? Since when does Emily bump and grind? In front of a crowd, no less? Kelly really should remove his fucking hands from my sister's fucking body if he wants to live to see another fucking day.

I left him to watch over her, and it seems he's taking that job pretty damn seriously.

Is this really fucking happening?

Does he not realize that I'm going to fucking kill him? Right here. Right now.

The God-forsaken song they are getting nasty to finally ends. I turn to bitch to Martinez and he's not there. I didn't even notice that everybody had left my table, and I'm standing here alone with my arms crossed over my chest seething. I see the moment Emily catches my eye and realizes that I just caught the show she and Kelly put on for the entire place to see. She's hauling ass over to me because she knows she has some damage control to do.

By the time she's standing in front of my table, worrying her necklace like she does, looking nervous as hell, I can't wait to bust her balls. I'll deal with Kelly later.

"So, Emmers... is there something you want to tell me?" I can hear the venom spewing from my grinding teeth, but I can't help it. I cannot fucking believe Kelly and my little sister were practically having sex on the dance floor.

"Mick, we were just dancing. Not sure what you mean?"

Let the lying commence. This is un-fucking-believable.

"I'm not stupid, Em, and if that was a just a dance... in public... at a wedding... then I am going to kill Kelly right here and now! But I think there was more to it than that. Are you guys together, Em?" Just as I finish asking the question, Kelly reaches us and is standing right behind Emily.

"What? No Mick! You know I don't do relationships. He's just some fun for now. He's a really nice guy and I deserve some fun, don't I?"

I look over her head and see the genuine hurt that crosses Kelly's face and realize this whole thing is a much bigger deal than I could have ever imagined. "Fuck this," Jonathan says as he turns and takes off out of the grand ballroom. Emily's face falls. There is clearly much more going on here than just a dirty dance at a wedding.

"I think somebody else may have had a different answer

to my question, Emmers." I can't help but feel kinda bad for her. But what the hell is going on here?

Emily turns and runs after him. Clearly, big brother is being left in the dark. Since when do Emily and Kelly have a thing so serious that he would be this upset and she would run after him? I was only gone a week, right?

Emily runs *out* the door just as Alex walks *in*. Bam! She is a fucking sight. I was so upset that she wanted to hook me up with her friend that I didn't even notice how great she looked tonight. She always looks great, but shit, she is killing it in a green dress that seems to wrap and gather at one side. It clings to her body and shows everything she has to offer without being slutty. She looks totally professional, yet sexy all at once. God, this woman is killing me. Her legs... her legs in those heels are simply... perfection.

I don't even realize that I'm staring until she's standing right in front of me.

"Mick, what's going on? Why did Emily just run out of here crying?" She asks breaking the spell I was under while I watched her cross the room.

"To be honest, Alex, I have no idea. Em and Jonathan were just out on the dance floor bumping and grinding and putting on a show for the whole place. As if that weren't enough when I asked her what was going on, she lied and said she was just having some fun. But the way he stormed out of here after hearing her say that leads me to believe there's more to the story."

I can tell by the look on her face that there most certainly is more to the story, and Alex knows all about it.

"You have got to be kidding me! You know? How have

you known this and not told me? I tell you everything, Alex. How could you keep something about my sister from me?"

She puts her hand on my arm to calm me, and as much as I want to push her off of me, I don't. She does calm me. Just being in her presence calms me, but when she touches me, all my anxiety seems to melt away and something different takes hold. I'm not sure exactly what it is, but it's different and fierce and it takes a hold of me. All of me.

"Mick, it's not my story to tell. There's a history there and I *do* know all about it, but it's not my place to tell you." As she talks, her hand slides down my arm and she takes my hand in hers. "You and I *are* friends and we share things, but it doesn't mean I can break your sister's confidence. I know you're upset right now. I also know you love Emily enough to realize her happiness is what's important."

I don't know how she does it, but I'm no longer seething. I'm more pissed that other people seem to know what's going on and I don't!

"Am I that much of an ass that she couldn't tell me about him?"

"No, but you are her big brother. You also think that nobody will ever be good enough for her, especially a cop. Not just any cop, but a cop that works in your department and that you call friend." I hate that she's making sense. "You also have been known to get into a fight or two in your day, Mick. Why would she want to put him in that position?" What is it about this woman? I was good and pissed and she has just sucked all the fun out of my current mood. I was ready to brawl, and now all that pent-up aggression is fading away.

"I guess you're right. But why does she have to date a

friend? A friend who's a cop on top of that? She knows what this life can be like, Alex." Saying what is really at the crux of the matter, I realize it's this life and what it can do to a person. I don't want Emily to have any more stress and worry than she already has. The life of a police officer can be scary at times, and I want so much more for her and Ireland. If he weren't a cop—and my friend—Kelly is exactly the kind of guy I would want Emily to be with.

"He's a great guy, Mick. You need to let her tell you her story and maybe you'll feel differently."

Her phone pings, letting her know she has an incoming text.

"Shoot, sorry Mick, but I have to go deal with the DJ. Listen, it's all gonna be okay and I think when you hear her story you might feel differently about all this." She lets go of my hand and dashes out the door. About ten steps away, she looks over her shoulder and says, "Text or call me tomorrow and let me know how things go with Amber."

And just like that, she deals me another blow.

I have no interest in this Amber chick. Come to think of it... I haven't had an interest in anybody in weeks. The only woman I think about is the one in the green dress currently walking away from me. The view is fan-fucking-tastic, but I feel an instant loneliness when she leaves. I'm really not sure how much more of this I can take.

How did this night go from great to miserable?

I feel so far removed from my own life and those I care about. I would never set Alex up with somebody else. How does that seem okay to her? Does that mean that she wouldn't mind if I was going out and hooking up with randoms like I used to? My ass hits the nearest chair, and I rub my hands over my face, trying to shake my disbelief. I just don't get how we could feel so differently about each other. I mean, I know we aren't 'together' but there is still something there. Isn't there?

My situation with Alex is at least something that is somewhat familiar to me. I have always felt as though I was floundering when it comes to this woman. But not my little sister! Emily and I have always been close. How is it I have no idea that she has a thing with my co-worker? A thing that apparently goes back further than this past week. What the hell? What's next? Is my mom going to tell me she ran off and eloped with somebody I've never met? I mean seriously, what is going on with the women in my life?

The reception is winding down, and Wesley and Tricia are preparing to leave. Just as we're all about to gather by the ballroom doors to send them off with bubbles as they make their way out of the hotel, Emily walks back in. She looks lost. I leave the line of guests to help her find her way. Right now, that way is to me, her big brother. I'm tired of being out of the loop and I need to get to the bottom of all of this. When I reach her she looks up at me while her blue eyes sparkle with tears.

"Come here, Emmers." I can tell that she's worried that I'm still upset, but how can I be? She's my baby sister and she's clearly in pain. I take her into my arms, rub her back and tell her it's going to be okay. Because my sister is one tough cookie, she inhales a deep breath and blows out a shaky one. She wipes her face and stands tall. I keep my arm around her shoulders and we join the other guests to watch the bride and groom leave.

After we cheer on the happy couple and watch everybody blow bubbles in their direction, I keep my arm around Emily and guide her back to her table. There we find Cami and Emily's purse.

"Hey Cam, I'm gonna give you and Emily a lift home."

I can see the confusion cross Cami's face. She didn't see what went down with Emily and Jonathan, but as soon as Emily looks at her friend, her eyes start to well with more tears.

"Oh, chica. What happened?"

"Cami, I messed it all up again. I don't want to talk about it here, though. I just want to go home." Emily turns her gaze to me and pleads with me. "Can we please leave?"

"Of course. Cami, you ready?"

Cami walks over to my heartbroken little sister and links arms with her. "Let's get our girl home, Mick."

I let the girls walk at their own pace and I walk ahead of them so that they can talk. I have the truck ready and waiting for them when they get there.

"Mick, your truck is dumb!" Cami says as she struggles to climb into the cab of my lifted 2500 in her dress and heels.

"Hey, didn't your mother teach you that if you didn't have anything nice to say, you shouldn't say anything at all? Besides, I'm not a short stack like you and I have no problem getting into my truck. Here, let me give you a boost."

"Mickey Jacobs, if you cop a feel helping me into this god-forsaken truck, you will be sorry."

"Only in your wildest dreams, Cameron Holsted." I say as I grab her by the waist to lift her into the back of the cab. Before she can sit down, I can't help myself and I give her a little slap on her ass.

"Mickey! Damn you! Keep your hands to yourself!"

I chuckle as I hop into the driver's seat. That is until I look at Emily in the passenger seat, back to looking lost. She looks like the love of her life has just left her, and I cannot for the life of me figure out how she can look like she does. I was only gone a week. I reach over and tug on one of her long curls, but she doesn't even turn to look at me.

I catch Cami's eye in the rearview mirror, and she just shakes her head back and forth.

The drive to Cami's is a quiet one. Once we get to her place, I help her out and shut the door. "Cami, what is going on with Emmers and Jonathan?"

"Mick, you need to let her tell you. She told me what happened tonight and she feels horrible. She's ready to tell you. You just have to give her a minute to breathe. Just continue being that amazing brother you are and support her, Mick. Remember that her happiness is what's important. She deserves to be happy more than any of us."

"I agree, Cam. I promise to hear her out and I won't push. I've just never seen her look so lost."

"I have. She'll get through this and they'll figure it out. You may not realize how important your role in her life is, though, Mick. What you think means the world to her, so please be cool." She beckons me with her finger and I bend down to get closer to her level. She places a kiss on my cheek and says, "Take good care of our girl. She needs you tonight."

I wait until Cami's inside and then I jump back into the truck. "Emmers, you wanna talk about it?"

That was all it took. I hadn't even started the engine yet. Once she started her story that started just over five years ago in San Clemente, she didn't stop. I'm turned in my seat, staring at my sister in disbelief. Disbelief that my friend and co-worker turns out to be the love of her life and that she met him years ago. Hearing that she met him the week after she found out she was pregnant with my niece and that she was too afraid to tell him or try to be with him after that week; my heart breaks for her, and quite frankly for him too. To hear how badly our father's treatment of our mother has affected her isn't a surprise to me, but I am a little stunned that it could stop her from being in a relationship with somebody that meant so much to her.

To know what was happening at Kells that night while I was preoccupied with Alex blows my mind. So much was happening right under my nose and I missed it all. When she tells me, she finally told Jonathan about Ireland and that he still wanted to try and to get to know her, but she let Courtney and her own insecurities get in the way. I'm suddenly frustrated. I keep my mouth shut and let her carry on with her story.

To find out that in a way it's because of me that Jonathan ended up spending the week with Emmers, and that this gave them another shot at getting to know each other, makes me want to give my sister one of her famous high fives. At the same time, knowing her fear that I wouldn't approve or that I would want to kick Jonathan's ass is what caused her current state of heartbreak makes me feel like a dick.

She assures me it's not my fault, and that it's really more about her fear of relationships and her own insecurities, yet I know that a small piece of this is because she was worried about my reaction. She finishes her story by telling me about their one-sided fight in the parking garage and how hurt and betrayed Jonathan felt. I have to say; I get it. He has really put himself out there, is willing to give her a chance at something real, and knows that Ireland is part of the package. I don't say it out loud, but I am leaning towards Team Kelly right about now.

On a heavy puff of air, my heartbroken sister, who has been staring out the windshield, turns to face me. She's waiting for me to react, but I only have one question.

"Do you love him? Right now, sitting in this truck, after hearing the things he said to you tonight, before he took off. After everything, do you love him?"

"He's the love of my life, Mick."

That's all I need to hear. "Well, then, what are you going to do to make this right?"

"You're okay with this?"

"It'll take some time to get used to, but he's a good man, Em. I knew he had been through a lot, but now knowing that he lost you along with everything else... I don't know how he's kept it together. I know what it's like to have you in my life, and I can't imagine if you just disappeared on me. Jonathan's willing to give you a chance. He's ready to take on a single mom and her daughter. I love you, little sister, but I get why he's so pissed. You need to give him some time to cool off, but I know he'll come around."

"You think so?"

"Of course he will. You and Ireland are hard to resist. He would be crazy to walk away from the two of you. You need to tell him how you feel, though. Stop being afraid to share yourself with him. You both deserve to be happy. Stop getting in your own way."

"Wow." She seems shocked by my reaction. "Thanks for being so supportive, Mick. It really means a lot."

I start the engine and set us toward home. All this talk of

finding the love of your life has my mind spinning. Of course, Alex is all that I can think of. I've never thought of what I feel for her as the L-word, but I know I feel strongly for her. I know that tonight, when she tried to set me up with that Amber chick, it hurt. It hurt badly. I can't imagine how bad it would hurt to be in the situation that Emily and Jonathan are in.

To think that my dad had love like this and threw it all away is truly mind-boggling. I'm so pissed at him right now. I wish he knew what he's done to Emily. Not that he would care. All he cares about is himself.

I'm starting to think that all of my dad's talk about men not being made for monogamy is a bunch of bullshit. I always looked up to him, but the older I get, the more I realize he really messed up, and what he's done to our family is unforgivable. Yet, I forgave him. I feel like such an idiot.

Out of the corner of my eye, I can see Emily watching her phone. She must have texted him and he's not replying. I have a feeling it's going to be a long night.

Chapter 8

Alex

Setting Mick up with Amber and acting like I thought it was the best idea in the world was enough to make me want to throw up. Telling him to call me and let me know how it went with Amber nearly gutted me. I just had to keep walking without looking back. The tears that were pooling in my eyes weren't for him to see, and they weren't for me to shed. I gathered myself as I approached the DJ booth and did what I always do. Put on my mask and act like my life was perfect.

What was I thinking? Did I really think setting him up with somebody was the smart thing to do? What the hell is wrong with me?

He was right at the reception when he said that we tell each other everything... because we do. I realize now that I don't remember him going on any dates or mentioning any girls. That's odd and something that didn't cross my mind until after I made my faux pas and set him up with Amber. Why would I give him something like a night with Amber to add to our daily conversations? I have been in love with this man my entire life and have had to hear about his exploits for years now. Why would I want to help add a notch to his bedpost? What the hell was I thinking?

I haven't had a chance to talk to Mick at length since the wedding. I have no idea if he and Amber hit it off. After the wedding, Mick took Cami home and then Emily told him her truth about Jonathan. He now knows everything,

But not telling him the truth backfired. Jonathan heard her lie, which led to a fight, and he wasn't speaking to her. Jonathan had finally agreed to talk to Emily when there was an incident at work and he was shot. Jonathan survived and is healing. Unfortunately, another officer didn't make it.

Now poor Mick is busy consoling his sister and worrying about his brother-in-arms. I saw him at the hospital the night of the shooting, and he was devastated. Emily was in Jonathan's room and I found Mick pacing the floor as he and what seemed to be the entire police department waited in the waiting room. When he saw me, he grabbed hold of me and didn't let go. Feeling him tremble in my arms trying to keep it together was difficult, to say the least. I didn't know what to say or do. All I could do was hold him and just be there. I can only hope it was enough.

I never thought that I would be glad to hear that some-body was dead, but hearing the news that the assailant had been shot and killed in a standoff when the other officers arrived, I was so relieved.

Bob, the officer that was killed, was actually the training officer that was with Mick the night my dad had his stroke. I didn't know him well, but he was kind that night and Mick is heartbroken. He was a mentor to him and now he's gone. He hates he wasn't on duty that night. I tried to tell him that even if he had been there, things may not have been any different, though I don't think he could hear that in that moment. I could tell he was trying to stay strong for his sister and for Jonathan. He genuinely is a good man, and he puts so much focus on taking care of everybody else that I can tell he's not going to take the time he needs to grieve for Bob himself. He'll take care of everybody else instead. That's what Mickey Jacobs does.

With all of this going on, the timing really hasn't been right to ask him if he liked Amber. It shouldn't even be on my mind... but I can't help it. We still check in with each other every day, and I've been over to see Emily, but we haven't had a chance to actually talk.

To make things worse, Amber has been on vacation all week and I can't ask her how it went, either. I'm making myself crazy, wondering if they're going to see each other again. I'm also starting to feel this overwhelming cloud of depression that follows me everywhere I go. After going a week without communication, while he was hunting, and now with the shooting, I haven't really been able to talk to him or see him. Our texts are just check-ins and he hasn't been around when I've gone to see Emily.

I miss him.

Not having any communication with him that isn't a text about Jonathan and Emily or the funeral arrangements has been hard. I know I should be grateful that during this stressful time he's still thinking of me enough to text me with updates, but my insecurities and depressed state have crept in enough that it's messed with my headspace and my frame of mind isn't what it should be.

This is why, when Kevin walks into my office, my guard is down and I agree to happy hour with him and several other co-workers.

The next day, he takes me to lunch.

Then it's dinner with co-workers and him giving me a ride home. The walk to the front door comes with a kiss on the cheek.

How in the world did this happen?

Before I know it, it's Thursday night, and Kevin is knocking on my door with a bottle of wine in his hand and a sweet smile on his face. With my messed-up headspace and my current down-and-out state, I let him in. I know I shouldn't, but I do. Part of it is the depression and part of it is fear. I just don't want to deal with a scene and he scares me just enough to not push his buttons.

"So, Alexandra, are you seeing anybody?" He asks as he pushes my hair behind my ear.

"Nothing serious, Kevin. How about you?" I ask him, but I really don't care. It's my lame attempt at trying to keep the peace during his unexpected visit.

"Nope, just like you, nothing serious."

He's pushing himself towards me, and as he does, I step backwards. I'm trying to keep my distance, but my back is against the wall after just three quick steps.

His hand snakes up my body, to my neck, and then to my face. He gently caresses my face and says, "I've missed you, Alexandra."

The chills that run down my spine are not ones of lust or passion. His touch. His words. They bring nothing but fear and disgust to the forefront of my mind. I'm unsure of what to say or do, but I know I have to get out of this situation.

He gently kisses me on the lips and says, "Have some wine with me?" He bends down and kisses me on the neck, and I think I might be sick.

"I was going to call it an early night. I have to get up for an early morning meeting and I should really get some sleep. It was nice of you to stop by, though." I manage to squeak out.

I try to pull away from him as he presses his body flat against mine so there is no space between us. I'm stuck against the wall, and my mind is racing, trying to figure out how I'm going to get out of this situation.

"Oh, come on, Alex. I have to go home tomorrow, let's just have one night to remember the good old days."

Without waiting for me to reply, he shoves his tongue down my throat. Then he takes my left arm and raises it above my head and holds it there by my wrist.

He finally rips his mouth from mine, then whispers in my ear, "You still taste good. God, I've missed you."

"Kevin, I really do have an early morning."

"Well, let's get you ready for bed, then. Shall we?" He asks—but he doesn't want me to actually answer him—as he takes me by the wrist and lowers my arm from the spot where it was pressed against the wall. I try to pull it out of his grip but he just grips tighter. I pull harder, with no luck.

Trying to sound strong and not as panicked as I say, "Kevin, no. Please, I really need to get some sleep." It makes no difference and he ignores my plea.

Trying again to escape his grip, I pull so hard that I lose my balance and slip to the ground with him standing above me, still holding me by the wrist with my arm in the air above my head.

"Ah, ah, ah, Alexandra. Please don't be difficult." He says as he drags me down the hallway and to my bedroom.

I don't know why I don't try harder to pull away from him after this, but when I hear the venom in his voice, I shut down.

I do what I did in my childhood and block out what happens next. The only difference between then and now is that this time I'm not listening to my parents in the other room. This time it's happening to me. This is one of the only times in my life that I appreciate this skill of mine. The skill of blocking out the unpleasantness of life. Escaping into nothingness. Shutting out all of the things that are too hard to deal with in the moment.

I feel like I'm having an out-of-body experience and watching what's happening to me from afar. I feel everything, but not all the way on the surface. I've shut it all off enough... enough that it's like I'm a spectator and not a present participant.

I'm not present when he lets go of my wrist and drags me by my hair, or when he lifts me roughly and pushes me to the bed. I'm also not present when he pushes my skirt to my waist, pulls my panties so hard that they cut into my skin and rip to shreds. I don't make a sound when he pushes inside me, not caring that I'm not ready. I barely notice that when I try to turn my face to the side to avoid his stare, that he fiercely grabs my face and turns it back to him. It hurts, but I don't really feel it. Just like I don't really hear him say, "Look at me while I fuck you, bitch."

Luckily for me, in just a matter of minutes, he completes

his task, gets up, dresses himself and says, "Thanks for the walk down memory lane, Alexandra. I'll see you next week."

And just like that, he saunters out of my room, back down the hall and out my front door.

I force myself out of my bed and slowly drag myself to the front door. I lift my hand in slow motion and lock it. I don't feel the metal of the deadbolt in my hand, though. I don't feel anything. Something in me registers that I should check the peephole to make sure he's gone and thank God above he is. I turn so that my back is against the door as my body numbly slides down the door until my butt hits the floor. It's then that I realize that I am still dressed. He simply lifted my skirt, ripped off my underwear, and found his release.

I sit on the floor, but I don't cry.

I don't panic.

I do nothing.

I just sit on the floor of my entryway. Numb.

Why did I just let that happen?

Why didn't I fight back?

What the hell is wrong with me?

I need to get to a meeting. I know it will be hard to admit my situation, but group meetings are a safe place. I haven't been in a long time and I know now is the time.

The one thing I do feel right now is shame. I am filled with so much shame.

Thank God he's going home for a couple of days and I'll have at least two days to myself to figure this out. This won't happen again. I have to make that clear to him. I need to make him see that I am not interested in a relationship with him.

I lift my sore body off the floor. The top of my head is

stinging from where he grabbed me and pulled me down the hall. I'm walking gingerly as the pain from where he entered me when I wasn't ready is starting to burn. Feeling the damage he's done to my body brings me back to the present. And now I'm feeling too much.

I feel weak. Full of shame, disgust, fear, and guilt. I'm confused and I feel hollow.

I manage to make it to my bathroom just in time, unable to stop the convulsive vomiting that follows as all of my feelings take over. I may be present again, but I am not in control of much of anything.

How have I let myself become a spectator in my own life?

* * *

"Alex, he's here. I just saw him down the hall with Pam and it looked like they were headed this way." Olivia warns me as she walks back into the office we share with Amber.

I didn't tell her everything that happened, but she knows I plan on ending things today.

Again.

"Thanks for the heads up," I say as I get up and grab the manila folder on my desk. I can't get out of here fast enough and decide that I'll head out to the consultation I have starting in 20 minutes. I don't need to leave just yet, but I'm not ready to see him. I'm a person who avoids confrontation at all costs. Especially at work. It feels like the safest place to have an unpleasant conversation with a man like him, but it still isn't something that I'm looking forward to.

Just as I cross the threshold of the office door, I have to

jump back as he steps into my space. As always, just a little too close for comfort.

"Where are you off to, Alexandra?"

"Hi, Kevin. Just heading out for a consultation that I have in a few minutes," I say, hoping he doesn't hear the panic in my voice.

"Do you have time to chat for a minute or two before your appointment?" He asks, but I can tell it's not really a question. It's an order. Even though I already know the time, I still look at my phone like I'm checking—I'm doing anything at this point to stall long enough to avoid alone time with him.

"Um, sure... but only a few minutes. I don't want to be late," I answer, trying my best to emphasize I have work to do, but I might as well get this over with.

He pokes his head into the office and gives his hello to Olivia. Then he puts his hand on my lower back and walks me down the hall and into the mail room. The mail room that, much to my dismay, is currently empty. I really don't want to be alone when I tell him Thursday night can't happen again, but at least we're at work. He is our HR manager. He won't cause a scene, will he?

As we walk further into the room, he turns me so that my backside is against the counter. His hands are on my hips while his fingertips press into me. "Thursday night was great, baby. When can I see you again?"

The nausea begins to build.

I'm looking at the ground when I say, "Kevin, I don't think we should continue seeing each other outside of the office."

One of his hands leaves my hip and grabs my face, a little

too hard—just like the other night—and he brings my attention off the ground to his threatening eyes.

"Now why is that, Alexandra?"

"I just need to focus on my work and I don't want anybody to think that I'm getting preferential treatment because I'm dating somebody in management. Corporate management at that," I say, just like I had rehearsed in my head all day long.

"Oh love, you don't need to worry about those sorts of things. I'm kind of in charge of Human Resources, and I don't think you have to worry about any of that."

"But my reputation and my work are really important to me, Kevin,"

Now his hand holding my face is squeezing even harder as he growls, "Alexandra, you don't get to brush me off again. I let you do that once before, but it's not happening again."

Not letting the fear get to me, I jerk my face out of his grip and stand my ground. "I really don't think it's a good idea, Kevin. It was good to see you again, but now really isn't a good time for me."

"You really are cute, you know that?" He says as he looks at the door to make sure that we're still alone. Once he sees the coast is clear, he grabs my hair and pulls it so hard that I let out a surprised squeal and tears form in my eyes. Not from emotion or fear, but from the stinging sensation I'm feeling on my scalp. "I don't recall asking you if it was a good time for you. I did ask you when I could see you again, and I expect an answer."

When I don't reply, he pulls even harder. "Don't make me ask again, Alexandra. You want to keep your job, don't you?"

Trying to appease him and get out of the room, I say, "How about lunch tomorrow?"

"That's a good girl," he says, releasing my hair from his grip. "It's not the correct answer, but since I have plans to drink and hit the strip clubs with the rest of senior management, I can't see you tonight anyway."

There are voices in the hallway, so he steps back. I quickly brush my hands through my hair and over my clothes and stand up straight while I try to gain control of my nerves.

Just as my manager, Pam, enters the room I say, "Okay, well, I'm off to my consultation with the Pattersons. I'll see you tomorrow. Have a nice night."

"Yes. See you tomorrow, Alexandra," he says, but I don't look back to acknowledge him.

I rush down the hall and to the bathroom.

How did I let this happen? How did I get myself into this situation? How did he go from overbearing and a bit rough to this?

I check my phone for the time and find that I have less than five minutes to gather myself and get to the hotel lobby for my appointment. I'm doing my best to push aside the fact that my boss essentially raped me last week and that he's now threatening me. He basically just told me that if I don't let him do it again, I'll lose my job. I have this undeniable urge to vomit, but I don't have time for that. Instead, I stand in the bathroom stall leaning against the closed door and do what I do best.

Compartmentalize.

Block it out.

Put myself back together again.

Stop my body from shaking.

Present to the world the version of me I want them to see.

I always told myself I would never let a man treat me this way.

I would never be this weak, and yet here I am.

I clearly am my mother's child.

Chapter 9

Mick

"**W**hat the fuck?" Sitting in the cab of my truck in my driveway... this is the only response I have to the words in front of me.

SWEET THING

> Mick, I don't think it's a good idea for us to communicate anymore. I'm seeing Kevin again, and out of respect for him, I won't be texting or calling you.

Why would she ever go back to that douchebag? I saw how he was with her, and I don't trust him not to hurt her. None of this makes sense. I don't understand what could make her go back to him. I've had so much going on with losing Bob, Jonathan getting shot, Emily's broken heart while Jonathan recovered and then the break in. I know I haven't had much time to see or even talk to Alex, but I still don't understand how she could go back to somebody who treats her so poorly.

> Sexy Beast

> WTF?! What do you mean you're back with that asshole?

SWEET THING

You wouldn't understand.

SEXY BEAST

> Try me!

SWEET THING:

Mick, it doesn't even matter. He found our texts and he got pissed and asked me to stop talking to you.

SEXY BEAST:

> Why him, Alex? Why can't you go out with somebody else? Not him!

Why would she want to be with some tool that manhandles her in public? This is not the Alex that I know.

SWEET THING

I don't love him or anything, Mick. I just don't want to be alone right now and at least my heart is safe when I'm with him.

Her last message nearly stops *my* heart. What does she mean by that? Is she referring to me? Is she saying that she would be with me but that her heart wouldn't be safe? If she is, she's probably right. I don't know how to date one person or how to be in a relationship. That doesn't mean that she needs to go back to her asshat of an ex.

SEXY BEAST

If he lays a hand on you, I expect you to call me. You call me day or night and I'm there, Alex.

SWEET THING

Thank you. Bye, Mick.

And just like that, she's gone.

My friend.

My *more*.

I've always known it, but today, I'm certain. She's my more. She's the one that I should try with. The one that I should give up all the others for, but she doesn't feel the same way. She would rather be with cufflink wearing, uptight, manhandling douchebag, Kevin.

Fuck this! I need to go out and get drunk. Riley's working tonight, so I'll start at Kells and see where the night takes me.

* * *

I know the minute I walk into Kells that I'm not in the mood for a night out. But I'm here. I'll just sit at the bar and keep Riley company. It's a weeknight, so it's not too busy.

"What are you doin' here, Mick?" Riley asks.

I take my seat at the bar. "Just need a lot of alcohol and to get laid," I say matter-of-factly.

Riley throws his white bar towel over his shoulder, crosses his arms in front of him and just stares at me. Looking me in the eye without blinking.

"I know I'm pretty, Ry, but you're really not my type. I mean, I like 5' 10" brunettes, but beards aren't really my thing." I say, trying to deflect the fact that he knows something's wrong and is looking for an explanation.

"Did something happen with Alex?"

How the fuck does he do that? I can't hide shit from him.

"What does Alex have to do with anything, Riley?" I snap back at him.

He steps away to help a customer and, after serving up two whiskeys and opening a tab; he heads back my way and slides me a *Kells Lager*, my favorite Irish beer, and carries on like our conversation had never stopped. "I don't know, Mick, let's see... you guys are playing this 'friend' game, but I don't remember the last time you hooked up with anybody. You guys text all day every day and now here you are acting like you want to get drunk and get laid. Two things are wrong with this equation. One... you aren't a big drinker. You have always said you don't want to be like your dad and for me to put the brakes on if you ever seem like you're imbibing too much. Here you are, wanting to do just that. Two... since when does Mickey Jacobs have to announce he wants to get laid?"

"I think you're looking a little too deep into things, my friend. It's just been a rough day."

I drink down half of my pint, set my glass back down and look anywhere except at Riley. Thank fuck he has to walk away to help some more customers. These new patrons happen to be two hot blonds. Their skirts are a little too short and their shirts are a little too low cut for their own good. I think the second part of my equation is going to be easier than I thought.

I watch as the girls pay for their drinks and head back to their table against the wall on the opposite side of the bar.

"So, what happened?"

Slowly turning my head to Riley, who has returned from his bartending duties, I say, "Don't be a dick."

"Mick, since when can't you talk to me? I know how you feel about the girl. I've watched you, watching her, for years. You finally have her in your life, but you're *just friends*. I don't understand this little game you're playing with her. Why are you doing the friends thing? This doesn't seem to be your usual style, dude."

He really does know me better than anybody. He knows my stance on dating. Shit, he knows everything there is to know about my life. We've been best friends since first grade. The problem is, I haven't even admitted to myself what this is really all about. Today, for the first time, it really hits me.

"I want more than friendship, Riley, but you know that. You just love to torture me and want to hear me say that shit myself."

"So, what's the problem?" He asks with his arms crossed in front of his chest yet again. He's standing there like I'm in trouble and he's my dad, just waiting to dole out my punishment. Dick.

"Leave it alone, Ry."

He continues standing there, but doesn't say a word. I know how damn stubborn he can be, and he will stand there all night if I don't start talking. Why the hell am I friends with him again?

"Jesus Ry, just get me another beer and stop with the third degree." On that note, he picks up a glass and fills it with another beer. I didn't even notice that the taps were right in front of me and he didn't have to walk away to get me my beer.

Shit!

"Anything else I can get for you? We don't sell panties here, but I can recommend a nice place down the road that may just have your size. I think it's called *Pussies 'R Us*."

"Fuck you, Ry. I really don't need your shit tonight." Rubbing my hand over my face, I let out a big sigh and finally blurt out why I'm so miserable. "Alex said she's seeing that douchebag, Kevin, again. She said she has to stop talking to me out of respect for him or some shit like that."

I can see his genuine concern for her cross his face. I had told him about Kevin manhandling her, and his protective side has kicked into gear just like mine did. He's known her as long as I have, and my feelings for her aside. Neither of us would let anything happen to Alex if we have anything to do with it.

"Shit, Mick. What is she thinking? He sounds like a real piece of work," Riley says, with both hands on the bar in front of me.

"She said I wouldn't understand and that she doesn't want to be alone. She says she doesn't love him and knows she doesn't have to worry about getting her heart broken," I say, repeating back the gist of our text messages.

"I just don't get it. She's a smart girl. She's beautiful and sweet as hell; she could have any guy she wanted. Why this suit?"

In my head, I think back to the night that I pulled up to her house, and found her with a black eye and saw her bruised and battered mom. I can't help but wonder if it's the only pattern she knows? I also know what she means when she said that he wouldn't break her heart. She's implying that she can't have more with me because she knows I'll break her heart.

"Fuck, Riley. She's the one girl I've ever wanted more with. And I can't have her," I say as I look into my best friend's eyes and see the sympathy that he has for me. I hate it.

"Why is that, Mick? You had her for a night. Why can't you have more than that?" He asks.

"Emily, for one," I say, making my first and most obvious excuse.

"Mick, that is some bullshit right there and you know it!"

"How is that?"

"Hello, Dickhead! Emily of all people wouldn't hold you back. You haven't said a word about her and Jonathan. He's a cop and a co-worker of yours, and you let that shit go. You know that her happiness is more important than your caveman feelings, and you aren't getting in the way. Emily is a much better person than you, my friend. She loves you both and wants you both to be happy. Even if that meant you were happy together. Got any other lame ass excuses up your sleeve?"

One point for Riley.

"She doesn't think that I'm the relationship type. She thinks I'll break her heart and she's probably right, Ry. I've never been in a relationship or had to stay committed. I would have no idea what I was doing. She deserves better than fucking Kevin, but she also deserves better than me."

"I get it. She's watched you break hearts all of these years. I can understand why she'd be hesitant, but dude, it doesn't mean she's right."

"Ry, I did not break hearts. I never made any commit-

ments and I always made it clear I wasn't looking for a relationship. How could I break any hearts? Besides, you're just
like me. What's the difference between the way you behave
and the way I do?"

"Dude, just because a girl says she understands all your
little rules doesn't mean they didn't fall for that pretty boy
face of yours. You get them all *dickmatized* and then they'll
agree to anything you say. Trust me, you left plenty of girls
crying in their cereal the morning after, Mick. You just
weren't there to witness it. And the difference between you
and me? I have always known I didn't want this lifestyle to
last forever. I know the one is out there and I'll find her one
day. Until then..."

"I think you're wrong, and even if it's true, I promised
nothing to anybody." I reply, knowing that I sound indignant
and I'm ignoring his last comment about finding the one, but I
can't help it. I've always told myself there wasn't just one
person out there and because I made my intentions clear,
girls wouldn't get hurt when I didn't stick around.

"You may think I'm wrong, but you have broken plenty of
hearts. Just remember... payback's a dirty bitch Mick, and her
stripper name is Karma." He walks away and leaves me to
mull over his last statement about karma and to fill another
drink order. I sure do wish it was busier in here tonight, but
it's a Wednesday. It's steady, but not busy enough to avoid
Dr. Johannson and his therapy session and movie quotes.

A few minutes later, Riley is back with another lager that
he sets down in front of me.

"Last one, Mick. You don't need to get drunk, you need to
figure out how to get the girl."

"I don't want the girl, Ry."

"Mick, who do you think you're talking to?"

I know he's right, but fuck, I don't know what I'm doing. "She has a boyfriend."

"Bullshit. She told you she was just lonely and that she didn't love him. She's waiting for you to grow a pair and make a decision."

Feeling lost and knowing he's right, I look my best friend in the eyes, and see the concern projected from them. This isn't just about him trying to give me a hard time; he cares. "What the hell do I do, Ry?"

"Do you want more?" He asks, already knowing the answer.

I simply nod my reply.

"Well, then...Go. Get. Her. One thing you need to remember though... she's not just any girl. She's Alex. We all love her. If you do this... shit, Mick, if you do this you need to be sure. She's like a sister to me and if anybody hurts her, you know I will step in. All three of those girls are family to me, and I want them to be safe and happy. Do you think you can give that to her? Can you take care of her like she deserves to be?" he asks and again I just nod. "You hear me, brother?"

"I hear you," I say as he moves a few feet to my left and helps one of the blondes again.

I do hear him. Hearing him lay it out like that makes it even clearer that I really don't know what I'm doing, and that this is a bigger deal than I had even considered. Can I do this? Can I do more? My mind is now more of a mess than it was before I set my ass on this stool. I need to get out of here.

I am just getting ready to tell Riley to close out my tab, when one of the blondes walks over and introduces herself.

"Hi, I'm Jessica," she says, extending her hand to me.

"Mick, nice to meet you," I say as I take her hand in mine.

She sticks around for a few minutes and I try to make conversation with her, but it's painful. It's nothing like talking to Alex. With Alex, talking is one of the easiest things I've ever done. This... making small talk with a stranger... this is difficult. It always was in the past, but for some reason... every girl I meet these days bores me.

I see Riley out of the corner of my eye, lift my hand and motion like I'm writing something—the universal sign I want to pay my bill and go. "It was really nice to meet you, Jessica, but I'm getting ready to head out."

"Well, that's too bad," she coos as she touches my shoulder and then glides her fingers down my arm. "Can I give you my number?" Wow, this girl has no shame. Did I really go for this shit in the past? Yes, I did, and I would have jumped on this chick in a hot second if she was this willing just weeks ago. Now, if I'm being honest, it feels kinda gross.

"Ah thanks, that's real sweet of you, but no thank you," I say as Riley hands me my credit card, bill, and a pen. I sign the bill, leave him a big tip as always—he does give me an employee discount—and give him a wave goodbye.

I hear Jessica say, "What a dick." As I walk out the doors that lead to 2nd Avenue. I cannot disagree with you, darling. I am a dick; I just didn't realize it until tonight.

Chapter 10

Alex

December

I t's been a month since Mick and I have seen each other, and to say I was excited, yet nervous, to see him would be an understatement. The last time I saw him was at Bob's funeral, but we didn't have time to talk as he was doing Honor Guard duty. The wedding seems so long ago, and I can't help but picture him with Amber. I remember seeing them talk at the reception and it hurt. It hurt more than it should have. Even though I'm the one that set it up, and Amber told me that nothing happened between the two of them, I still remember how it felt. I know that if I don't keep my distance, I'll end up feeling that way over and over again.

Kevin is still making his presence known, but I've only had to endure him a total of eight days in the last month or so. Those eight days have left their mark. He hasn't left any physical evidence, but his abuse is real. He has made it perfectly clear that I am his. He has also made it crystal clear that he is not mine, and that he can do what he wants, when he wants and with whomever he wants.

He disgusts me.

I disgust me.

Luckily, there are no immediate visits planned and I feel like I can breathe again, if only for a little while. If he knew I was going to be spending my evening in the same house as Mick... well, I don't even want to think about that.

I can't wait to see Cami and Emily at Ireland's party. Just like the horror that lived inside my home growing up, they don't know anything about Kevin's abuse. Just like they never knew about my dad. I don't know why I don't tell them. Pride? Fear of seeing the pity in their eyes? Shame? I don't know exactly why, but for some reason I have never trusted my two best friends with the things in my life that aren't pretty.

I hope that my weight loss isn't too noticeable. I haven't had much of an appetite this last month. The stress of Kevin and the madness of missing Mick have my appetite playing a disappearing act. Not to mention the 24 hours or so after each of Kevin's visits where I spend endless hours with my head in the toilet trying to repel every touch, every threat, every degrading word.

As I pull up to Mick's house, I give myself a moment to prepare. I need to walk in and act like I don't miss Mick every single day. That thoughts of him don't occupy nearly every second of every day. That it's not the thought of him that gets me through the horrible nights with Kevin. That I don't wish his voice was the last I heard every night. I also need to be sure that I don't clue the girls in. I know that Emily's world is Ireland and Jonathan right now, but she is still pretty perceptive and rarely misses a thing. Then there's Cami. She's trouble. If she does notice something, she will call me out, right then and there. That girl doesn't pull any punches.

I finally step out of my car and nervously make my way to the front door. I have Ireland's gift in one hand and my digital 35 mm camera around my neck, like usual. Having the weight of my camera around my neck brings me the balance that it almost always does. It has always been my security blanket. Hopefully, it will keep me distracted and away from Mick tonight.

I can hear Ireland giggling the moment I walk in and the sight that I see in the family room takes my breath away. Instinctively, I raise my camera up and capture the moment. A moment where the most devastatingly handsome man I have ever seen has the cutest little girl in the world in his arms, and he is tickling her mercilessly. She's laughing so hard she can barely catch her breath, and the smile on his face is picture perfect; one I will never forget.

Taking the friendship I shared with Mick before Kevin came back into the picture, the support he's given his sister during all that she's been through with Jonathan and her stalker, our amazing night all those years ago and add the scene before me to that equation, Mickey Jacobs seems almost perfect.

"Hey Alex," Mick says, breaking the spell that seeing the two of them together has me under.

He sets Ireland down and helps fix her princess dress. She comes running over to me yelling, "Auntie Alex!" I squat down, drop her present and move my camera just in time to catch her as she jumps into my arms and gives me one of her awesome Ireland hugs. This little girl really is something special.

"Hey Ireland! Happy birthday, little lady!" I let her go but take her by the hand and spin her around and say, "You look beautiful! I love your dress. You have got to be the prettiest five-year-old I know!"

"Thank you, Auntie Alex. You look pretty too," she says as she takes my hand and tries to spin me around too. I help her out by just turning on my own. When I come back around to face Ireland, I see Mick hasn't moved from the spot where he was previously tickling his niece and he's staring at me.

I can hear Ireland chatting away, but I don't really hear her. Outwardly paying attention, I throw in a "Really?" and a "Uh, huh." But I don't hear a word. It's impossible to hear anything with those chocolate eyes staring back at me. We just stand there with our gazes never leaving one another's while Ireland continues to swing my hand while she talks a mile a minute about her party.

Finally, Emily saves the day and comes over to give me a hug. "Baby Girl, I know you're excited but you need to take a breath and let Auntie Alex get through the front door."

Emily pulls my eyes from Mick's and to my friend. "She's fine, Em. Just a little excited. I get it. You only turn five once, right, Ireland?" I say, looking around Em and down at Ireland's chocolate eyes that match Mick's. No wonder she's a special kid. When Emily is your mom, and Mick is your uncle, you know you come from some outstanding stock.

Pulling myself out of my head and remembering where I am and why, I ask. "So, where do the presents go, Em?"

She points to the table set up across the room and I head

in that direction. I drop the present off and pause as I look at all the cute wrapping paper. Man, the creators of *Frozen* are making a pretty penny if this table and Ireland's dress is any indication.

I take a couple of pictures of all the presents, and just as I'm about to walk away I feel his presence. He doesn't have to touch me to know he's there. I feel him any time he's in close proximity. It's not like when Kevin is near and I feel cold and sick. No, when Mickey Jacobs is around, I feel warm. Excited. Happy.

"Hey Alex, you gonna say hi?" he asks, standing right next to me... pretending to look at the presents.

I turn my head to look at him and say, "Hey Mick. How's it going? Your place looks great all decked out like it is today. You might want to consider keeping some of this princess stuff up after the party. It's you," I say with a wink. A wink! I just winked at him. Am I flirting with him already? So much for keeping my distance!

"Oh, you think so, do you? Well, maybe I'll consider it. Ireland seems to think you have impeccable style and I do agree with her... you look very pretty today, Alex," he says this as he ever so lightly bumps his shoulder into mine.

I can feel myself blushing and quietly I say, "Thank you." I know I need to get away from him, so I say, "I'm gonna go see if Em needs any help. Talk to you later."

He says nothing and lets me walk away.

For the rest of the party we keep our distance, but I catch him watching me several times. When I do catch him, he doesn't look away. He makes it perfectly clear that he wants me to know that he's watching me. Besides the stares we only exchange a few words in passing. I continue to document the day for Emily and marvel at the love in the room.

Ireland is one lucky little girl.

While in the crowded kitchen helping Emily hand out cake, he puts his hand on the small of my back to scoot by me so that he can get a plate out of the cupboard. The feel of his touch on my body, even through my clothes, was all it took to let my guard down. As he stood behind me with his hand on my back, I couldn't help but lean against him. As my back ever so lightly pressed against his chest, his hand curved around my hip and he gave me a squeeze. The moment only lasted seconds, but it was more than enough to forget the many reasons why moments like these shouldn't happen. Feeling me pull away, he gets his plate and steps away.

A little later, I'm leaning against the kitchen counter, eating my cake when Mick joins me. He leans against the counter just a couple of feet away from me. Although he isn't touching me, I can feel him. He has always had this effect on me. It started when we were kids, but it's different now. It's not a school-girl crush, it feels real. It also seems like the feeling intensifies each and every time I'm around him.

"So, I was wondering if you would do me a favor?" Mick asks while intently watching me pull my pink plastic fork out of my mouth. He even turns towards me with one hip on the counter, and I know it's so he can get a better look.

"What's up, Mick?" I ask as he continues to stare at me. Or maybe it's my fork he's into?

He brings his thumb up to my lips and says, "You got a little frosting right here." As the words come out of his mouth, he drags his thumb over my lower lip, then puts that same thumb in his mouth and eats said frosting. "Got it," he says.

He sounds like his usual, carefree self, but his deep brown eyes seem to darken as his gaze locks on mine once more, and his tongue slowly wets his lips. Damn. Is it hot in this kitchen?

Trying to remove myself from this intimate situation, I ask, "What kind of favor did you need, Mick?"

He steps away and leans in front of the kitchen sink. Is *he* trying to distance himself from *me* now? I am so confused.

"Well, you know how I hate to shop, right?"

"Um... Yes, I do. You whine like a little baby at the mere mention of it."

"Right, that's where the favor comes in to play. It's Christmastime and I have to shop for Mom, Emily, Ireland and Sidney. I'm not sure I can do it on my own. Would you please come with me?"

"Mick, I told you it wasn't a good idea."

It's not just because of Kevin. I know that as long as I keep Mick in my life I'll never find happiness elsewhere. I'll never be able to find somebody that will make me happy the way I should be. The way only Mick can.

He pushes off of the counter and takes a couple of steps until he's standing right in front of me. "Please don't make me beg, Alex. You know I have a lot of pride, but I need you. I cannot go to the mall alone," he says with puppy dog eyes. He's really working it. I'm not sure, but he may be the one turning five today. Not that I mind hearing him say that he needs me. I dreamed of those exact words leaving his mouth throughout my high school years. But still... he is such a big baby.

"Mick, you don't need me to go to the mall," I say back. I

want nothing more than to spend time with him, but I know it's not a good idea.

Taking my hand in his, he gets down on bended knee and says, "Dearest Alex, eleven days from today, will you please do me the honor of accompanying me to the mall of your choice, Saturday, December 12th?"

And... because Mick always gets what he wants, and I don't want anybody to see his display here in the kitchen, I cave and yell-whisper my reply.

"Yes, Mick! Now get up off of the floor, would you? You are so ridiculous!"

I can feel myself blushing.

I can hear myself giggling.

If I listen real hard... I bet I can hear my heart breaking.

"It worked, didn't it?" He says as he stands up with a look on his face that says he knew he would get his way in the end.

He was right. And because he's Mickey freaking Jacobs I'm going Christmas shopping with him in 11 days.

Kevin can never know, and I am going to have to figure out a way to make sure that Mick doesn't think that things are back to normal.

"Cool, I'll pick you up at 10:00 a.m. on the 12th and we'll make a day of it. It's really great to see you again, Alex."

"It's good to see you too, Mick. I'll see you in a couple weeks," I say as I start to leave the kitchen.

As I walk past him he gently grabs my wrist and asks, "Is he treating you right, Alex?" His hand slides from my wrist to my hand and he entwines his fingers in mine.

Heaven.

"Tell me he hasn't hurt you? Tell me that if he did lay a hand on you, that you would tell me."

I can see the concern in his eyes and feel the warmth of his hand, and it makes me feel more than I've felt in weeks.

With Kevin, I simply turn off my emotions. I feel nothing when he's around. This has always been my coping mechanism. But with Mick, it's impossible not to feel. I may feel more with Mick, but not enough to tell him the truth. I lie and tell him I'm fine and that, of course, I would call him if Kevin were to hurt me.

I can only hope that he believes me, but I don't stick around to find out, as I regretfully let go of his hand and walk out of the kitchen.

I instantly feel the loss of him.

Missing him starts all over again.

Chapter 11

Mick

"What the hell is wrong with me, Frank?" I ask my most trusted, four-legged confidant. He just looks up at me with his tongue hanging out like he's been on a run.

We haven't been on a run, but I *have* been keeping him busy. He's out of breath because he's my shadow and he follows me everywhere. That means that he has been pacing the living room with me for the last thirty minutes. I think I must be losing my mind or possibly even growing a vagina. I am full of feelings right now, and I don't know what the hell to do with a single one of them.

"Buddy, we need to get you in shape. I have a feeling this pacing isn't going to end anytime soon and you've got to keep up with me. You can't leave me hangin', dude."

Yes, I am talking to my dog... like he's a person, but anybody with a soul treats their dog like family. If you don't like dogs, I probably won't like you. Simple as that.

Talking out loud to Frank is the least of my worries right now. It's been five days since Ireland's party, but it feels like it's been years. Seeing Alex again has made the itch to be around her that much stronger.

She's finally texting again. It's not like before, but there have been small pieces of communication. I generally start my day with a good morning to her and she replies back, but after a couple more texts back and forth, they tend to drop off.

I don't know why, but I feel like there's something more to her needing to end our friendship. I know that it has to do with Kevin, but I can't help but feel like there's some sort of turmoil that I'm not aware of.

She did promise to call me if he hurt her, and she hasn't called, but my gut tells me there's more to it. My gut tells me something is wrong and she needs me. Part of me thinks that I just want to play her knight in shining armor and rescue her from her suit. But I know that's not what this is.

She's different.

Seeing her at Ireland's party made things clear for me. I miss her and she misses me. She may have been trying to hide her feelings, but I know her, and she feels the same way I do. I don't know if she wants more from me than the friendship we shared... but I do. If all she misses is my friendship, I can live with that as long as she's in my life. If that little light in her eye that I saw a few days ago is a sign, she feels the same way I do. She's shutting me out for a reason. I need to figure out just what that reason is. I don't think this sick feeling is going to go away until I do.

"What do I do, buddy?" I ask Frank as he plops on the ground not able to keep up with my furious pacing any longer. He looks up at me with those big bulldog eyes and I know he's thinking about what a pussy I am. "Hey, don't look at me that way. I don't know how to do this. I don't know how to worry about a woman that's not my family. What do you want from me? I don't know what to do with these... these... feelings!" I don't usually have feelings, so this is freaking me the fuck out! "What would you do, bud?"

Frank lets out a heavy sigh of disappointment and closes his eyes, no longer wanting to deal with me.

"Whatever. Who are you to judge, Frank? You don't even have balls. You do not know what this is like."

I mean, for fuck's sake. I'm currently pacing my living room floor and asking my dog for relationship advice.

I don't know why I thought asking her to go shopping with me, 11 days after the party, was going to do the trick. I didn't lie. I do hate shopping. Shopping with one of my best friends—who just happens to be more beautiful than I have words for—might just make the god-forsaken task a bit more bearable. The truth is, I was desperate to make sure she didn't leave my house that day without knowing when I was going to see her again. Desperate times call for desperate measures.

I don't know why I keep telling myself that I'm okay with just being her friend. I know that it's not true, but I don't really know what to do about it. I'm out of my league, my depth and my mind, for that matter.

I feel anxious.

I have never had much patience, but when it comes to this woman, I feel like I have shown more than ever before. I can't do it anymore. This patience thing and following all her little rules about our 'friendship' is making me a crazy person.

Enough.

I know from the text she sent me earlier today that she's

not going anywhere and she's home. It's time to find out what's really going on with Miss Alexandra Stotts.

Alex

I'm so happy to be spending a Saturday at home with Blazer. My poor cat spends so much time alone. Being in the event planning business means working a lot of hours and often weekends. I love my job, but I love my weekends too.

I know I should be taking advantage of my free time by going out with friends, but that is the last thing I want.

I. Am. Exhausted.

Between my hours at work, sleepless nights thinking about Mick and how much I miss him, and the constant antagonizing texts and calls from Kevin—I am emotionally spent.

How did I get here?

How I could have turned into my mother?

I always thought that she was weak for staying with my dad. I vowed I would never be her; be that weak. Yet, here I am. Kevin doesn't even live on the same side of the continent and I am letting him control me. Is it because in some strange way, he almost feels safer than Mick?

I know Mick would never hurt me physically, but the damage that he could do to my heart is something that I'm not so sure I could recover from. Just the small time I was with him on Tuesday, and the few texts we've exchanged since, have made me happier than I've been since Kevin came back into the picture.

Yep, Kevin is on the other side of the country, Mick is back in my life—even if in small doses—and I am home on a Saturday night in my yoga pants, baggy sweatshirt, my hair up in a high ponytail, a pint of Ben & Jerry's in my hand with my cat purring in my lap. I'm watching *The People's Couch* and laughing my ass off, feeling content.

Just as the hysterical family of three on my television is bringing me to tears with laughter over their reaction to the *Empire* season finale, there's a knock at my door.

Dang it, I knew my peace and quiet couldn't last forever, but thirty minutes is just not long enough. Let's see what they're trying to sell and get back to my couch, my ice cream and my show.

Not thinking, I unlock the door and throw it open without looking through the peephole.

I should have looked.

I'm not prepared for the person who I see standing before me. If I had looked... I would have never opened my door.

"Alexandra, good to see I caught you at home," Kevin all but sneers.

The expression on his face and the tone of his voice sends an ice-cold shiver down my spine. I'm not sure why, but I have a feeling that this visit is going to be even worse than those that have come before it. Something feels off.

Gathering myself, but not moving aside to let him in, I say, "Kevin, I wasn't expecting you. I didn't know you were coming into town."

"I didn't know I needed a reason to visit. I am curious about something though..."

Not really wanting to know, I play along and ask, "What's that?"

"Why the hell am I still standing outside? Are you not alone, Alexandra?"

His comment is confusing me, and I'm not sure what exactly he's implying. "Oh, sorry, I didn't mean to be rude. Come on in. There's nobody here but me, unless Ben & Jerry count?" I joke, trying to lighten his mood, but he doesn't bite.

As I step aside to let him in, he storms past me. I shut the door but don't lock it. I always lock it, but for some reason I feel like leaving it easy to open is a good option to have at the moment.

Again, something just feels off.

I follow behind him and see him checking every room in my tiny townhouse. He even checks behind the shower curtain in the bathroom. Who is he looking for?

"Kevin, what's wrong? Who did you think would be here?"

He walks back into the living room and heads right for me. Just as I bring my usual fake smile to my face—the one I save just for him—he backhands it right off. I wasn't prepared for the hit, so my balance is thrown and I fall to the ground and land on my hip.

Before I have a chance to get back onto my feet, he's grabbed me by my hair and is dragging me through the house. He lets go of my hair and then grabs one of my wrists and is trying to pull me up and onto the couch. I decide to help him with this and push myself up on my feet before he does any real damage to my arm.

Once he's thrown me down on the couch he squats down

in front of me and grabs me by the chin and forces me to look at him.

"I thought I warned you, Alexandra. I thought I had made myself perfectly clear when I said you are mine. Did I not?" he asks, still gripping my chin so hard that there is no way that I could pull away.

"You did make yourself clear. I haven't been with anybody but you," I say, growing more and more confused.

In a syrupy sweet voice that slowly turns sinister, he says, "Oh sweet, Alexandra. I knew you were a slut, but I didn't know you were a lying bitch, too." And with those words, he backhands me on the same side as before. As the momentum from his hit sends me falling on to my side, I curl myself up into the fetal position and wish that the couch would just swallow me whole and take me away.

"I saw the pictures on Facebook. I made it clear I wanted you to stay away from that Jacobs asshole, but no, there you are at his house having what looks like an intimate conversation in his kitchen. Now, would you like to try again, or do you have more lies to spew out of that pretty little mouth of yours?"

Still curled up, I don't even look up when I yell into the couch, "It was a birthday party for a five-year-old. He's my best friend's brother. I can't help that the party was at his house, but I promise you nothing happened."

"I saw how close you two were. I can see how that pretty boy looks at you. He looks at you like he's fucked you. Has he fucked you, Alexandra?"

Just as I'm trying to come up with an answer that wouldn't grant me another slap to the face, there's another knock at the door. Oh, thank God! In my head I'm screaming to whomever is out there that the door is unlocked and to please just come in.

"Don't think you're getting out of answering that question, my dear. We'll get back to that in a minute."

He grabs me by the biceps and pulls me off of the couch and uses his other arm to cover my mouth. He sets me down at my kitchen table and whispers in my ear that he'll kill me if I make a sound. With that being said, he takes his hand off of my mouth and heads down the hall to the front door. Thank god he doesn't notice that my cell phone is sitting on my table right in front of me.

As I pick the phone up, the first thing I do is turn off the sound just to be safe. As I go to dial 911, I hear a familiar voice at the front door.

"Uh, hey. How ya doin'? Is Alex here?"

It's Mickey! He's here!

The last thing I want is for him to see me like this, but thank God he's here.

I hear 911 answer and I pick up the phone and simply whisper, "Please help me." I know that they will have my address on their computer screen shortly and I have to hope that my plea for help and leaving the line open is enough.

I get up from my chair and take two steps so that I can look down the hallway to the front door. Kevin doesn't have the door open wide enough for Mick to see me, but it is open wide enough for him to see that for some reason, Kevin has his shirt and shoes off. What the hell is going on?

I step back to the table as I hear Kevin explain that I'm 'indisposed' at the moment, but that he can take a message for me.

I don't hear what Mickey says, because all I can hear is

my heart pounding in my ears. I look at my phone and see that 911 is still connected. I set it face down but move it to the other side of the table so it isn't right next to me.

Kevin steps back in the room, and I take in his appearance. His shirt is missing, as are his shoes. His hair is messed up; his pants are unbuttoned and he has a smile on his face that has victory written all over it.

He can see the confused look on my face, so he explains himself. "That's right, you lying slut. Your big, tough, boy next door looking boyfriend was just here. Unlike you, I check the peephole before I open the door and thought I would make him see he wasn't the only one that's fucking you. Now, since I'm already practically undressed, I think I'll fuck you like the whore you are."

I jump up from the chair and try to run past him and to the hallway that leads to the front door; to Mick. I'm not fast enough. He catches me by my arm and pulls it behind me and slams me face first into the wall as I let out a scream.

"Where did you think you were going, Alexandra? Jacobs isn't going to help you. He seemed pretty pissed at what he thought was happening here and stormed off. Looks like you're all mine," he breathes into my ear.

Tears silently stream down my face as I look down the hallway at the front door. The front door that leads to freedom and to Mick. Knowing he was just on the other side of my door moments ago and I didn't yell for him or even try to get his attention was so stupid. Why didn't I scream? What is wrong with me?

Now, here I am up against this wall. My arm feeling like it's about to break as Kevin struggles to pull my pants down. I know what's about to happen as my pants are dragged down my legs and he presses his other arm against my neck to press me even closer to the wall.

His forearm leaves my neck, and I think he may have changed his mind, but it's simply replaced by his hand around my neck. While he's choking me with one hand, he grabs my head and pulls it back and then slams into the wall. Just as he kicks my feet further apart—to grant himself easier access—I do what I do best. Stop feeling. I shut down all my emotions and disappear from my current reality. Sometimes, when I'm in bed with Kevin, I think back to my night with Mick all those years ago.

Not today.

Today, I just shut down and I don't think about anything.

I do my best to just disappear.

* * *

Mick

This is why I don't care!

This is why I never want more!

What the fuck was I thinking coming over here?

I'm back in my truck, but for some reason, I can't seem to leave. When Kevin answered the door my entire reason for coming over here completely evaporated. I am honestly dumbfounded. I knew she was with him, but seeing it thrust in my face like that isn't sitting well.

I don't know why I'm still sitting here in front of her place. I know that I need to put myself out of my misery and leave, but I can't seem to start the damn truck. I have this sick feeling in my stomach and I don't know if it's from seeing him clearly in a state of undress and knowing he had been in bed with Alex, or if it's my gut telling me that something here isn't right.

Maybe I'm just a glutton for punishment, but I decide to go with my gut.

I've seen him get a little too rough with her myself, and something just doesn't feel right. I need to see her face and have her tell me that everything's okay, and then I'll go.

I've just jumped out of the truck and taken two steps toward her door when I hear her scream and my heart nearly stopped. Without thinking, I haul ass up to the front door and start pounding. I give it about three-seconds and when nobody answers the door; I try the handle and can't believe my luck when it turns and the door opens.

My lucky feeling instantly drifts away as I take in the scene at the other end of the hallway. Kevin has Alex by the neck and her arm bent behind her back. Her face is pressed against the wall and there are tears streaming down her face. She's looking right at me, but that I'm here doesn't seem to have registered. Her expression hasn't changed. The next thing I notice is that he's got her pants down and he's positioned himself behind her. He's about to force himself on her.

Red... that is all I see.

The rage that fills my body overcomes me. What happens next is as close to an out-of-body experience that I have ever had.

I slam the door shut to get his attention and storm down the hallway. I can see the sneer on his face the moment he sees me. It's almost like he's glad that I caught him. Like he wants me to see him hurting her. Touching her. Ruining her.

His pants weren't quite down all the way when I walked in so it only takes a second for him to pull them back up, and as he does he lets go of Alex and she falls to the ground. My instinct is to go to her. I'll deal with him, but first I need to be sure she's okay. I kneel next to her and ask her just that. When her eyes finally connect to mine, I can see the moment she comes back to reality and realizes that I'm here.

Trembling, she says, "You're here?"

"I am. I'm here, Alex. I need you to look at me and tell me if you're okay? Are you hurt?" I need her to answer me before I leave her on her own and beat Kevin senseless. "Alex, please answer me!"

"Yes, I'll be fine. Thank you for being here."

Out of the corner of my eye, I see the asshole putting his shoes on like he thinks he's just going to saunter out of here like nothing happened.

"She's fine, Jacobs. Girls like her have to be kept in line. I'm done with her now. You can have her. She's damaged goods anyway."

And with those words, he has just signed his own death sentence.

He's sitting in a chair at the dining room table and is bending over to tie his shoes as I walk up to him and punch him in the side of his head. He falls off the chair and onto the ground, and I am instantly on top of him. He's flailing about and trying to push me away with his hands, but I have no problem getting several more shots off to his face. He can fight all he wants. There is no way he can stand up to my fury. And that's just what this is. The need I have to inflict my wrath upon this piece of shit is out of my control.

Just as I raise my fist to take another swing, I feel somebody grab my arm and pin it behind my back, just like Alex's just was. I struggle to pull away from whoever is on top of me, and manage to get my arm out from their grasp, but instantly feel another set of hands on me. Even though I continue to struggle, the hands pull me off of him and I feel cuffs trying to be placed on my wrists.

"Mick, calm the fuck down, man! I don't want to cuff you if I don't have to!" It's then that I realize that the voice yelling at me to 'calm the fuck down' is a police officer. Not just a police officer, but one of my best friends.

How the fuck did he get here?

"Let go of me, Martinez! This fucker needs to die!" With my threatening words, I feel Emmett's hold tighten, and he drags me away from the bloody mess that I was making of that fucker's face.

Emmett drags me across the floor and pushes me, not so gently, against the wall. With his hand on my chest to keep me in place, he says, "We got this. He's already in cuffs. You need to take care of Alex." He can see the confusion on my face and knows that I don't know how he got here. "She was smart enough to call 911 and leave the line open. Dispatch heard everything. We got this."

As I sit on my ass against the wall, I realize that he placed me next to Alex. She's managed to get her pants up, but she's just sitting with her knees pulled into her chest and seems to be in shock. I shove Emmett's hand off of my chest and scoot over to Alex and place myself in front of her. I put my legs on either side of hers so that I can get as close to her as possible.

"Alex, baby...you okay?" she isn't looking at me so I try to move so that my eyes are level with hers but she doesn't reply. "Hey, sweet thing... I need you to talk to me. Tell me where you might be hurt. I'm here, baby. You don't need to be scared. I'm here."

She finally lifts her eyes to mine and she simply says, "Mick?"

"Yep, I'm here baby. You okay?" I can feel myself panicking. Bruises are already forming on her face, and I need to know if there is more damage that I just can't see.

"You're here?"

"I'm here. So are the police, and they've got him, Alex."

Just then the paramedics walk through the front door and I signal for them to come to Alex first. That fucker can wait.

"Alex, the paramedics are here and they want to check you out, okay? Just be sure to tell them anywhere that you might be hurt." I turn to the familiar faces of our fire department and tell them we'll meet them in the living room. "Baby, I'm gonna pick you up, okay?" She replies with a small nod of her head.

I scoop her up in my arms and walk her over to the couch, and gently set her down. I start to move away so that the paramedics can look her over, but she grabs my hand and finally looks me in the eye. It's clear she's asking me to stay with her and there isn't anything that could pull me away. Whatever she needs, I'm here.

I sit down next to her, and as I settle I feel her slide her fingers between mine and she holds on to my hand with all she's got. My bloodied hand that just moments ago was feeling the crush of that low life's bones... that same hand now feels the trembling fragility of a woman who has once again been shattered and abused.

"Ma'am, can you tell us where you were hurt?" Johnson, a paramedic I've worked with for several years, asks.

I'm glad it's him here and not some newbie fresh out of class.

"It's mostly just my head," she says, lifting her hand to the side of her head.

"And what happened, ma'am? Do you remember what might have happened to cause your head to hurt?"

"Um... Kevin... he um..." she looks up at me with pools of unshed tears in her eyes.

I let go of her hand and put my arm around her to pull her into me. "It's okay, Alex. You can tell them. I'm right here and Kevin is gone. I've got you, baby," I whisper into her hair.

She reaches for my free hand—that is also cut and bleeding from beating that prick's face in—and intertwines our fingers again before moving her gaze to Johnson. "He slammed me against the wall and then pulled me back by the neck and slammed my head into the wall." At this admission, the tears begin to fall and her sobs come falling out. She brings her arm around my waist and buries her face in my chest. I squeeze her to me and hold on for dear life. God dammit! I wish I had been given just a couple more minutes alone with that asshole. I want to kill him or at least maim him. The picture that has been painted in my head of him smashing her head against the wall is one I'm not sure I will ever forget.

"Ma'am, I know this is hard, but we're going to need to check your eyes and make sure that you don't have a concussion."

"Her name's Alex and let's give her just a minute, Johnson."

He stands up and walks away, giving us a couple feet of space. Whispering into her hair once again, I ask, "How you doin', sweet thing? You gonna be able to let them look at you in a minute?"

She pulls her face from my now wet t-shirt and says, "I'm so embarrassed, Mick. How did I let this happen?"

"This isn't your fault, Alex. I don't want to hear you say anything like that again. Do you hear me?" She doesn't reply and just stares at me, looking lost and defeated. "Let's just get you checked out and then we're going to have to talk to the officers as well. Nobody here is going to judge you. In fact, they're all friends of mine. You're in a safe place, with safe people. Don't be embarrassed. Let's just be glad it's all over."

With a newfound determination, she sits up straight, wipes her eyes with the sleeves of her sweatshirt, takes in a big breath and exhales loudly. "I'm ready."

As Johnson approaches us, I go to scoot over and give him space to examine her, but she squeezes my hand and panicked eyes stare into mine. "Hey, I'm right here. I got you," I say as I hold up our connected hands. "I just want to give him some space."

"Sorry, I'm being silly," she says, trying to release my hand.

I don't let go, though. I kiss her forehead, give her a little wink, and scoot over.

I sit with her while Johnson shines his light in her eyes and has her follow his fingers. He also cleans the cut on her cheekbone, but says she shouldn't need any stitches. Her head is another story. He gives her two little steri-strips just above her right temple. If they don't stay, she'll have to go to the hospital to get stitches. The worst part for her is when Emmett has to take pictures of her injuries.

She does seem a little foggy from the concussion that Johnson has confirmed, but she keeps it together.

Next, Emmett has to come take our statements. As he's explaining that he's going to need to separate us and take our statements individually, Emily arrives. I can see Alex's eyes go wide as she sees her enter the room. Her lifelong fear of her friends knowing her secret is about to come out, and it scares the shit out of her. I can see it all over her face.

"It's okay, Alex. She loves you and she'll want to be here for you. She will not judge you."

In a rush, Emily collapses on the floor in front of Alex and looks between the two of us. Alex, with her cuts and bruises and tears streaming down her face. Me, holding her hand and sporting bloodied knuckles.

"What happened, Mick? Alex, are you okay? What's going on? Emmett called me and told me to get here as soon as I could. Alex, are you okay? I saw Kevin in the back of one of the squad cars. Did he do this to you?"

"Emmers, take a breath. Why don't you sit here with Alex while she gives Emmett her statement?" I say, pleading with my eyes for her to stop with all the questions. The last thing we want right now is for Alex to clam up because Emily's here. "Alex, I'm going to go give my statement right over there, and Emily's going to sit with you while you give yours. I'll be as fast as I can be. Okay?"

"Okay."

"Hey, you are not weak. You are one of the toughest women I know. You don't need to have any more secrets. You've got this. Tell them your truth. You've got me and Emily. We aren't going anywhere."

Just like that, her tears stop falling and she sits up a little straighter again. Emily takes my place on the couch and takes Alex's hand in hers. I head over to the county officer that they've brought in to take my statement. Its policy to have somebody not in my own department take my statement. You just never know.

I know the drill, so I state my name, age and how I know Alex. I explain the situation from the time I knocked on the door until Emmett pulled me off Kevin. My interview is over rather quickly. I know that there will be more of an investigation, but it's enough for now.

It took Alex some time to start explaining what's unfolded here in her own words and she's just gotten started. As I listen to her describe what happened, and that her pictures with me were the reason for his visit, I feel sick. Not to mention imagining him dragging her by her hair, hitting her and slamming her head against the wall. I am relieved to hear that I stopped him from raping her. It's not much, but at least I saved her from that. I still feel like I could throw up. The only thing that stops me from doing just that is the fact that I'm hanging on every word that she says to Emmett.

After Alex finishes, Emmett asks her how long their relationship had been like this. Hearing her describe her relationship with this asshole takes me back to that night at the hospital. The night she told me her secret, and I sat next to her, shocked that none of us knew. Here we are again. How didn't any of us know?

She explains how he first came back to work and threatened her in the mailroom after he had already shown up here and raped her. He raped her and she didn't reach out to me.

He raped her.

I'm nearly knocked on my ass by the wave of emotions

that hits me. Somehow, I feel like this is my fault and I should have known. I should have saved her. Why didn't I save her? Seeing her sitting on the couch recounting these last weeks, she is clearly ashamed and embarrassed. I should have saved her. I can tell she feels weak, and in a way, so do I. I don't know if I'm strong enough to take all of this in and know that I didn't help her. I can't believe all of this happened to her. How did none of us know? Right now, she is what is important, and I have to keep my shit together. She needs me and this time I'm gonna be there. That she can count on.

Hearing her tell her story connects all the dots for me. I wish she had told me, but I do understand. I know that with the way she grew up watching her mom as an example of how to deal with a man like her dad, this is what she knows. Put that with the fact that this jackass was also management. Corporate HR Management, to be exact. She had nobody at work to go to, and she was raised to keep her private life... private.

After she finishes her story, she looks over at me and I know she knew I was listening. She wanted me to know where she had been these past weeks and why she had ended our friendship. I give her a brief nod so she knows that I heard her and I understand.

Emily pulls Alex's attention away from me and, with tears cascading down her face, says, "Alexandra Stotts! You are never to leave something like this to yourself again! You have too many people who love and care about you and are always here for you. I love you so much and I am so sorry that I've been so wrapped up in my own life that I missed this. I should have seen that something was off, and I am so sorry for letting you down."

"Emily, you didn't let me down. I didn't want you to know. I was embarrassed. I don't know how I let myself get into this position. I didn't want you to know how weak I was," she says to my sister with her eyes looking at the ground. She looks defeated.

"Alex, you ended up here because a man with power used his position to threaten your job and do you harm. It's not your fault. He's a piece of shit. I hope he knows how lucky he is that he only got Mick's wrath because Cami and I would know no limit to the pain we would inflict on this fucker if given the chance!"

At the mention of Cami, I see fear cross her face again. She doesn't want Cami to know, but Emily sees it too and doesn't let her say a word.

"No! No more secrets! Cami deserves to know. She and I both need to be better friends. The three of us have always taken care of each other, and it's time Cami and I did a better job. When you're ready, the three of us will get together and have a night to catch up. A night to catch up on all of us, not just with you. It's needed."

I love my sister. She is pretty freaking amazing and Alex is lucky to have her, but at the moment she looks like she's overwhelming Alex.

"Hey Emmers, thanks for sitting with her while she gave her statement. You can head home if you want. It was cool of Emmett to call you, but I got this."

"What do you mean, you got this? Why are you even here?"

"Alex and I are friends, Em. I came by to check on her because it seemed like something was wrong at Ireland's party." I pull this out of my ass and hope that it flies.

Emily turns to look at Alex. "I am such a shitty friend. Mick noticed something was off and I didn't. I am so sorry, Alex. It won't happen again."

"Thanks, Em. You really don't have to stick around. I'm just tired and want to get some rest. I'll be fine and I promise no more secrets."

Emily pulls her into a hug and then looks between me and Alex like she's still trying to figure out why I'm here. She walks by me and I can see the look in her eye that tells me she knows. She knows that there's something more between us, but she's leaving it alone... for now.

"Take good care of her, Mick." My little sister orders as she gives me a hug. It's a request and a threat all wrapped up in one. *Message received loud and clear, sis.*

Sometime later, after all the crime scene pictures have been taken, cuts have been cleaned, questions have been asked and information has been given, we're alone.

Timidly she asks, "Mick, I'm gonna take a shower. Do you mind hanging out until I'm done?" She looks tired and still a little scared.

"I'm not going anywhere. You take your shower and I'll pick up the mess that everybody left behind. Take your time. I'll be here when you get out. If you want to stay at my place tonight, it's perfectly fine with me. No ulterior motive."

"Nah, that's okay, Mick. I'd rather just stay here. Thanks though."

* * *

"Blazer sure seems to like you," she says, referring to the sleeping cat in my arms. It's thirty minutes later and she's just joined me on the couch. Wet headed and blurry eyed.

"Did you really name your cat after a Chevy?"

Giggling, she says, "Mick... hello... this is Portland... duh!"

"Wow, I'm impressed. You named your cat after the Trailblazers. I didn't know you were such a big basketball fan. We'll have to get to a game before the season's over."

"Mick?"

"Yeah?"

"Thank you."

"No need to thank me. I'm glad I got here when I did. Seeing you like that, Alex... I don't even know what to say. I am so sorry you had to go through all of this. Not just today, but the last weeks and when you were a kid. You've dealt with way too much. I'm just glad I could help today."

"You shouldn't have done that today, Mick."

"What the hell are you talking about? I should have killed him!" Is she trying to protect this asshole? I feel myself getting pissed. So does Blazer, because he jumps out of my arms when I yell my objections.

"Mick, what if he presses charges? You could lose your job."

And there it is. She's thinking of me.

Not herself, but me.

Why does she not know how to put herself first?

"Don't you worry about me. I'll be fine. He can press charges if he wants, but with the 911 recording and your statement, I don't think we'll have to worry about that. I doubt you'll be seeing him at work anymore, either. I don't think these kinds of charges work well in HR management."

"Shit! This means that everybody at work is going to find out! God Mick, this is all so humiliating."

She leans forward and puts her face in her hands. I rub her back and try to reassure her the best I can. "Hey, this doesn't mean that your co-workers are going to find out. He works in the corporate office on the other side of the country. I doubt he's going to advertise it. It's going to be okay, Alex. And to be on the safe side, Monday, we're going down to the station to file a restraining order." There's no hiding the fear in her eyes at the thought of my last statement. "Alex, I'll be with you every step of the way. You don't have to do this alone."

"Thank you, Mick. For everything."

Just then there's a knock at the door and she jumps. "Sorry, I should have told you I ordered pizza. It's all good. I'll be right back."

I get the pizza, salad and soda all set up on the kitchen table and she joins me. I steer the conversation away from today and to the frivolous topics of Portland basketball, our mutual hatred of the Los Angeles Lakers, the latest Tarantino movie and, of course, her love of Ben & Jerry's. She tells me about her favorite show, *The People's Couch,* that is about watching other people watch TV. When I tell her that it sounds lame and I can't believe she would watch that crap, she makes me promise to watch 30 minutes of it and tell her if I still feel the same after watching it.

Two hours later, I pick up our empty pints of ice cream and concede that she was right. Her show is hysterical, and in my head I'm thinking, *if it distracted you, that's all that matters.*

I head to the kitchen and throw away our garbage and put our spoons in the dishwasher. When I return to the living room, she stands and says, "Thanks for sticking around, Mick, but I'm exhausted. I think it's time I turn in."

"No problem, lead the way."

"What do you mean, lead the way? The way to the front door?"

"Sweet thing, if you think I am going to leave you tonight, you are sorely mistaken. There is nothing you can say that would get me to leave you right now. I know you don't want more than friendship from me, and that is a hard pill to swallow, but that doesn't mean that I don't still care. I know you've always taken care of yourself, but you don't have to. You don't have to do everything on your own. Please know up front, though... I am not even going to pretend to be chivalrous and sleep on the couch or the floor. I am sleeping in your bed, with you in my arms, where I know you are safe."

"Mick, you don't need to do that. I'll be fine."

"You might be, but I won't. This isn't for you, Alex, it's for me."

Reluctantly, she relents. "Okay."

I turn off the lights and follow her to her bedroom. She turns on the bedside lamp and then heads into the primary bathroom. I stay back to give her some privacy and a few seconds later she calls me into the bathroom.

She hands me a brand-new toothbrush and as I take it out of its plastic container, she puts toothpaste on her toothbrush and then hands the tube to me.

"Thanks," I say as we both go about our business, like it's

something we do together every night. I watch her go through her routine in the mirror, but she doesn't look my way.

Once she finishes, she heads out to the bedroom and crawls under the covers. I take my time and let her settle before I join her. I turn off the light and take everything but my t-shirt and boxer briefs off. I join her under the covers and say, "Come here, Alex."

"What?" she asks with her back to me.

"Alex, I told you that I needed to sleep with you in my arms. Please don't make this difficult."

She rolls over and puts her head on my chest and her arm around my waist as I pull her as close to me as I can get her.

"Thank you," I say into her hair.

"Thanks for staying, Mick. I'm glad you're here."

"Me too, Alex."

Lying in her bed, with her in my arms... I take in the day. How I went from pacing my family room and talking to my dog to finding Alex being attacked to lying here with her in my arms... it's a lot to take in.

I deal with domestic abuse regularly at work, but today was different. Today, it was somebody I care about. Today it was Alex. My Alex. My Sweet Thing. I called her that years ago when we had our night together and it stuck. In my mind, that is what I've always called her. And just like the song says, she's my everything. It took me a while to figure it out, but there is no doubt in my mind. She's it for me.

I hear her breathing even out and realize that she's sound asleep. I'm sure with everything that's happened, she's exhausted. As for me, I'm not sure I'll sleep at all tonight worrying about her concussion. Not to mention the fact that I hate every second that I'm in this bed where I know he violated her. It's almost too much to take. Besides that, I'm not sure I could forgive myself if I were to miss a minute of having her here, in my arms.

She stirs and nuzzles even closer to me as her long leg weaves around me. Nothing has ever felt so right. If I was unsure before, this moment has solidified everything for me. She's not just my Sweet Thing. She's my *more*.

Chapter 12

Alex

"I don't know why I care so much, I just do!" I say to Blazer as he weaves around my ankles, meowing.

"I know it's just Mick. And I've known him forever, but he does something to me, Blaze." Moving the hangers back and forth in my closet, nothing seems good enough for a day of shopping. "I wish he wasn't Mick and he wasn't being so perfect lately. He's making it extremely hard to keep my distance." Blazer lets out one last meow and then curls up amongst my shoes and falls asleep.

"Okay, good talk." I can't believe I've been dismissed by my own cat.

Finally, I settle on a cream sweater, dark jeans, and tall brown boots. As I touch up my hair and make-up one last time, I can't help but recap this past week in my mind as I sing along to Marian Hill.

Waking up in Mick's arms on Sunday morning was like a dream. It was a dream that only existed because of the nightmare that was Kevin, but it was worth it to end up there. Mick's arms, and waking up in them, are stuff that dreams are made of. In fact, every day since that horrific Saturday has been better than the last.

On Sunday, Mick made me breakfast and hung out at my place most of the day. We binge watched the first season of Orange Is the New Black and ate leftover pizza. I sat on one end of the couch and he sat on the other with my feet in his lap. He was always touching me somehow, and it felt so natural. I think I missed half of what was happening on the show. Every time his hand would lightly glide up my leg or he would gently rub my feet, it was all I could focus on.

I could tell he didn't want to leave me on Sunday night. I think I was recovering from the day before, better than he was. Standing at my front door, he gently cupped my face in his strong hands and said, "If you need anything at all, you call me. I don't care how big or small you call. If your headache gets worse... call. If you get scared... call. If you can't sleep... call. I'm here for you, Alex. No more secrets, deal?"

I can barely make an audible sound when I reply. "Deal."

Letting go of me, he opened the door to leave, but still had his eyes trained on mine. "Lock the door behind me, Alex. I'll call or text you later." And with that, he shuts the door behind him and I know he won't leave until I lock it. So, I lock the door and then try to calm my giddiness, but it's impossible. I feel like pulling a 'Tom Cruise' and jumping up and down on my couch, but I digress. Sorda. Instead, I run down the hall and throw myself on my bed and drown in his sent. I don't even care that my face hurts from yesterday and that jumping face first into my bed was probably not the best decision. The giddiness releases itself in the form of a squeal when ten minutes later I get a text from him that includes a picture of him pouting.

SEXY BEAST

Do I have to go to work?

SWEET THING

You do. Just be sure to tuck your cape in nice and tight.

SEXY BEAST

My cape?

SWEET THING

Yes, your superhero cape. The one with the big SB on it. You've rescued me twice now. Thank you.

SEXY BEAST

I wish I had known you needed rescuing when we were kids, but I'm glad I could be there yesterday. I'm no superhero, though.

SWEET THING

Well, we will have to agree to disagree.

SEXY BEAST

Just curious... SB??

SWEET THING

Sexy Beast, of course!

SEXY BEAST

LOL! I'm never gonna live that down, am I?

SWEET THING

Nope. ;)

SEXY BEAST

Well, I better suck it up and get ready for work. Get some rest and if your headache gets worse, we're going to the hospital. I'll leave work if you need me. Do not hesitate to call!

SWEET THING

Yes, sir, Dr. Jacobs.

SEXY BEAST

Don't be a smart ass, Alex.

SWEET THING

Hey, I gotta stick to what I'm good at.

SEXY BEAST

From what I remember… you happen to be good at some other things, too. Very good. If my memory serves me correctly???

Shocked at his change in conversation, I don't know how to reply. Minutes go by and I'm still just staring at my phone like it will bite me if my thumbs touch the screen. Finally, another message appears.

SEXY BEAST

Alex… DO. NOT. FREAK. OUT.

SEXY BEAST

I know you don't want to go there, but give a guy a break! You just spent the night in my arms and I didn't cross any lines. I will always want to cross those lines with you, but if you aren't on the same page, I get it. That doesn't mean that I don't hope that you'll skip a couple chapters and catch up to me. I would love to be on the same page because I think my place in the story is better than yours, and I'm hoping you'll catch up. If you're a slow reader, that's okay. I'll wait.

SWEET THING

Mick...

SEXY BEAST

I'll wait.

SWEET THING

What if I never catch up?

SEXY BEAST

I'll wait.

SEXY BEAST

Gotta go to work. I'll check in later.

True to his word, he did check in later. He also showed up at my office the next day just in time for lunch. It wasn't just a social visit, though. He went with me to file my restraining order and *then* took me to lunch. There was no talk of pages or chapters or books of any kind.

He worked Monday and Tuesday night, but there were text messages throughout the day and night just like after he left on Sunday.

Wednesday night, he took me to *Legend*. Not only did I

get to sit next to Mick at the theater, but I got two versions of Tom Hardy up on the screen. Mick gave me a hard time when I confessed that I chose that movie because Tom Hardy happens to be my celebrity crush. He admitted he thought he was pretty badass, so he was fine with my selection. It was a great movie, but there was a lot of violence and one scene that depicted domestic violence. As soon as the scene started, Mick grabbed my hand and didn't let go the rest of the movie.

He has surprised me every day.

He has been present every day.

Always checking in or just sending a picture of Frank and pretending that he wanted to say hi.

On Friday night, he met me at *On Deck* after work for happy hour. We spent another night playing our little game of make-believe. Mick is surprisingly good at creating alternate universes for strangers. He gets pretty creative too. My favorite has to be the elderly couple that looked to be in their eighties and a bit out of their element. According to Mick, they have a sex dungeon at home. She's the dom and he's the sub and they still get their groove on regularly.

He makes me laugh.

He makes me feel safe.

He makes me happy.

Checking my watch, I see that it's time to hit the road. I need to be at the mall in twenty minutes, so I do one last check of my appearance before I leave. I can't help but notice the smile that's smiling back at me as I take one last look in the mirror. It's new. I like it. Happy looks good on me.

I'm not sure that I'll be this happy down the road, but I'll take the happy while it's here. Besides, I didn't stand a chance after spending the night in his arms. Follow that night up with every day this week and the deal was sealed.

* * *

Mick

Well, this is a first.

I've never taken a date to the mall before.

But then again, I guess this isn't really a 'date'.

I made it clear Sunday night that I want more than friendship. I'm not sure if she thinks I just want sex or if she realizes I want more. It's only been a week since I told her I would wait. It feels like an eternity. But I told her I would wait, and I will. If she doesn't catch up, I'll have to grow a pair and bring the topic up again. This time not like a pussy via text, but in person. I have a feeling I can be a bit more persuasive up close and personal. God, I want to be up close and personal with Alex.

This whole shopping thing isn't my style. I know I could have just shopped online, but it was an excuse to spend time with her.

Holiday music is playing; the mall is lit up with decorations and people are rushing by in every direction. All of that evaporates the minute I see her walking across the parking lot. Sweet Jesus, she is beautiful. She's wearing tight jeans and sexy as hell high boots. I can't see what's going on under her jacket, but I know it's hot.

She lifts her head and sees me waiting for her. She gives me a little wave and practically skips the rest of the way to me. Without hesitation, she slips her arm through mine and says, "Let's shop!" Does she realize what she's doing to me? Having her body against mine is already making this whole shopping thing a much more pleasurable experience. *This* kind of shopping I can do.

"Well, good morning to you too!"

"Sorry, I'm excited! I love to shop and I am determined to make this fun for you!"

"How exactly do you plan on making this fun?" I ask as I hold the door open for her.

"You're with me. How could this not be fun?" She says with a wink as she knocks her shoulder into mine.

"No truer words have ever been spoken. Lead the way, sweet thing,"

"Stop it Mick," she sighs.

"Stop what?" I ask, genuinely confused.

"Don't call me that."

"Call you what? What did I say?"

"You called me sweet thing. You did it that night at Lola's and you did it Saturday night when you were taking care of me." She's no longer walking with her arm in mine. She's pulled away and has her arms wrapped around her waist, almost like she's trying to soothe herself.

"Shit, sorry, it upsets you. Is there a reason I can't call you that?"

"I don't want to be like all the rest, Mick. I don't want you to use your charming little names on me. Please don't treat me like everybody else. We're friends, Mick. I'm not one of your 'girls' and I hate that I'm on your list of Sweet Things. I don't need the reminder."

What the hell?

Stopping in the middle of the crowded mall, I turn and

face her, pull my phone out of my back pocket and hand it to her.

"Alex, there are no other Sweet Things. I called you that at Lola's all those years ago and in my mind, it stuck. Check my phone. Look for your name. I don't have an Alex or an Alexandra in my phone... but I do have a Sweet Thing. It may sound cheesy, and it may sound like a line, but in my head, that's what you've been to me since that night." She's still holding my phone in her hand, but she isn't looking at it. She's looking right at me and I can tell that there's something she wants to say. I think she may be stunned silent. "Here, let me show you," I say, taking the phone back.

I go to my contacts and scroll down to her name. I turn the phone around and show her that her number is attached to the name Sweet Thing. She still hasn't said a word, so I go to my text messages and pull up our last exchange and show her my screen once again.

"See, every time we text or talk, that's what I see. It's not my go to pick up line. You are not just some girl on some imaginary list you seem to think I keep."

"Mick... I don't know what to say..."

Her head drops and she looks to the ground. Shoppers are bumping us with their overflowing bags of gifts as they scurry by. Men who don't want to be here on a Saturday curse us as they fight through the crowds to get around us. I don't care about any of them. I only care about the woman standing in front of me. The woman who currently won't look me in the eye. The woman who I know wants more but won't allow herself to catch up. Nothing is more important than making her see that she means more to me than she seems to know.

"Alex, I think you know that I want more. And I don't mean sex. I know we aren't on the same page when it comes to what we want from each other. Hell, we aren't even on the same chapter. I just hope we're at least reading the same book. I promised not to rush you. *I* am here... here waiting for you to catch up. And just so you know, I'm not going anywhere. Now, give me my phone and take me shopping, woman!"

I stick my arm out so that she can take it again. She smiles, puts her arm through mine and all is well in the world. Putting that smile on her face makes me feel like a superhero. A superhero who can handle a day at the mall as long as his Sweet Thing is by his side.

* * *

Alex

"No way! You have got to be kidding me! How was this going on in my own home and I never got to witness it?"

"Mick, you were never around. You and Riley were way too cool to be hanging out with your little sister and her friends. You were out in the big bad world being...well, being Mickey Jacobs. You didn't have time to hang out with a bunch of thirteen-year-olds."

"If I had known that there were choreographed dance routines to Jennifer Lopez and Gwen Stefani happening, I would have found the time... I promise you that. You have no idea what kind of big brother gold mine that would have been. I would have had reason to give Emmers a hard time for the rest of our lives!"

"I think you might have been surprised at how good we were, especially Emily. I have to say that our Lady Marmalade was the best. You have no idea how sorry you are that you missed that one!" I laugh.

With tears coming out of his eyes from the laughter the image the three of us lip syncing and dancing has brought to his mind, he asks, "Please tell me you were Pink!"

"Why would I be Pink?"

"She's the hot, feisty one. I would much rather imagine you as Pink," he says with a lift of his eyebrows. "Christina was already 'dirty' and Maya was too timid. Oh wait, there's Little Kim too... hmmmm...."

"Oh, just stop it! I wasn't Christina. I wasn't Maya or Lil' Kim either."

"Ahhhhh, yes! I was right! Do I know you or what? Please tell me there is video of you doing your best naughty version of Pink! Oh, sweet Jesus that needs to exist. It sucks that there was no such thing as *the cloud* back then. Maybe if I'm good, I can get you to repeat it someday." He smiles and takes a bite of his pizza.

I ruin his appetite when I remind him that a recreation of the routine would also result in him seeing his sister as timid Maya but also as raunchy Lil' Kim crawling around on a big four poster bed. He spits his pizza out and curses me for putting the image in his head.

"I guess I'll just have to conjure up my own video replay of only you as Pink in my head."

"Well, if that's the case, maybe you should pick a different song."

"And what song would that be, Sweet Thing?"

"I think *You and Your Hand* might be a more accurate

Pink song for me to sing to you," I say with a sassy little smile on my lips. I don't think that was the answer he was expecting. When an olive hits me in the face and he tells me to shut up, my suspicions are confirmed. I just stick my tongue out at him and he gives me a gentle smile.

"Thanks for today, Alex. I really appreciate the help."

"Of course, Mick. You know I love to shop. Besides, you're shopping for three of my favorite ladies, so that makes it that much more fun. I have to admit, I know little about Sidney. Emily never talks about your half-sister. What's she like?"

"I know. Emily really hasn't been able to forgive our dad. I don't think that she likes that I have a relationship with him. It's not much of a relationship, but I do talk to him and try to stay in touch so that I don't lose contact with Sidney. It's not her fault that her dad is a philandering drunk. She's a pretty sweet kid and I think you'd like her. I can't believe she's twelve now. It seems like yesterday that Emily and I were watching Mom pick up the pieces of her life. It would be so much easier to hate him, but he's my dad."

"Trust me, I understand."

"Alex, I don't know how you do it. How do you go visit him and help take care of him after what he put you and your mom through all those years?"

"My mom. That's the answer, Mick. If it wasn't for her... well, if it wasn't for her, I doubt I would have any contact with him at all. But we aren't talking about me. Tell me more about Sidney," I say, trying to get the conversation on anything other than my parents.

"I get it, Alex. I do. I know you don't want to talk about it, but if you ever *do* need to talk, you know I'm here, right?"

"I do. Thank you. Now tell me about your sister."

He gives me a smile and a small shake of the head. He knows I'm deflecting, but he lets me get away with it by picking up where we left off talking about his little sister.

"Let's see... Sidney. She's pretty cool. I think she and Ireland would have a blast together. They both have those blond curls and big brown eyes. Sidney's hair isn't as light as it used to be, but it's still blond. She's really athletic. She plays sports all year-round. Volleyball and Softball are her favorites. I'd love to take Ireland to one of her games sometime, but it might be awhile before Emily's ready for that."

Not giving it a second thought, I reach across the table and grab his hand. "She'll get there, sweetie. I know she will."

"You think?" he asks as he turns his hand over and I rub my fingers over his palm.

"I do, Mick. Now that she's back home with everybody that loves her, her life is going to feel more stable. Having Jonathan as a part of that foundation will make her that much stronger. Don't get me wrong, she's the strongest person I know, but having his support and ours is going to give her a confidence that she didn't have before."

"What about you, Alex?"

"Of course I support her. Emily is like a sister to me."

"No, Alex. What about you? Who supports you? Who gives you all of your strength?"

His words squeeze my heart and steal the air from my lungs. If only he knew what he was doing to me. He makes it so hard to not want to move things to the next level.

"Alex. Talk to me."

Why does he keep bringing the conversation back to me? He knows that this is a loaded question. He knows that *strong* is not a word that has ever been used to describe me. He knows this better than anybody.

"Mick, I think you know I haven't found my strength yet. If I were strong like Emily, would I have let Kevin into my life? I've been cheated on, lied to and now... well, you know what else. I'm not strong, but I'm trying Mick. I am trying."

"Alexandra Stotts, you are strong. Your entire childhood you dealt with what was going on behind the walls of your home without telling a soul. You went to school, got good grades, played basketball, ran track and had a social life. You never let it stop you from living your life and you did it without leaning on those closest to you."

"Mick, don't."

"Alex, you are just as strong as Emily, if not stronger. Everybody knew Emily's secret and she had all of our support. Imagine how much stronger you could be if you let those that care about you in. Emily and Cami would do anything for you. Alex, I'd do anything for you." He turns our hands so that he can interlace our fingers. "I would love to be the person that gives you that extra strength. I know you don't need it, but it doesn't mean that I wouldn't like to be the person that you lean on. That person that gives you that strength."

"Mick, you *have* been there for me. You were there that night at my parents' house and you stayed with me at the hospital all night long. You saved me from Kevin. You've helped me more than anybody ever has," I say, avoiding the fact that he basically says he wants to be with me and wants more than friendship.

"Alex, I don't want to rescue you again. I don't know if I

could survive seeing you like I did when I walked into your place the other day. I don't..."

"I'm so sorry, Mick. I know rescuing me over and over again isn't your responsibility..."

"You didn't let me finish. I wasn't done. Can I continue, please?" I nod my head to grant him the sarcastic permission he's seeking. "Thank you. What I was going to say was that I don't want to rescue you again... but I *will* rescue you over and over if that is what it takes to keep you safe. I know we aren't on the same page, Alex, but I'm not going anywhere."

Our server interrupts our talk to drop off the check, thank God. At his arrival, I pull my hand back and reach for my purse. Before I can get my wallet out, Mick has already put cash down and tells him to keep the change.

"Mick, you didn't have to get lunch. How much was my part?"

"It's the least I can do. Shopping hasn't been so torturous with you on my arm," he says with that classic Mickey Jacobs smile I know has broken many hearts.

"Well, thank you, but you didn't need to. I'm having fun and I think I finished all of my shopping today too. What's left on your list?"

"I know what you're doing, Alex. It's the holiday season and for that reason, and that reason only, I will let you get away with ending our conversation. I've put it out there and you know where I stand. I don't want to pressure you, but I know you feel something too. I know you have a list as long as your arm for the reasons why we shouldn't try this." He motions the space between us with his finger. "But I'm here anytime, day or night, if you decide you want to discuss that list. Until then, I'll still be here... waiting for you to catch up. Got it?"

"Got it," I whisper. My eyes never leaving his. His eyes convey the sincerity with which he just spoke. Mickey Jacobs has just laid down the gauntlet. He wants me. How did this happen? What do I do?

Not letting me sit and contemplate what his words truly mean to me, he stands and offers me his hand. "Come on, sweet thing, let's finish this shopping trip up and get the hell out of here."

And just like he always does, he lightens the mood. He knows that in my head I'm analyzing everything he just said and could very well start panicking. But doing what he does best, he changes the tone and makes things casual again. I take his hand, and as we walk out of the restaurant, he brings his arm around me, pulls me in close, and kisses me on the top of my head.

God, I love this man.

I love him and I do not know what to do about it.

Chapter 13

Alex

"Hi, sweetie! Look who's here!" My mom says with more excitement than I've heard from her in years.

Walking into my dad's room here at Cascade Assisted Living, I look to my left where my dad's bed and recliner sit and see the smiling face of my Aunt Lena.

Rushing to her, I exclaim. "Aunt Lena! It's so good to see you! What are you doing here?"

Throwing her arms around me, she says, "Oh, honey. It's good to see you too! Now let these old eyes take a look at the most beautiful niece in the entire world."

Shaking my head but taking a step back, I say, "I'm your only niece. Nice try though."

"You are still a vision and I am so glad you got here when you did. I've come to take you ladies to tea! I have hats and everything!" She says, clapping her hands together.

"Tea? Hats? What?"

"Yes, isn't it great, Alexandra? Lena wants to take us to holiday tea at the Heathman!"

Yes, it is great, but I also know that Mick has a date there today. He booked this date months ago and now he's going to think I'm there stalking him.

"That's great, Aunt Lena, but how did you get Christmas Eve reservations? You have to book months in advance for a chance at a table during the holidays."

"I've been planning this for ages. I knew you two would just be sitting here with Randall, so I thought I would surprise you! I know we'll see each other tomorrow with the rest of the family, but I thought some girl time might be nice. Besides, this is our last chance. The Heathman is closing the tearoom after the holidays. I just had to get us in there before that happened. So, good surprise?"

"It's a great surprise, Aunt Lena. What time are our reservations for?"

Please don't say noon.

"1:00. So, we have a couple of hours before we have to get going. I'm so glad you two ladies have kept with your tradition of dressing up when you come to visit Randall for the holidays. I was just telling him how much I love the little Christmas tree you've brought in for him." She says referring to the two foot, pre-lit tree that sits on his dresser.

"That's all Mom. You know how she is about tradition and the holidays," I say as I put my arm around my mom and give her some love. I don't know how or why she does it, but she still takes care of my dad as if they had the most beautiful marriage in history. That's the only reason I'm here. This tiny, silver-haired woman who took so much for so many years.

The day my dad had his stroke was scary, sad and liberating.

When we were given the diagnosis of paralysis on his left side and a loss of speech, Mom was devastated. Dad was the bread winner for our household, but in my mind my mom should have felt relief. Relief that she wouldn't have to live in fear of being beaten or berated on a daily basis. Even once she had a job, made new friends and got to have a life for the first time in twenty years, she was still depressed. Turns out she really loves my dad and can't seem to find herself without him. She visits him most days after work and we spend every holiday, big and small, with him. We've had to move him a few times due to his cantankerous ways, but I'm really hoping he gets to stay here. He doesn't always treat the staff well, and this has been the fourth home we've put him in. I don't blame the facilities that have asked us to find a new home for him. I know exactly how they feel. They just don't know how lucky they are that he can't talk.

"Oh, honey. You know how much it means to your father to have us here. I know your dad is thrilled right now to have his three favorite girls here together. Isn't that right, Randall?"

I finally have to acknowledge the man in the recliner. My mom is leaning over him and kissing his cheek while my father stares right through me. He's given up. He can't berate us anymore and he isn't the powerful force over us that he once was. In general, I no longer have any feelings for my dad. Good or bad. I don't have a resounding anger towards him, nor do I have an outpouring of love for him. If it wasn't for my mom, I would never see him again and I would have erased him from my life. When I'm here with Mom and I have to watch her dote all over him, I feel sick. I feel sick that she takes such good care of a man that made her life a living hell for decades.

It's also a rude awakening. It shows me what would have been my future if Mick hadn't saved me just a few short weeks ago. I see the depths that I had sunk to with Kevin.

Shame.

Seeing my parents together makes me feel shame and regret. I don't do regret, and having Mick in my life is making me realize that it's time I start doing something about that.

"Hi, Dad. How are you?" I finally ask him.

Playing the role of the caring daughter is one that I have perfected. Aunt Lena doesn't know the truth about our lives, so I play my part. I set down the small gift in my hand and place it on the table next to his sad little *Charlie Brown* tree.

After making small talk for about twenty minutes and watching my mom feed him his lunch, we finally get ready to leave. Every time I leave his room, I feel a frisson of fear slowly melt away. I'm no longer afraid of him, but I am still haunted by the feelings of the little girl that I used to be. These last couple of months, I seem to be haunted by the ghost of what could have been.

No more.

I'll continue to show up on holidays for my mom, but that is all he gets from me. No more than that. I have to make better decisions for myself and those that I have in my life.

"So, ladies... are you ready? Let's go eat tea and crumpets! I have our hats out in the car and I'll drive! Today is all about me treating the two of you!"

I don't even wave goodbye as my aunt rushes us out the door. I feel stronger leaving today than I did when I arrived. The only thing that was different was me. My eyes have been opened and

I saw the scene in front of me with fresh eyes. Eyes that Mick has helped to open. I see what I don't want. Who I don't want to be. I realize that I am in control of my life. I owe that realization to the sweet man that wants to give me more. I am stronger, but I'm not strong enough to give my heart and soul to Mick. Not yet.

I need time.

Time to be the strong woman that I want to be on my own and not just because I have Mick there to hold my hand. I've always let men dictate my life, and even though I know Mick is different and would never intentionally hurt me, I still need to do this on my own. I don't want to, but I know it's what I need to do.

Or is this just another excuse to push him away?

Climbing into my aunt's backseat, I see the hats that we will apparently be wearing to tea. "Oh, Aunt Lena! These are so cute. Please tell me I get to wear the black one with lace along the brim?"

"It's all yours, my dear. I'm so glad that you like it. I know they're all silly, but I thought it would be fun," she says as I grab the pretentious hat and place it on my head.

It's nice to hear my mom happy and excited. She and my aunt are Chatty Cathie's all the way to the Heathman. My aunt goes all out and forgoes trying to find downtown parking and pulls right up front to the valet. Wow, she really is doing it up today! Valet, ooh la la!

The Heathman is famous for their doormen who are dressed in full English garb. The doorman that opens my mom's door is fully outfitted in his red doormen's coat and pants, along with his high white socks and his fancy black hat. The Heathman is beautiful in all of its holiday splendor.

The tearoom is always fabulous with its large, ornate tapestries and paintings. The addition of all the holiday lights and Christmas trees in every corner just adds to the grandness of the room. But the enormous tree in the corner that reaches the second floor is the showstopper. The Heathman is a Portland classic, and it is such a shame this is the final year of the English holiday tea service.

After we're seated at our corner table and left with our list of teas to choose from, I scan the room. I know that Mickey's date was at noon and I am sure that he's gone already, but I have this feeling that he's near. It doesn't take long to see that I should always go with my gut. Over at a small table for two next to the grand tree is the most precious sight I have ever seen. Dressed to the nines for his date in a dark grey suit, is Mick. He's engaged in an intense conversation with the cutest blond I have ever seen. He's attentive and hanging on her every word.

I wish I had my camera with me.

In the middle of the animated story she's telling, I can see when she sees me out of the corner of her eye. She gasps, her eyes get big, and she exclaims, "Auntie Alex!"

Mick turns to look over his shoulder and the grin that was already on his face stretches even wider. Deciding it's rude not to go say hello, I excuse myself and walk over to their table.

Before I get there, Ireland is out of her seat and runs right to me and wraps her arms around my upper legs. "Auntie Alex, I love your hat!"

"Why thank you, sweetie. I love your dress. You look beautiful, as always."

"Thank you. Look at Uncle Mickey! He dressed up fancy too!"

Mick is now standing next to us. He leans forward, kisses me on the cheek and on a hushed whisper that only I can hear, he says, "You look beautiful, Sweet Thing."

I feel his kiss and his words all the way down to my bones. Oh, what this man does to me. Standing in the middle of a tearoom with a five-year-old attached to me and he still makes me hot and bothered. All it takes is his touch or hearing him call me 'Sweet Thing' and I lose control of my senses. Every touch and every word is etched into my soul where I keep everything good that Mickey has ever given me. It takes the five-year-old standing in front of me to wake me from my dreamlike state.

"Auntie Alex, are you here on a date too?"

"Yes, Auntie Alex... are you here on a date? I didn't know you were going to be here. You didn't mention it when I told you about *my* date," he asks inquisitively. If I were a betting woman, I would say that I sense some jealousy in his question. But this is Mickey Jacobs. He doesn't get jealous. Does he?

"Well, not really a date. I'm here with my mom and my aunt. My Aunt Lena surprised us today. She made the reservations months ago. She knew we would just be hanging out at my dad's place, so she decided to take us out. She wanted to be sure that we could have tea at the Heathman before it's gone."

"You're lucky, just like me, Auntie Alex! Isn't it bootiful?"

"Yes, it is beautiful, Ireland. We are both very lucky ladies," I say as I bring my attention up to the man who makes this room even more exquisite than all the fancy artwork and

162

holiday lights. He lights up every room he's in. I wish he didn't light me up as well. He's getting harder and harder to resist as each day passes. Seeing his love and devotion to his niece is incredibly endearing. It's actually kind of sexy too. He really is a good man. If only he could give me what I need. I know him too well for that though, even if he says differently.

"Well, I better let you two get back to your date." I look down at Ireland and say, "Merry Christmas, little lady. Make sure you get to bed early tonight so that Santa can pay you a visit. The sooner you go to bed; the sooner he'll be here. Don't forget to leave cookies and milk too," I say as I tap her cute little button nose with my index finger.

"Merry Christmas, Auntie Alex. I promise to go to bed early and Mommy and me already made cookies. I can't wait!"

I bend down and give her a hug and then when I stand, the handsome man in his perfectly tailored suit takes me in his arms and says, "Merry Christmas, Alex. I'll call you later, okay?"

"Okay, Mick."

Before he lets me go, he says, "You really do look beautiful. I love your fancy hat. I'll call you later." He kisses my cheek and takes my breath and another piece of my heart away with him.

Chapter 14

Mick

Dude, *don't be a coward.*
Since when are you afraid of a girl?
Just get out of the truck, pick up the packages, and walk to the front door.

I've never had to give myself a pep talk to approach a girl. Maybe the difference here is that she's not just a girl. She's a woman, and not just any woman. She's my *Sweet Thing.*

I used to think what I felt for her was that protective instinct that I've had since that night at her house. The night when she was a scared eighteen-year-old whose family secret was being revealed and she felt like everything was crumbling down around her. Staying by her side that night felt right to me. There was nowhere else I would have been. Knowing she needed somebody and that I could be that somebody for her made me feel like a man. That protective feeling has turned into so much more. I still want to protect her, but now I have this overwhelming need to make her happy, too.

I know she isn't the kind of person who you can buy with gifts. That's not what I'm doing here with my arm full of gifts and a Santa hat on my head. I just want to make her smile. It's something she doesn't do enough, but when she does... it is a sight to behold. Just the thought of seeing her surprised face at seeing me at her front door on Christmas morning makes it hard to contain my smile as I approach her front door.

Well, here goes nothing.

I knock and wait. When I hear the first lock start to turn, my heart beats faster than it has in a long time, and I feel an excitement that I haven't felt since I was a kid.

Maybe it's the Christmas Spirit?

Maybe it's something else?

I hear the second lock and the door swings open and my heart sinks.

I feel sick.

I feel pissed.

I feel stupid.

"Hey bro, nice hat," says the guy in nothing but a towel.

"Thanks *bro*," I reply with a mix of sarcasm and fury that I have no intention of hiding.

Having no shame in his appearance, he lifts his arm and holds the door open. "You here for Alex?" I just stare at him. Everything inside me wants to throw my arm full of gifts to the ground and tackle his skinny ass and beat the shit out of him. "She's in the shower, but you can come in and wait if you want."

This is why! This is why I don't do relationships and don't ever want more than sex!

Fuck this!

"Nah, that's okay. Just give her these and tell her Mick

says, Merry Christmas." I shove the gifts at him and storm my way back to my truck.

I practically rip the door off when I swing it open. I slam it shut, rip the stupid fucking Santa hat off my head and yell, "FUCK!!!!!!!!" at the top of my lungs.

Merry Fucking Christmas to me!

I take a few calming breaths and start the truck. I turn the music up as loud as I can. I usually lean towards hip-hop, but right now, I need something loud. I opt for some old-school Rage Against the Machine to get me through my drive back home. I don't want the girls to see me upset on Christmas morning. Besides, it's really my own fault. She has always said she wasn't on the same page. She's never promised me anything or said she wasn't seeing other people—or *fucking* other people, for that matter. Nope, this is all on me.

Turning into my driveway, I turn the music down and shut the engine off. I take a deep breath and try to get myself back into the Christmas Spirit. I reach down and grab my phone out of the center console and see that I have a text. A text that I didn't hear come through because I was too busy having a mantrum and decided I had to blast loud music like a fucking teenager. The text is from Alex. I don't really want a lame ass explanation, but I need to know what she has to say, so I open the text with a shaky thumb.

SWEET THING

Thank you so much for the gifts. I'm so sorry I missed you. I have a present for you too! I'll be sure to bring it to your NYE party if I don't see you before then. I have to run to my aunt's for Christmas brunch so I'll FaceTime you later today and open my presents. Does that work?

Sweet Thing

Oh, and my cousin said you looked cute in your Santa hat. Sorry I missed it. Will you wear it when we FaceTime later tonight?;)

Relief isn't a strong enough word to explain how I feel when I read the word *cousin* in her message. Not only was towel boy her cousin, but I believe Alexandra Stotts was just flirting with me! She was flirting and she wants to FaceTime so that I can see her open her presents. Hell yes, I'll wear my Santa hat for her. I'd like to see her in a Santa hat too. Just a Santa hat.

This day just went from bad to fucking great!

SEXY BEAST

Sounds perfect. Just text me when you're done at your aunt's.

SEXY BEAST

Merry Christmas, Alex.

With a newfound energy, I bound out of my truck and look forward to the rest of my day with the other ladies in my life. I burst open the front door and am greeted by Frank in his red *Naughty but Nice* holiday shirt. I never thought I would be one of those people that would put clothes on their dog, but when the shirt is a gift from Ireland, well, I'd put him in a tutu if that's what had been in that gift bag. I have to admit... he looks like a stud in his shirt, and he seems to like it.

I give him the attention he's looking for, and then I see Ireland still prancing around in her nightgown. She's playing with her multitude of presents, and Emily and Jonathan are watching her from the couch.

They couldn't look happier.

And I couldn't be more envious of Jonathan Kelly in this moment. He has it all. Emily and Ireland are moving in with him and he'll get to see them each and every day. I know that he only lives minutes away, but I'll miss them. Not only will he get to see these two every day, but he's got what I'm beginning to realize I want.

A partner.

A family.

I've known that I wanted more from Alex, but now I realize this is what I want.

I want it all with her. She's my best friend, but she's so much more. I don't know if I feel scared, sick or elated.

She's the one. The one that I want to have a family with. The one that I want to sit on the couch with and watch our children play with their presents on Christmas morning.

Well, fuck me!

* * *

Alex

It's early afternoon and I've had a great day with my family, but I can't wait to get home! I can't wait to FaceTime with Mick. I hate that I missed him this morning, but just knowing that he was here started my day off just right! I can't wait to hear how his day went. Emily was finally going to spend time with their little sister, Sidney. It's a big day for him. I know how much Emily getting to know Sidney means to him, and I think Em will be glad she did it and sorry she waited so long.

The elation from seeing his gifts on my dining room table to Teddy telling me how cute he looked in his Santa hat has kept me going all day. I was even happy to see my Dad. I feel like there's nothing that could darken my skies today.

I've just dropped Teddy and Mom off at Aunt Lena's and am headed home to change and meet up with the girls at Cami's later when I get a text that darkens those sunny skies of mine. It's from my neighbor, Jean.

JEAN

> Merry Xmas, Alex. It's Jean and I just thought you would want to know that the guy the police took away from your place a few weeks back is here. He's knocked on the door a couple of times. He left once, but he's back and parked across the street.

It appears my skies are not only dark, but stormy as well.

I pull my car into an empty parking lot and text a thank you to Jean. Next, I try not to do what I do best... close myself and my feelings off. My elation is gone, and now I am filled with fear, anger, and exasperation. These aren't feelings I want to feel, but getting back to my group meetings has reminded me I can't shut down. I need to feel these things, but I need to not let them take over. I need to use my brain.

Remembering my promise to Mick, I pick up my phone and call him.

He answers on the second ring. "Hey Sweet Thing, you ready to FaceTime?" He sounds so freaking happy and I hate to ruin his day but...I promised him.

"Mick..."

"Shit. Alex, what's wrong?"

"I am so sorry to ruin your Christmas, Mick, but you told me to call you if he came back. Well...he's back."

"Do you mean Kevin? Is that fucker there?"

I can tell he's trying to keep his cool, but he's barely keeping the illusion together.

"It appears so. My neighbor just texted me to let me know he's parked across the street from my place. He's knocked on the door a couple of times and he seems to be playing the waiting game now."

"Where are you, Alex?"

"I pulled into the Fred Meyer parking lot off Hwy 224. I know I can't go home; I guess I'll join my mom at my aunt's."

"No! Alex, you are coming to my place. I don't want to hear anything about it. You turn that car of yours in my direction. Once you're here, Kelly and I will go pay your guest a little visit and remind him about your restraining order," he says with a powerful authority that I can't argue with.

"Okay Mick, but I don't want to ruin your Christmas. You don't have to deal with him. Can't we just call it in and have him arrested?"

"Oh, I'll call it in, and he *will* get arrested, but I think a conversation is in order first. You don't worry yourself about it. Just get here."

"Thanks, Mick. I'm on my way."

"See you soon."

Minutes later, I pull up in front of Mickey's house to see him sitting on the front steps. The moment he sees me pull up, he rushes off the steps and is opening my car door before I even get the chance to turn the car off.

Stepping out of the car, I can feel the tension radiating off of his body. He looks me in the eyes and then seems to take quick inventory of me to make sure that I'm really there. He takes my face in his hands and his eyes are on mine with more care and concern that I have ever seen from them.

"You okay?"

Grabbing on to his forearms as he continues to hold my face, I reply. "I'm okay, Mick. I'm just so grateful that Jean texted me. Just the thought of being face to face with him again makes me sick to my stomach. Thanks for letting me come over. I know it's Christmas and you're probably enjoying time with your family."

"Alex, I've been wishing you were here all day. I'm gonna be even happier with you here. I wish it were for a different reason, but I'm happy nonetheless. Now, let's get you inside where it's warm."

He kisses me on the forehead, shuts my car door, pulls me

into his side and walks me up the front porch steps and to the front door.

I didn't notice the crowd in the front window as we made our way to the house, but once we're through the front door, I see it. Emily, Jonathan, Ireland, Mick's mom Cheryl and Cami all witnessed Mick's greeting at the car and the way he held me as we walked up to the house.

As if reading my mind, he turns me so that I'm facing him and quietly says, "Jonathan and I are going to go take care of things. I think now may be the time to tell those that love you your secrets. Tell them everything, Alex. Tell them about your childhood, Kevin, and since it seems the cat is out of the bag, tell them what you want about us. I don't ever want to be one of your secrets, Alex. Remember... I'm just waiting for you to catch up. You tell them what you want, but I think they deserve to know the real you and what you've been through." With another kiss to the forehead, he asks, "You okay if we go? You need anything?"

This man surprises me every day. As I look over at my friends, who I know love me unconditionally, I know that he's right. They deserve to know the real me. They also deserve to know why it is I called Mick today and not one of them. That part almost seems harder than the rest. I don't know exactly how to tell them about the two of us. I don't really know what we are, but it's clear that we're something. He's Emily's brother. Will she hate me? Will they all tell me how stupid I am to think that Mick could really want more than a one-night stand?

"Alex?"

"Sorry, I'm fine, Mick. Thanks for everything. Please be

careful and don't do anything that could get you in trouble."
Looking over at Jonathan, I say, "And that goes for you, too."

"Yes, ma'am," Jonathan says as he ruffles Ireland's hair
and gives Emily a chaste kiss. He walks out the front door
and Mick gives me a small smile and says, "I'll be back, baby.
Now go talk to the girls and remember... I got you."

Mickey Jacobs has me.

In what world?

I remember that I'm not alone when Cami's voice chirps.
"Yes, chica. Why don't you come over here and talk to the
girls? I have a feeling there's a lot that we need to be filled in
on. I was just picking these two up to meet you at my place,
anyway. Here seems like just as good of a place, so let's stay
put and chat, shall we?"

After Emily gets Ireland set up in her room with all of her
new presents and a movie, Cami pours some wine and
Cheryl asks if I would rather she leave. I tell her I'd like her to
stay. She's like a second mom to me and she deserves to know
my secret.

Two hours later and it's all out there. The three of them
now know everything about my childhood, my time with
Kevin, and my friendship with Mick. There were tears.
There were angry words. Most of that anger was towards my
father and a little towards my mother for staying. There were
also words of anger for not trusting my best friends with the
truth. I know they think they could have helped, but I really
don't think that's true. There wasn't anything that anybody
could have done without a public scandal. There was also
some anger towards Mick, too. Emily is pissed that he never
told her about the night of my dad's stroke or about his bad
vibes about Kevin.

In the end, it feels good to get everything out. No more secrets from those that matter most to me. The only thing that they haven't made too many comments about is Mick. Emily doesn't seem mad, but she seems concerned. Cami... well, she seems shocked.

"So, what you're saying is that Mickey Jacobs... lifelong playboy... king of the one-night stand... wants a relationship... with you? No offense to you, Alex and Cheryl. I know that he's your son, but I'm just keeping it real."

"I understand, Cami. It's true that my son has never been in a relationship and has never thought that he wanted to commit. The thing to remember is he is a good man, and I've always known it would take the right woman to help him find his way." Cheryl sends a small smile and a wink my way.

"You're right, Cheryl. Mick is a good man. Look how he's stepped up for Emily and Ireland, and he'd do anything for any of us. The thing is, I don't want Alex to be an experiment. Alex deserves more than to be something that Mick tries out."

Emily speaks up and says, "Cami, you do realize that Alex is sitting right here. Why don't you ask her how she feels about Mick?"

Cami's startled when Emily calls her out, but she recovers and says, "Sorry, chica. I didn't mean to talk about you like you're not here or to hurt you. You just deserve the best, and I would hate to have to kick Mick's ass if he hurt you. Tell us how you feel."

How do I feel?

Looking Cami straight in the eye, I continue telling my truth. I feel safe here and it means a lot to me that she cares, that they all care. "The truth is... I don't know, Cami. I've been in love with Mickey since we were kids. He was always my secret crush. When he showed up that night at my house, I was mortified. But not only did he stay with me the whole night, he kept my secret. The night I spent with him a year later was one of the best nights of my life. Sorry, Em. Sorry, Cheryl. I know you don't want to hear about that, but it's the truth."

Emily and Cheryl look like their heads are about to explode, listening to my confession.

"Now, years later, he's become one of my best friends. I was so afraid of ruining that friendship by taking things to the next level that I let Kevin take over my life. Then, just like before, Mick was there to rescue me. Not only does he rescue me, but without knowing it, he tells me he wants to make all my childhood dreams come true. He wants to be with *me*. That dream becoming reality... it scares me almost more than anything my dad or Kevin have done to me. I don't want that dream to end in heartbreak. It's not worth it. He's too important to me now. I don't think I can take that risk. He may not know it, but he already has my heart. I just want him to keep it in one piece."

Because I haven't taken my eyes off of Cami during my little confession, I don't realize that Emily's eyes still look like they are about to pop out of her head until I look over to see why everybody is so quiet.

Emily and Cheryl stare over my head in stunned silence. Slowly, I turn my head and, much to my dismay, Mickey and Jonathan stand behind me. Mick has a mixture of emotions crossing his face. One of those emotions is smugness.

Without missing a beat, he says, "Sorry to interrupt, ladies. Alex, I hope you don't mind, but I packed you a bag.

You're not going home tonight. We need to be sure that we get a security system installed at your place. Because of the holiday, it's going to be a day or two before that can happen. I texted you but didn't get a reply, so I took it upon myself and asked your neighbor Jean to take Blazer for you. I hope that's okay? I wasn't sure how he would get along with Frank. Might be a little safer with Jean."

I can't believe he's letting what he overheard slide. Since when does Mick not have something to say? And why does he look so smug? It's actually starting to piss me off.

"Sorry, I didn't see your texts. Thank you for doing all of that. I'll call Jean and make sure that she's fine with taking Blazer."

"No problem. I'm gonna put your stuff in Em's room for now and we'll figure the rest out later."

Now that it's all out there, I don't have to be afraid of everybody hearing Mick's answer when I ask him what happened at my place.

"Alex, I don't think he's going to bother you again. He's in custody, but we're gonna get that security system installed just to be safe. You should have had it all along. That goes for you too, Cami. If you don't have it, we're getting it installed. I would think after what happened to Ireland's room, we all would have been smart enough to make sure that all of you girls were protected. We didn't do that and that's my bad. We'll have this remedied by the new year, though. *That,* you can count on."

"Mick, what did Kevin want?"

"Don't you worry about it. Kevin won't be a problem in the future."

"Mick! I'm not a child! What did Kevin want?" I yell, as I push my way up from the table and stand in front of him.

With his arms crossed in front of him, he says quietly. "You don't want to know, Alex."

"Mick..." I start but am interrupted by Emily.

"Mick, you need to tell her. After everything she's told us today..." Emily stands beside me and grabs my hand and gives it a squeeze. "She can handle it."

I can see him warring with himself, and just when he's about to speak, Ireland comes running out of her room. "You're back! Yea! Mommy, can I have a snack?"

Jonathan scoops her up and says, "Let's get you back in your room. I'll get you some fishies to tide you over before dinner, and then we'll play with your new toys. Deal?"

"Deal, Jonafon."

"Okay, Princess. I'll be right there. You go get ready for me." As he passes by, Jonathan gives me a look that says he's sorry and that I'm not going to like what I'm about to hear.

"Thanks, baby," Emily says to Jonathan, still holding my hand.

"Why don't we sit down?" Mick says.

"I don't want to sit, Mick," I say indignantly.

Cami and Cheryl are now standing and Cami takes my other hand.

"Well, I need to sit down." He sits down on the couch and puts his hands together and drops his head between his shoulders and lets out a heavy exhale. He brings his head up and looks me in the eye and says, "Alex, that fucker was going to try to take you and God knows what else."

"What do you mean, take her?" Emily asks, so I don't have to.

"He was wearing gloves, which wouldn't be odd in December except... we found things... in his trunk." He puts his head down and then, on a growl, he pushes himself up. With venom in his voice, he says, "Duct tape, zip ties, large garbage bags and chloroform. We know he was planning on drugging you with the chloroform and we can only guess what his plan was from there with what he had in his trunk. Needless to say, I think we might just owe your life to Jean. If she hadn't reached out... fuck... I don't even want to think about it." Not caring that Cami and Emily are holding my hands, he barrels into me and takes me in his arms and hugs me with everything he's got.

The girls step aside and I wrap my arms around his strong back.

He's trembling.

My superhero is trembling.

I try to step back to look at him, but he won't let me. He just holds on even tighter.

"Hey, it's okay, Mick. I'm here. I'm safe." I squeeze him back and repeat. "I'm here."

He finally steps back, and his eyes are red and full of unshed tears. The moment he sees my shocked expression at seeing his emotions. His tears seem to evaporate, and the stoic man I have come to know is back. "You okay?"

"What? Yeah... at least I think so. I don't think it's quite sunk in yet. I don't know how I can ever thank Jean enough."

Emily approaches and asks. "Do you need a minute to take this in? What can I do for you, Alex?"

Feeling the strength from the four people surrounding me with love, I say, "You know what, I don't need a minute. I wanna know what I can do to help with dinner. I know that

I've thrown a monkey wrench into everything, and I want to help in any way that I can."

Emily looks at her brother with a small smile and says, "See, I told you she could handle it."

Cheryl steps up, puts her arm around my shoulder, gives me a motherly look and says, "Alex, honey. I've been working on dinner all day. There isn't much to do. We need to eat sooner, rather than later though, so Jonathan and the girls can head to Devon and Gabby's for dessert. Come with me. You can help set the table."

With that we set the table and have an enjoyable meal with no mention of abductions, abusive fathers or being an experiment to Mick. After we eat, Emily, Ireland and Jonathan leave for Devon's, and Cami and Cheryl both head home. Cami says that I can come stay with her, but Mick shuts that down real fast. He blames her lack of security, but I know better. He wants some time alone after our crazy day. I wouldn't mind that right about now, either.

After saying goodbye to his mom, he shuts the front door, locks it, and then turns around with his back pressed to the door. His gaze penetrates right to my heart as he speaks a thousand words without saying a single thing. He's glad we're alone. He needs to decompress after everything that happened with Kevin and I see a fire. A fire that says he knows exactly how he'd like to decompress.

From his spot against the door, he lets out a one-word growl. "Alex."

As soon as my name crosses his lips, he pushes off of the door and with an intensity I have never seen from him before, he crosses the room. One hand goes around my waist and pulls my body flush with his as his other hand gently cups the back of my head. "I know we aren't on the same page, but I need this for me. I'm asking you to please let me take this right now. Please, Alex?"

"What do you need, Mick?"

"You. In my arms. I don't need sex, but I do need you in my arms and if you don't mind... I'm going to kiss you right now."

"Mick..."

I don't get to finish my sentence as the softest, gentlest kiss I have ever felt touches my lips. I can feel all of his emotion in this kiss. It feels like he's worshiping me as his lips caress mine. He's gentle, careful and slow. He now holds my head with both of his hands tangled in my hair as he ever so lightly bites on my bottom lip. I hear myself let out a small whimper and this fuels his fire. His tongue seeks entry as it traces my upper lip and I part for him. Our tongues find one another and are in a beautiful dance of passion. A dance that is filling me with everything I never knew I needed. I know that in this moment; I am experiencing the most perfect kiss of my life.

He brings one of his hands to my face, strokes my jaw with his thumb, and then slowly drags his hand down my neck and to my chest. He stops his hand over my heart and then, much to my dismay, removes his lips from mine. I'm relieved when his lips continue their journey down my neck. He stops his kisses and is almost nuzzling my neck when I hear him moan. "Still my favorite spot."

His favorite spot?

His lips find my collarbone and his tongue outlines it, and then he drags his lips back up my neck and to my ear. "Sweet Thing, I want nothing more than to make love to you all night long, but I know now is not the time. I know today has been emotional for both of us and I have no intention of taking advantage of that. Thank you for giving me this. You have no idea how much I needed it." I start to pull away so that we can continue the conversation, but he doesn't let me. Instead, he pulls me tighter and buries himself deeper into my neck and says, "Not yet, baby. Just let me have this moment."

I don't even know what to say. No matter how many times he tries to tell me, I still cannot believe that he feels this way about me. All I can do is hold on as long as he needs me to. I need this moment just as much as he does. If only I was strong enough to admit to him that I need this too. Hell, I wish I could admit it to myself. It's so easy for him to just put it all out there. A man who has never done this before.

Why can't I?

Chapter 15

Alex

"Oh, Auntie Alex, I can't wait for you to see my new room! It's the most bootiful room you'll ever see!" Ireland says as I help Emily pack up her room.

I couldn't be happier for Emily and Ireland. Watching the two of them with Jonathan melts my heart. The three of them were meant to be together, and I'm so glad that Jonathan has asked them to move in. He didn't just ask them to move in, but he made a room fit for a princess for Ireland. He also redecorated his bedroom and office just for Emily and has done all he can to make his house *their* home. Now all he needs is the two of them home with him and that's just what's happening today. Nobody deserves this more than they do, and I must say Jonathan is a great addition to our little family that we've put together over the years.

"I can't wait to see it, Ireland! You'll have to give me a tour when we take your things over there. Are you excited about moving?"

"So excited! I'll miss Frank and Uncle Mickey, but I

will see them lots still. Plus, I get to live with Frances! Frances and Frank are best friends, so we'll have to have play dates. I love Frances, I hope she gets to sleep with me!"

Emily walks into the room with more boxes and says, "No dogs in the bed, baby girl."

She turns to leave to get more boxes and Jonathan pops his head in. With a wink he says, "There's a dog bed in your room too, Princess. We'll have to wait and see about bedtime."

And with that, he's gone. I hear a little giggle come from the other side of the room and when I get a look at the smile on her adorable little face, it's clear that Ireland is just as head over heels as her momma is. Too cute.

It's Monday, and I'm still at Mick's. Christmas was on Saturday, so we had to wait until today to get the security system installed. Mick is at my place with the contractors that are doing the install, and I'm here helping Emily and Ireland get packed up and moved.

The last couple of days have been pure bliss. I know it's not reality, but I'll take it while I've got it.

After Mick took his 'moment' on Christmas night, he light-ened the mood and gave me my presents. He saw them on my kitchen table when he went into my place to pack me a bag. He didn't do a great job packing my bag and we had to go back on Sunday to get a few more things, but it's the thought that counts.

Saturday night we sat in front of his Christmas tree and he gave me my presents, but not before he put his Santa hat on.

Damn, he is one hot Santa.

With the glow of the tree lights in his eyes, his red and

white hat slightly askew on his blonde head and the glee-full smile on his face, I am a goner.

No gifts required. My heart is his. Just. Like. That.

With the excitement of a five-year-old on Christmas morning, he pushes a perfectly wrapped box in my direction and says, "Go ahead. Open it."

"Mick, I feel so bad. I don't have your present. This isn't fair."

"Don't even sweat it. I'm excited for you to open your gifts. I don't need anything. Now get to it!"

Before digging into the beautiful paper, I burn this memory of Mick into my heart. I don't ever want to forget the way he looks at this moment.

Happy.

He looks happy.

To think that any of that happy shining back in my direction is because of me warms my heart. I don't ever want to forget how I feel right here in this moment.

"Wow, this wrap job is pretty nice. You do this?"

"As a matter of fact, I did, smartass."

"I'm impressed. You have mad skills,"

"Oh, you have no idea, sweet thing."

I set myself up for that one, and I feel the warmth of my embarrassment as well as the lust I have for this man on my cheeks. I would love nothing more than to throw these gifts to the side and have him show me his 'mad skills' right here in front of the tree. He sees my blush and throws a wink in my direction.

The moment I peel the paper back, the laughter that tumbles out of me is surprising but welcome. I feel like I haven't laughed in years. Leave it to Mick to break that cycle. After I catch my breath, I say, "You know me so well!"

Not serious enough to change the mood, but with levity, he says, "I do."

He really does. And the fact that I am holding a full-size JC Chasez doll in my hands is proof. "How did you find this? They haven't made these for years! You really are a superhero!"

"No cape necessary. Being that it's 2015 and all there is this thing called the internet and it is quite a magical thing. It's amazing the things you can find on there." He wags his eyebrows up and down and I just roll my eyes at him. "Nah, he was easy to find, and I know he was your favorite. I'm sure a love as strong as yours was for *NSYNC and JC never dies."

"I love it, Mick! And you're right. A love that strong never dies and let's face it... Justin got all the attention, so I'm proud to be the new owner of this JC doll. I can't believe you bought me a doll, though."

"Not a doll, an action figure." He corrects me.

"Oh, well, then that makes me feel a little better. I guess you're never too old for an action figure."

"Never. Here, open this one," he says as he pushes a square box my way.

"Hmmm... it's not big enough to be a doll house.... I wonder what memory from my youth this gift will evoke?" I peel the paper off and see the silver Nordstrom box underneath. I lift the lid off of the box and pull the tissue back and see proof, yet again, that he does know me. "Mick, this is the hat I tried on when we were shopping the other day. I can't believe you remembered. Thank you, I love it!" I'm sitting on my knees, so it's easy to lean forward and throw my arms around him and thank him with a hug.

"I know you were playing around when you tried it on at the mall but...damn, Alex...you just looked so good in it. I may or may not have dreamt about you wearing that hat, and only that hat, but I cannot confirm nor deny that." He takes the hat out of the box and places it just so on my head. *"This one's a little sexier than the one you had on at the Heathman. Just sayin'."*

Did he really just say all that?

"Thanks, Mick. It really does mean a lot that you remembered and that you may or may not have thought of me in it. See the mall isn't so bad after all. I bet you can't wait to go back again."

I can tell he's surprised by my reaction, but he recovers well. *"For you, I will brave the mall yet again."*

He slides a larger box over to me but doesn't say anything.

"Mick, you've done way too much. Please tell me there aren't any more after this one?"

"Just open the box, Alex."

This gift isn't wrapped in paper but instead is in a beautiful red box with a sparkling gold bow on top of it. I take the bow off the top and gently place it on a snoring Frank, who's lying next to me. It doesn't phase him and he continues his deep Christmas slumber.

Slowly, I lift the lid and peel back the tissue paper. I gasp when I see what's inside. I lift my eyes to the radiantly proud man sitting before me.

"Mick."

I can only whisper his name. I can't believe he's done this for me. Why has he done this for me?

"Did I do good?"

"Did you do good? Mick, this is a Nikon F2 Titan 35mm. You did too much."

"Nah, it was my pleasure. I thought you'd like it. There's a bunch of information about it underneath. It was made in 1979 and..."

"Mick, this is too much. I can't accept this. I can't even imagine how much it cost or where you found it." I cut him off while I continue staring into the box like the Hope Diamond is inside.

"Hey," he says, trying to get my attention, but I can't look at him right now. I'm suddenly overwhelmed with emotion and I'm not sure how to deal with it. He repeats himself when he says, "Hey." This time, he gently uses his finger to lift my chin so that my eyes meet his. "Alex, you haven't even touched it yet. Pick it up. It's yours and it's not too much."

"Mick, I've researched these and I know that this had to cost you a pretty penny. You didn't spend this much on your entire family put together."

Still speaking softly and sincerely, he brushes his thumb over my cheek to catch the lone tear that I didn't even know was falling. "Alex, please don't take offense when I say this, but...what I do with my money isn't really your concern." Searching my eyes to make sure that I haven't taken his honest reply personally, he says, "Okay, sweetheart. I work hard for my money and seeing your reaction when you opened your gifts was worth every penny. Nobody deserves to be happy more than you do. There is nothing in this world that I want more than to see you happy. Now. Please. Pick. Up. The. Camera."

Once again unable to find adequate words to express myself in this beautiful moment, I do what I'm told. I feel like *a kid in a candy store as I hold the classic camera in my hands. I examine every lever, button and feature that I can find. It is a true thing of beauty.*

"Mick, it's beautiful! And it's in mint condition, too! Thank you so much!"

I jump up onto my feet and start pacing the room, holding the camera up to my eye and checking the view of everything in the room through the antique lens. When I finally stop moving and take the camera away from my face, Mick is standing in front of me with an alert and awake Frank at his heel. The smile that lights his face mirrors that which is on mine. We just stand there and smile at each other. We look like two grinning fools.

"Thank you again, Mick. Hey, can we run to my place real quick and get your gift?"

"No can do, Alex. You aren't going anywhere near your place tonight. There's just one thing I want to end the day."

Cautiously, I ask. "What's that, Mickey Jacobs?"

"Get your mind out of the gutter, woman! I'm not asking for sex. We aren't there yet, but what I want does involve you and my bed."

Relieved, disappointed and yet excited all at once he has my curiosity peaked.

"Does it now?"

"It does." He takes the camera from my hands and places it back in the box and then places the box on the dining room table. He motions for me to follow him as we walk down the hall to Emily's room. He lifts a finger as a signal for me to stay where I am and he reaches into the room and grabs my bag. He throws the bag over his shoulder and leads me past Emily's room and up the stairs to the loft that turns into his primary

suite. The room is filled with big, masculine furniture, but just like the rest of the house, there isn't anything on the walls. I sure would love to help him decorate this place. He heads to his dresser and pulls out a pair or boxers from his top drawer and a gray V-neck t-shirt out of the next drawer down.

Walking over to his bathroom, he places my bag next to the door and hands me the items he apparently has selected for me to wear. "Take your time getting ready for bed. Your toothbrush is in your bag and you can help yourself to anything you might find in there," he says with a thumb pointed over his shoulder. "I'm gonna go let Frank out once last time and close the house up for the night. Alex, I don't want anything more than to hold you in my arms. I promise I won't cross any lines. So, get that deer in the headlights look off of your face and relax." He brushes past me and, not letting me down, he leaves me with a smart-ass comment. "Besides, I don't bite. Well, not too hard."

That was two nights ago. And true to his word, all he did was hold me. I said that I was worried that another night sleeping in his arms might be crossing a line and to that he simply pulled me even tighter to his side. With my head on his chest, he kissed the top of my head and said, "Merry Christmas, Sweet Thing."

Sunday morning I woke to an empty bed and helped myself to a shower. After, I found him serving up our breakfast and acting as though this was our normal everyday routine.

We didn't talk about us, but we did talk about Kevin and the fact that if I wanted to see that he got prison time, I would have to testify against him. Mick was worried that I wouldn't be up for it, but now that I realize how strong my support system is, I feel strong. I tell him so and I can tell that he's proud of me.

Even though Kevin is currently in custody, Mick still won't let me go home. He insists I wait until the new security system is in. Because of this, I do convince him that we need to go back to my place so that I can get my make-up and other things that I simply can't be without. While we're at it, I make sure we grab his Christmas present as well. We also have to go by the police department to fill out some paper-work. It's not a fun task, but if it keeps Kevin behind bars, I'll do whatever I need to.

Mick didn't leave my side once, but he also didn't give me any more of his Christmas night kisses. I know it's for the best, but it's also all I can think about. His kiss was perfect. I know that I will never be kissed like that again.

We spent the evening with Emily, Ireland, and Jonathan and had a great time. After Jonathan left for the night, we all start getting ready for bed. Emily gets Ireland tucked in and then addresses the issue that I know has been on her mind all day.

"So, where are you sleeping tonight, Alex?"

She doesn't sound angry, but she does sound concerned. Before I get a chance to reply, Mick steps in and addresses his inquisitive sister.

"Emmers... don't start with Alex. This is all me. There is no parental guidance needed. I will sleep better with Alex next to me while she's here. Don't go thinking there is any sort of debauchery going on. I know she isn't interested in that, and I would never push her to do something she didn't want to do." Emily and I both start to speak, but he stops us both. Still looking at his sister but grabbing my hand, he says,

"We are both grown adults, and I don't get up in your business and your sleeping arrangements with Officer Kelly, so I would appreciate the same courtesy from you."

Sheepishly, Emily replies. "You're right, Mickey. I'm sorry. Seeing you together like this is just new for me."

Finally, finding my voice, I say, "There's nothing to be sorry about. I understand how it looks, Em, but I promise there isn't anything going on." I can feel Mick's grip on my hand loosen when he hears my statement. He doesn't let go, but he does pull me towards the stairs to his room with only our fingers still touching. I guess our conversation with Emily is over. I'm handed another t-shirt and boxers combo and he disappears behind the bathroom door and leaves me to change without a word. He comes back out in just his boxer briefs and gets into bed without saying a word.

After washing my face, brushing my teeth and changing into my assigned sleep wear, I slip under the sheets but stay on my side. As much as I want to find my place on his chest again tonight, I don't think I'm welcome. My words to Emily hurt him. How could I hurt a man who has done so much for me? I know that I haven't made any advances or said anything to lead him to believe that we're more than we were before our kiss, but it's clear that I've hurt him. I can't go to sleep with his pain thick in the air.

"Mick..."

"Don't, baby. Just get over here and let's get some sleep. I know where I stand. I may not like it, but you haven't made me any false promises."

"Mick, I don't want to hurt you."

"Then, get over here."

I can't help but feel confused as I take my place tucked

into his side with my head on his chest. I can't help myself when I turn my lips to his chest and kiss him. I can feel his beautiful heart beating under my touch and I want nothing more than to keep his heart for mine forever. I know how this will end. And I don't think my weak heart could take it. If I can continue to compartmentalize him as a friend and companion, I can hopefully keep him in my life.

This morning he was nothing but sweet, but down to business. There was a lot to do with my security installation and moving the girls. We didn't get much time to talk, but he seemed fine. I wish I felt the same. I don't like things down to business like this. I miss the flirty and fun Mick. If only I was a speed-reader and could catch up to him. I want to be on the same chapter as him more than he knows.

If only I wasn't so far behind.

* * *

Mick

I feel sick to my stomach.

I've just gone over the instructions to Alex's new security system with her, and I know it's time for me to leave. I keep finding every reason I can to draw out the evening. Right now, I'm having a conversation with Blazer.

"Now, listen Blaze. If anybody comes near this place, I need you to scratch their eyes out. You take care of our girl and make sure she locks the doors and sets the alarm every time she comes or goes. Got it?"

"Mick, I'm twenty-seven years old. I've lived alone for years. I got this."

"I know you do, but Blaze and I have an agreement. I just need to make sure that he's holding up his end of things."

"Mick, stop being ridiculous and get back to your life. You've given up the last three days to my stupid drama. I appreciate it more than you know, but I'm really starting to feel guilty."

Letting Blaze go, I brush my hands over my clothes to wipe the cat hair off—and to delay my inevitable goodbye. "Alex, I don't know how many times I have to tell you, but you weren't an inconvenience, and I loved having you around. Also, what went down with that prick wasn't stupid drama. I need to know that you're taking all of this seriously. What he meant to do to you... it wasn't stupid. It was serious. Please tell me you understand that?"

She steps closer to me and takes my hand in both of hers and says, "I understand, Mick. I don't mean to make light of the situation. I know that your confrontation with Kevin was horrible and you put your career at risk doing what you did. I will forever be grateful to you."

She's referring to her discovery of my bloodied knuckles the morning after my *conversation* with her ex. Thank goodness I had the smart thinking to clean up before I came back to the house. If she had seen all the blood on my hands after our *talk*, well, I don't even want to think about her reaction.

"Oh my God, Mick! Look at your hands! How did I not see that last night? What did you do?"

"Don't worry about it. It's all hunky dory."

"Mick, tell me what happened. Now!"

Now, if bossy, feisty Alex isn't sexy as fuck, then I don't know what is. I want to laugh at her, but I can see how serious she is. I don't think my amusement would be appreciated right now.

"Listen, when I found him outside your house, stalking his prey, I might have lost it just a little bit."

"What do you mean, Mick? Please tell me you didn't attack him... unprovoked? Mick, you could lose your job."

"The long and the short of it is that I knocked on his window and reminded him about the restraining order, and he found that to be humorous. I may or may not have badged him and asked him to step out of his car. Because he's an arrogant fuck. He got out of the car and spat at me. I may or may not have then pushed him against his car to make sure that he knew I wasn't okay with his behavior. He then tried to get away from me and took a swing. That was all I needed to get legal permission to swing back."

"How many times did you swing back, Mick?"

"Enough," I answer.

What she doesn't know is that after the arresting officers arrived and we opened his trunk to find what we found, I somehow got my hands on him again and may have grabbed him by the throat, hit his head against the car a few times and then proceeded to try to choke him to death. Kelly and the other officers on the call pulled me off of him. I proceeded to beat the shit out of the hood of his car, and that's what did the real damage to my hands.

"And you didn't get in trouble?"

"Nope."

"What if he presses charges?"

"Let's not worry about that right now."

"Mick?"

"*Alex?*"

"*Thank you.*"

"*Once again, it was my pleasure.*"

"As long as we're on the same page. You think you got all of this? You need anything else while I'm here?"

I don't want to leave. Playing house with her these last couple of days was better than I could have dreamed it would be. Everything with her is so easy. Her presence makes me feel lighter in some strange way. Having Emily, Ireland and Alex under my roof at the same time reminds me that there is still good in this world. At work, I deal with that 1% of people that aren't good, but when that becomes your norm, it's hard to remember that not everybody is that fucked up.

"We're on the same page and I don't need anything else."

She gives my hand a squeeze and goes to let go, but I pull her into a hug. "You call me or text me or FaceTime or carrier pigeon me, if you need anything at all."

"Mick, go. Go be Mickey Jacobs and rule the world. I'll see you at your place on Friday night to ring in the New Year. If you change your mind and I can bring anything, just let me know. And don't forget I'm gonna be late because I have to work the first half of Olivia's party that night. I'll be there before midnight, though."

"All you need to bring is yourself. Make sure you come straight from work so you don't miss the countdown."

"Will do. Now get out of here."

I pull her into a hug and find my spot in the curve of her neck and take a big inhale. I let her go and let myself out. The entire drive home, I'm on autopilot. I don't even know which route I took to get there.

When I enter the house, the cloud of loneliness that I feel

looming over me as I walk through all the empty rooms of my home is immense. All of my girls are gone, and I'm back to life with Frank. I don't want my old life back. I want a house full of noise and important people.

It's in this moment that I realize that it's been months since I've had sex. Since the night that Alex climbed into my lap at Riley's, I haven't been interested in anybody else. How do I make her see that I can change? I'm not my father. I refuse to be him.

There's a reason I don't go by Michael, Mike or Junior. I don't want to be associated with his reputation. He's an alcoholic womanizer. I watched him break my mom's heart and my baby sister's. I may have gone into his line of work, but I will never be him.

Walking through the house, I'm surrounded by reminders of my girls, thanks to Alex. I'm not sure if she realizes how much her Christmas gift meant to me. Well, it was more than one gift, but the way she packaged them together as one was pretty great.

"What the hell is that?" I ask as Alex brings an enormous stack of wrapped packages out of her room.

"It's your Christmas present," she says with a silly grin. Oh, this woman and her face. Every expression she makes fills me with a new emotion. I don't do emotions, so it's getting a bit exhausting to keep up with myself, but I never want it to stop.

"What in the world is it?"

"Well, that would ruin all the fun, now wouldn't it? Good thing you have a big truck and plenty of room. Now let's get back to your place so you can open it!"

Once we're back at my house, the girls and Jonathan are

back, too. Alex insists on carrying the gift inside herself, so I take her big, pink girly bag that she's packed. With the bag thrown over my shoulder, she gives me a little smile and I say, "Oh, I know I make this shit look good, girl." I blow her a little kiss and then open the door for her.

Once we've said our hello's Alex and I are back in front of the tree, only this time Ireland sits in Alex's lap while her mom and Jonathan watch from the couch.

The gift is a stack of different sized flat packages. Each is individually wrapped and then tied all together with twine. It looks too cool to unwrap, but with four sets of eyes on me; I don't think I have a choice.

"Come on, Uncle Mickey! Open! Open!"

"Hold your horses, Ireland. I was just admiring the nice wrap job Alex did here. Besides, I have to read the card first."

Mick,

Thank you so much for always being there for me and everybody else.

Your new home is beautiful, but it needs a little something.

Hoping these make your house more of a home.

Merry Christmas,
Alex

As I read her card, I can't help but think to myself that having the girls and Alex in my house made it feel like a home.

I take the smallest item from the top of the pile and unwrap the red paper to reveal a framed 5x7 picture of me holding Ireland in my arms while she laughs hysterically from the tickle attack I'm giving her. The picture is black and white and perfect. I pull my gaze from the picture and look into her warm, dark eyes. Beautiful eyes that take my breath away every time I find them staring back at me. She's smiling a shy, almost embarrassed smile. Holding Ireland in her lap... She. Is. Perfect.

"Uncle Mickey, show us!" Ireland begs as she bounces up and down in Alex's lap. I turn the picture around so that she can see it and she beams ear to ear. "It's you and me! And a tickle attack!" Looking over her shoulder at Alex, she says, "I love it, Auntie Alex!"

"Ah, thanks, sweetheart. You're the perfect model! Now, your uncle has lots more to open, so why don't you pass that over to your mommy so she can see it?"

Next, I open an 8x10 of Ireland, in one of her favorite princess dresses, blowing out her birthday candles. The way the picture blurs out the background and only focuses on Ireland's angelic little face and the glowing candles in front of her is extraordinary. After that, I unwrap another 8x10, but this one is of Emily. She's laughing and doesn't know that the camera is focused on her. Again, her work is extraordinary. The third 8x10 has two original pictures in it. One is of a Portland Police car and the other a Portland Police badge. Not only are these photos cool as hell, but a puff of pride fills my chest.

"Alex, these are amazing," I tell her, and mean every word. These aren't just snapshots. These pictures are pure art. I may

be biased because of the subject matter, but the way she captures the most endearing qualities of the girls is something pretty special.

"Thank you, but keep going!" She says, excitedly.

The next red package is even larger and contains an 11x14 of my man, Frank.

"Frank, looking good buddy!" I say as I turn the picture in his direction to show him just how much of a stud he truly is. As if that weren't enough, next is another big 11x14 that I unwrap to find a picture of Emily hugging Ireland from behind and kissing her on the cheek. Ireland has the biggest smile on her face and her nose is all scrunched up. Perfection.

Before I can even comment, Jonathan says, "Alex, I will pay you any amount of money you want for a copy of all of these but that one right there... I think I need a poster sized copy of that one."

Emily chimes in as well. "Alex, they are beautiful. We have to have copies!"

"I'll see what I can do," Alex replies with sass.

She's no longer looking shy and embarrassed. She looks proud. And she should be. Her work is exceptional and looks extremely professional. She should have her own gallery.

"Alex, they aren't kidding. You're a genius. To get these two to look this good... well, you are quite the artist," I say with a wink to Ireland, and I make sure to stick my tongue out and direct it to my little sister.

"Thank you, but you aren't even done yet! Keep going!" She says. This time she's the one bouncing Ireland up and down in her lap.

There is another 11x14 on the stack. This one is a black

and white photo of downtown Portland, but with some of the famous landmarks of the city in color. I freaking love it!

"Alex... where in the world have you been hiding this talent of yours? How have I seen none of your work before?"

She shrugs and says, "I don't know. It's always been something that I do for myself, but seeing all of your blank walls... well, it inspired me to share some of my work. Your walls are sad and need some love, Mick. Enough about me though, open your last one," she says, looking a little timid again.

This last one is even bigger and as I pick it up, I hear Emily say under her breath. "There better not be a picture of me in that huge ass frame. Just sayin'."

Emily doesn't have to worry about seeing her face in the gigantic frame because what is in this frame is so unique. I don't know when she did it, but in my hands I hold a massively cool picture of my house, including the front yard. Not only is it a picture of my house, but in the middle of this giant black and white photo, the only spot of color is Ireland with her arm around Frank as they sit on the top step of the front porch.

"Oh, Alex. It's so perfect," Emily says from the couch. Jonathan agrees with Emily and Ireland tells Frank how great they look together.

I haven't said anything yet. I feel like I've already used every complimentary word that I can to describe to her how great her work is. As I look at all the of the black frames filled with the things that mean the most to me, I... Michael Jacobs Jr.... am speechless.

Alex interrupts my thoughts of her and how well she knows me when she says, "Now, you don't have to put this here, but this is sort of what I envisioned when I made the one *of the house so big." She picks up the picture and then sets in on the fireplace mantel and leans it against the wall.*

She steps back and we stand shoulder to shoulder as we look at the picture in its new home. I put my arm around her and pull her into my side, placing a kiss on her temple. "Alex, it's absolutely perfect." Next, I whisper into her ear. "You. Are. Perfect. Thank you."

With tears pooling in her eyes, she mouths the words thank you to me. She rests her head on my shoulder and puts her arm around my waist. Our moment is brief but powerful.

Ireland pulls on her free hand and says, "Auntie Alex?"

"Yes, sweetheart?"

"I really love your pictures."

"Thank you, Ireland."

"Do you think you could take pictures of my Frank and Savannah in my new bedroom at my new house?"

Alex bends down so she's eye level with my niece and the light of my life and says, "I would love to, Ireland. Once you're settled into your new place, we'll set it all up. Then we can frame the pictures and put them on your new bedroom wall. If that's okay with Jonathan and your mommy?"

"Oh, thank you, Auntie Alex! I'm so excited!"

She told me to get on with my life. She acted like having her around the last three days was an inconvenience, but she couldn't be more wrong. I hate the reason we were together, but I loved every second that she spent in my house and in my bed.

I haven't hidden how I feel about her, but clearly I haven't fought hard enough to prove to her just how serious I am. I know that my past is something that is going to be hard to overcome. I know that I have been a bit of a man whore throughout my life, and I've never been in a committed relationship, but I know I can be faithful. It's always been Alex. That's why I haven't been able to commit to anybody else. *The One* has always been out there. Not only was she out there, but she was always around in some way. She was younger and my little sister's friend. She wasn't an option, but that didn't stop me from comparing every other female to her. Nobody else stood a chance with Alexandra Stotts in the world.

It's time to fight for what I want.

Chapter 16

Alex

January

Tapping the toe of my black high-heel, I wait, not so patiently, to be given the all clear that I can leave for the night. I promised Olivia I would come in and help her get her client's New Year's Eve party set up and make sure that things started off okay. Now it's 9:30 pm and I'm still here.

I'm itching to get out of here so that I can get to Mick's.

I don't know why I'm so excited. It's only been a couple of days since I last saw him. We text or talk every day, but I just can't get to his place fast enough. As per usual, when I know I'm going to see Mick, I made sure that I took special care with what I was wearing tonight. Not only did I need to wear something that worked for the party here at the hotel, but I wanted to dress to impress for after work, too.

I ended up going with a little Alfred Sung Fit and Flare wrap dress. It's black, sleeveless, V-neck and has a scooped back. The front of the dress is modest, with the V-neck and the little sash tied into a small bow on my left side. It's the scooped back that makes me feel a little sexy. My long hair covers most of my back, but I still love it. Because of my height, the hem of the flared skirt is about six inches above my knee. But the best part... the best part are the pockets! What is it about a dress with pockets?

I finally get Olivia's attention and when she sees me still standing over by the DJ—that is now spinning the party tunes that will be playing all over the world at every other New Year's Eve party—she checks her watch and her eyes open wide when she realizes how late it is and that I'm still here.

She skirts around the dance floor and makes her way to me. "Alex, I am so sorry. I completely lost track of time and the fact that you were still here. You look too damn good to be wasting your New Year's Eve here at work. Thank you so much for all of your help! I owe you one. Now, get out of here!"

"Thanks, Olivia. You did a great job with the event and I'm sure the rest of the night will go great. If you really are okay, I'm gonna go," I say, already walking backward towards the exit.

"Go! And thanks again!"

I run back to the office and grab my purse. I check my phone and see that I have one text and one voicemail. The text is from Cami.

CAMI

Chica! Your pictures are amazeballs! Mick's place looks so great! Hope you get to leave work soon! See you when you get here.

I can feel my face light up seeing her compliment. I can't wait to see where he put them all.

Just as I leave my office, my phone chimes and this time it's Mick. It's like he knew I was thinking of him. After the first chime, more chimes alert me to two more messages from him.

SEXY BEAST

WHERE ARE YOU?!

SEXY BEAST

It's 9:30 already! :(

SEXY BEAST

Hope you get to leave soon. Please drive safe! See you when you get here. I saved you a spot in the driveway.

I throw my coat on and text him I'm on my way and scurry down to the parking garage. I know it's silly, but after what almost happened with Kevin, I feel a sense of dread when I'm alone. Being in a big, quiet parking garage like this brings on an intense paranoia every time I have to go to my car after work. I don't know if I jog to my car because I'm scared or because I'm excited to get to Mick's. I know once I get to Mick's, I'll be safe. My closest friends are waiting for me, and with this knowledge I feel a rush of exhilaration pulse through my veins. I weave my way in-between cars, trucks, vans and motorcycles and finally reach the safety of my car. Once I'm in, I lock the doors, start the engine and make way towards freedom.

On my way, I listen to the voicemail on my phone. And I light up once again. Just hearing his voice—even if it is whiny—lights me up like a freaking Christmas tree.

"I can't wait to see you tonight, Sweet Thing. Hurry up and get that fine little ass over here. But drive safe! Can't wait to count down the year with you... anyway, see you when you get here. Please hurry."

It's clear there was something else that he wanted to say but didn't. I don't know what it is, but hearing his words echo in my ears makes my night, my week, my year. He didn't confess his undying love for me, but it was enough.

Pulling into his neighborhood, I can see why Mickey put letters in all of his neighbor's mailboxes. The street is packed with vehicles, and I'm thankful that Mick was thoughtful enough to save a spot for me in the driveway. I would have had to park blocks away otherwise, and with my newfound paranoia, that would have been a horrible walk in these kick ass heels. I can't help but chuckle when I pull into the driveway and I see a sign on the garage door in front of my saved parking spot. It says...

SWEET THING PARKING ONLY. IF YOU AREN'T SURE IF THIS MEANS YOU...THEN IT DOESN'T!

I park my car, and as soon as I open my door, I can hear the music. Mick is a fan of hip-hop old and new and it doesn't surprise me to hear Flo Rida pulsating from the house as I make my way up the front steps. Every time I walk through this front door, I feel safe. And happy. I never would have imagined that I would spend my New Year's Eve at Mick's house. I especially wouldn't have dreamed that he would be waiting for me to catch up. Me. Alexandra Stotts. How did this happen? The elation at just the thought of this makes me giddy as I walked through the front door.

The giddiness melts away the moment I enter the entry-way. I don't know what I expected. Did I expect him to be sitting in the corner by himself, waiting patiently for my arrival? No, that wouldn't be Mick. I know this is his party. I know that even though he isn't a big drinker, Mick is always the life of whatever party he's at. It still hurts to walk into my safe place and discover him in the middle of the room, surrounded by dancing women. He's in his element. This element does not include me and reminds me exactly why I can't give him more.

I close the door behind me, even though I really want to walk back through. I know that Mick is the ultimate party boy and ladies' man, but I'm not sure that I can stand watching it all night. I force myself to take a fortifying breath and look away from the scene in front of me. Cami and Emily are still here, and my new focus is finding my girls and getting through the night in a completely different room that does not have a view to the make-shift dance floor in front of me.

As I take my first step into the belly of the beast, I hear his voice bellow over the noise of the music and the crowd.

"SWEET THING! YOU MADE IT!"

He pushes his way through the sea of bimbos that surround him, and before I know what's happening, he's wrapped me in his arms and my feet are off the ground. He spins me around, places me back on my feet, and then places a sweet kiss on my cheek.

"So glad you finally made it. The party can finally start! Here, let me take your coat and get you a drink."

I unbutton my coat and turn my back to him so he can take the coat off of my shoulders. "Thanks, Mick. You don't have to stop dancing. I'll find the girls and grab a drink."

I turn back around to face him and his dark eyes are full of lust. Lust that is aimed in my direction and not at the bevy of beauties behind him.

"Alex...you look...phenomenal," he says with a husky whisper.

I feel my body flush with heat. When I walked through that door mere moments ago, my emotions and my body had gone cold. But with one look and one stuttered sentence, I'm filled with a heat that I can't control. I'm not sure my words are even audible when I simply say, "Thank you."

"CHICA!!!!" The sound of Cami announcing my arrival breaks the spell that this alluring man always seems to put me under.

I peer around Mick to see Cami dancing her way over to me. Cami is always full of piss and vinegar, but tonight she's on fire.

Cami pushes Mick aside, gives me a quick hug and then takes me by the hand and leads me in the direction of the kitchen. I look over my shoulder to see Mick still standing in the same spot, holding my coat. He's staring and his gaze almost looks primal as he follows my descent deeper into the crowd.

"So, what's your poison? Mick's got nearly everything here. It's already ten. You have some catching up to do."

Spotting a bottle of *Chateau St. Michelle*, I grab a wine

glass off of the counter. "I think I'm just gonna go with some wine tonight, Cam."

"You sure?"

"Yep, I'm sure. I gotta be able to drive myself home later so, a couple of glasses of wine will do me just fine."

"Whatever you say. Let's fill that glass and go find Em and the rest of the gang," Cami shouts as she bounces along to the Jay-Z song that reverberates off of the walls.

We join Emily, Jonathan, Riley, Devon and Gabby and spend the next thirty minutes yelling over the tunes that never stop spinning. Even though we have to yell to hear each other, we're having a great time. Cami referred to this group as our *gang*. If this *is* a gang, then it's a gang I would gladly be initiated into over and over again. Riley, Cami, Emily and I have been a *gang* for years now. Jonathan, Devon and Gabby may be our most recent members, but they are great additions to our little family.

The energy around me crackles, and I feel him before he's actually touching me. I watch the eyes of all of my fellow *gang* members pop out of their heads like cartoon characters at the same moment that I feel his powerful arms engulf me from behind. He rests his chin on my shoulder and whispers, "Hey."

Shocked at his public display of affection, I stand stock-still but manage to get out. "Hey."

Devon, Gabby and Jonathan can see how uncomfortable I am. They consciously turn away from us and start their own conversation. Riley has a smile on his face that could pass as smug, but I know he's proud of his friend. But I'm his friend too, dammit! Can't he see how scared I am right now? Cami and Emily are no help as they stare with their mouths hanging open.

With his chin still on my shoulder, he whispers into my ear. "Alex, can I talk to you for a minute?"

Wanting to do anything to escape being the current center of attention, I agree to his request to talk.

"Sure, Mick."

His arms release my waist and just as I prepare to miss the heat of his body against mine, he takes my hand in his. We bounce off the other partygoers like pin balls as he guides me through the family room and down the hallway. The hallway that leads to the stairs that lead to his room. The room that I slept in with him earlier this week. The room that I never wanted to leave. Right now, though...right now I feel like I'm entering a minefield as he opens the door and pulls me in behind him. He doesn't have to pull very hard. These days I think would follow him anywhere.

He shuts the door, locks it, and then turns in my direction a few feet in front of him. Like a wild animal, he stalks me like I'm his prey as he closes the distance between us. Standing in front of me, he lifts his hand and gently brushes his thumb over my cheek.

"Alex, we need to talk."

"Mick..." I try to interrupt, but he silences me with his mouth. It's a gentle kiss. There isn't anything forceful about it, but I follow his unspoken command and it quiets me.

Slowly removing his lips from mine, he says, "No, Alex. I get to talk first. Okay?"

I take a step back, hoping that putting space between us will clear my head. He knows he's cheating by kissing me and that I won't be thinking clearly enough to hear what he has to say.

"Alex, I know that I've told you I would wait for you to catch up, and I know that we still aren't on the same page. I also know that you've been through a lot and you may not be anywhere near my chapter. But after having you here this past week, a lot of things have become clear to me. They're things that I've always known but hadn't really let myself believe before now. Do you know what I've figured out, Alex?"

Taking another step back, I run into his dresser and exhale, "What, Mick?"

He strides towards my now trapped body and says, "I've never been in a long-term relationship. I've always told myself that it was because I believed all the bullshit that my dad fed me growing up. He would always say that men weren't made to be with only one person. It's not in our nature. The thing is, I've come to the realization that my dad is full of shit. It's all just a lame ass excuse to cheat and do whatever the hell he feels like. Well, Alex..." He searches my face to make sure I'm still with him. "I am not my dad. I finally realized the reason that I have never been in a long-term relationship is because of you. You're *the one* that I was always meant to be with, and you have always been right here. It's always been you, Alex. It's always been you, but... you were my little sister's friend. You were practically a member of my family. Yet still, it's always been you. Nobody else ever stood a chance because I've always compared them to you."

While he speaks, he seems so sure of himself. There is no doubt in his handsome face. This man has had my whole heart for my whole life and he just told me he feels the same. My heart is stuck in my throat, but I know that he deserves a reply. I inhale deeply to clear the shock from the corners of my brain and as I exhale to speak, he says, "I'm not done, Alex."

There's more. What he said was EVERYTHING! How can there be more?

"Sweet Thing, I have been watching you from across the room in this beautiful dress thinking of all the ways I could untie this pretty little bow right here," he says as he gives the end of the bow at my hip a tug. "All I want to do is send everybody home, strip you out of this dress, and make love to you all night long. The thing is... I can't do that until I know we're on the same page."

"Mick..."

"Honey, I'm still talking." He takes my long hair and pushes it over my shoulders. Then he takes a hand and scoops it all to one side. One side of my neck is now completely exposed. He slowly drags his finger down to the crook of my neck. "This right here. This is what I dream about. I don't dream of having sex with you—although I'll admit I do *think* about it often—I dream about this. This is my favorite place to be. This spot right here is my happy place. This is where I feel most at home." He bends down and nuzzles my neck and gently drags his lips across my collarbone. "I still remember how soft your skin was the night we found each other at Lola's. I remember thinking it was the softest skin I had ever touched. Then when you were in my lap at Riley's party and you let me hold you... I never wanted to leave this spot right here."

He kisses my neck just above the last kiss he marked me

with. He may not know it, but he *has* marked me. If only I wasn't so afraid that he'd leave my heart scared.

Standing to his full height, he looks me in the eye and says, "Alex. I want more. I love the friendship we have and I don't ever want to lose it but baby... I want more. You. Are. My. More. You always have been. Let me prove to you that I can be the man that you deserve."

My heart is beating so hard and so fast that I am sure he can see it himself. It must be beating out of my chest by now. I take in a big breath and slowly push it out through my mouth. I do this a couple of more times. Mick has always been what I want. I know he would never hurt me physically, but I know he has the potential to break my feeble heart. I'm tired of worrying about that, though. He just professed his feelings and has been nothing but open and honest with me. I need to stop being that scared little girl that I was growing up. I'm a woman now and it's time to take what I want. To take what he's offered to me.

"Mick."

"Yeah, baby?"

"Please kiss me again."

And kiss me he does.

This is a kiss that promises more than I could ever dream of. His hands are in my hair as he presses my back into his dresser. As if reading my mind, and with my head in his tangled hands, he guides me a few steps to the right and my back is now against the wall.

"Fuck, I love to kiss you."

His lips are back on mine in a fevered pace, and our tongues are dancing together.

There is no awkwardness.

213

It's as though we were made to kiss each other and have spent years perfecting the craft.

Pulling back from me, he places one hand on the wall next to my head while his other hand leisurely traces the curves of my body. He starts at what is apparently his happy place, then over my heart and to my breast. He cups my breast in his hand and leans over and places his lips on my chest where my heart is pulsing at a steady pace. As his hand floats down my rib cage and meets the bow on my hip.

"I have been wanting to unwrap you all night, baby."

He pulls on the ends of the bow and it comes undone. Much to his dismay, my dress doesn't fall open as the bow is just for decoration, but it doesn't slow him down.

Lifting my leg so that it wraps around his waist, he growls as he leans back in for an animalistic kiss. The kissing is so impassioned that I can no longer hear the party taking place downstairs. All I can hear is his heavy breathing. All that I feel are our hands everywhere. Exploring. One of his hands continues to travel up my leg, under my dress and all the way to my barely there black lace panties. He lets out another growl when he feels my practically bare backside. He brings his hand over my hip and finds the front of that same piece of lace.

His hand stops just above the top of the lace when he says, "Is this okay, baby? Do you want me to stop? Tell me if I'm going too far."

"Please don't stop, Mick."

His warm, cocoa colored eyes, outlined with long, thick lashes, reach all the way to my soul. He never takes his eyes from mine as his hand slowly finds its way into my lace. His fingers slowly but deftly explore and he finds that spot that makes me close my eyes and throw my head back. While continuing his assault on my senses, his skilled fingers enter me.

"Alex, you are so hot and wet for me, baby." He takes his fingers from my lace, and brings them to his mouth and one by one, he sucks my arousal from his fingers. If he thought I was hot and wet before, he should put his hand back where it just was and see what he's done to me now. He drops my leg and takes me by the hand and leads me to his bed. We stand in front of his bed and he interlaces our hands together. "Alex, we aren't going to make love tonight. Not with a houseful of people, but I would like to be doing this at midnight. Seems like a perfect way to start a new year."

Every time this man speaks, he gets hotter. Sexier. This time, it's me that initiates things. Releasing his hands and stepping closer to him, I boldly reach out and stroke his more than evident hard on through his jeans.

"Hmmm...it's bigger than I remember Mick," I say with a wink.

"Oh honey, don't even play. You know, you remember every second that we were together. There's no way you could forget the big man you've got in your hands right now. Trust me when I say I haven't forgotten a single second of that night. If you think you need a reminder, though, I am more than willing to take you there tomorrow. But like I said, not tonight."

"I look forward to it. How long do we have until we ring in the New Year?"

"About ten minutes. We better not waste any more time. Come here baby, give me my happy place."

He takes off his shirt and nuzzles into my neck again,

while his hands take a journey to my back where they discover my zipper. Teasingly slow, he unzips my dress and it falls to the ground. Leaving me standing in my matching black lace bra and panties and my four-inch black stilettos.

"Oh, God damn woman! You are a sight to see. You exceed any memories or fantasies that I could have ever conjured up." He gives me his hand so I can step out of my dress. The moment he's sure that I am steady on my feet, he lets go and his rough hands roam all over my body. His tongue caresses the swell of each of my breasts. He pulls the cups of my bra down and my breasts are now on display; pushed up by wire and material. "Fuck," he says as his tongue darts out across one of my nipples. "Seeing you trussed up like this is the hottest thing I have ever seen." He takes my other nipple into his mouth and twirls his tongue over it. I can feel both nipples tighten with excitement.

His hands are on my ass and my breast is in his mouth when we hear a knock at the door. Hearing a sing-songy female voice come through the door instantly throws a bucket of cold water on our moment of passion.

"Mick, I know you're in there. Open up so I can help you ring in the New Year again like we did last year."

And just like that, my libido disappears. I fix my bra and bend down to pick up my dress. A wave of realism rushes through me and I can't help but wonder how I got here. I knew better. Mick is the kind of guy that has random girls knocking on his door to 'ring in the New Year'. He did this last year with somebody else.

"I can't do this, Mick. This is why I've always said we can't cross this line. There are just too many girls out there knocking on your door." I pull my dress up and over my shoulders and turn to signal to Mick that I need help with my dress.

Zipping up my dress, he brings his lips to my bare shoulder and says, "There aren't too many girls. I haven't been with anybody in months, Alex. Since Riley's party, I've had no interest in anybody but you. Just give me a minute to get rid of whoever this is."

Retying the bow on my dress, I huff. "See, that's just it, Mick. You clearly were with her this time last year and you don't even remember who she is. How is somebody like that going to be a one-woman man and give me what you say I deserve? I know I deserve more than this. This was fun Mick, but it shouldn't happen again, okay? Let's just keep things how they've been. I don't want to lose you, but I can't deal with this. I won't be this woman." I feel defeated and lost.

"Baby, I swear there isn't anybody else. I don't want anybody but you. Please don't let this ruin the night. What can I do to be enough for you? How can I prove myself to you? Tell me and I'll do it."

"You're Mickey Jacobs, and I think that will always be too much for me. It's not that *you* aren't enough, but your past may just be too much."

There's another knock on the door as the girl on the other side coos his name.

"Baby, please just give me a minute to get rid of her and we can talk this out."

"Mick, as much as I might love it, I have to ask you *not* to call me, baby. It's just too hard."

As I brush past him, I reach for his face and guide his cheek to my lips and whisper. "Happy New Year, Mick."

With that, I take myself and my new resolve to the door

and make my way past the perky blond who I know to be a member of Courtney's merry band of whores.

"He's all yours."

I speed down the stairs and to the hall bathroom door that is mercifully open and lock myself in. I'm exhausted after going from the highest of highs to feeling so low I don't want to leave this bathroom. I don't want to see anybody. I don't want to explain where I went with Mick. But I have perfected my mask, and I can fake it just like I have my entire life. I just need to get my shit together and get back out to my friends. I see my make out hair in the mirror and do what I can to put myself back together again. I know I can't stay in here and dwell on things too long because the countdown is about to begin and I don't want to miss it, even if it isn't with Mick.

I hear the first number of the countdown to midnight chanted by the other partygoers just as I open the door. And there he is. Standing with his hands in his front pockets and with his t-shirt back on is Mick.

He looks right at me and continues the countdown. He isn't moving from the door frame and he has no intention of letting me pass. When he gets to five, he takes a step towards me and I take a step back. With each number that he says, he takes another step. Leaving the door open, he says, "Two... one..." He leans in and gives me a kiss that says everything he's feeling. I can't help but take in everything he's saying with this kiss. It should feel like a goodbye, but it doesn't. It feels determined. I left his room with a much different kind of resolve than he did. "Happy New Year, Alex. I think I'm going to need a little bit of time before I can hang out again. Text me if you need anything, but I need a little space."

He leaves me standing alone with only my reflection in the bathroom mirror, looking back at me. He seemed determined, but also solemn. I have never wanted to hurt him. Am I making a mistake? I know he's a good man, one of the best men I have ever known. I also know that nobody will ever be able to hurt me like Mick could. Maybe a little space will be good for the both of us.

Chapter 17

Alex

It's been a week since Mick walked out of that bathroom.

A week with no contact.

I haven't smiled in a week. Well, I haven't smiled a genuine smile in a week. From the moment I stepped out of that bathroom, my mask was back in place. My heart was breaking, but there was no way anybody would ever know it. Being unhappy but appearing happy as a clam is what I'm good at. It's what I know.

I left shortly after midnight and cried all the way home. I cried myself to sleep. I didn't leave the house the next day. I didn't answer my phone when Emily called. She said she needed to talk to me about something, and I knew that something was her brother. I didn't want to talk about it.

I know I'm doing this to myself. He's put it all out there. He's ready to commit. But I keep breaking both of our hearts because I won't even give us a try.

When I did finally talk to Emily and Cami, they were kind enough not to mention Mick. I don't think I could take whatever they would have shared about him. If he's hurt and upset, I will feel horrible that I could make the one person who always rescues me and makes me feel safe and cared for feel less than adored. If he is happy and back to dating, I will be heartbroken. No, it's best that they don't share. My heart and my soul couldn't take it.

If I have to find a bright side, it's that this time away from him is making me move on. I have no option. I know that there will never be anybody else, but I have to try to move on.

Move on from what?

We weren't even in a relationship, but it feels like I've just been through the worst break up of my life. Imagine how badly it would hurt if we *were* together. No, that is not an option. I have to live my life and for that reason, I've let Olivia set me up with a friend of hers. But that's not what I want. I want to not be me. I want to be carefree. Go to a random club, meet a random guy, don't ask his name and bring him home so he can help me forget. That's what I want to do, but that's not me. Instead, I'm going on a blind date.

Standing in front of my closet, I just stare blankly. It's not that I don't have anything to wear. It's the fact that I have no desire to go out with anybody. I don't want to do this. All I can think about is Mick. He's my best friend and I want to call him and talk about tonight. But I can't. He wants space.

Enough! Get your shit together, Stotts!

It's Portland, so I don't have to dress up for a place like *Trifecta*. Some skinny jeans, flats, light sweater and infinity scarf will do. It's not in a great area, but it's a hip place with great food and drinks, so you just overlook the interesting surroundings as you walk from wherever you may find street parking. Tonight, I only have to walk a couple of blocks and through twenty or so hipsters to get to the restaurant. Not too bad.

When I enter, I'm greeted by a hostess and before I say I'm meeting somebody here, Keegan is standing up from a booth waving.

"Thank you, but I think I see the person I'm meeting." I make my way over to the first booth on the right and say, "You must be Keegan?"

"That's me. I knew you were you the moment I saw you. Olivia sent me a picture of you and you look just like your picture." He shakes my hand and it's like a dead fish. There is nothing behind his handshake and I can tell he's nervous.

"Nice to meet you, Keegan. You look just like your picture, too." And he does. He's tall, thin, blondish-red hair, and glasses. I guess he's kinda cute, but he's not really my type. I only have one type. I only want one person. But he needs space. So, I push on.

"Have a seat and we'll order you a drink as soon as the server comes by again."

"Thank you," I say as I take a seat.

"So, you work with Olivia? She said you were beautiful, but she really didn't do you justice."

Feeling uncomfortable after his compliment, I reply, "Thank you. Yes, we've worked together for a year or two. How do you know her again? She said you had some mutual friends."

"Yes, I used to date a friend of hers, but I stayed friends with her boyfriend Bryce after the breakup."

"Oh, how long has it been since you've been out of a relationship?" Seems like a good place to start since he's talking about a breakup, right? Oh God, I so don't know how to date.

"It's been about a year and a half. She was the love of my life and she left me for somebody else. She moved to the other side of the country to be with him. I still can't figure out what happened..." And just like that, we spend an entire meal talking about his ex and everything that went wrong and what he could have done differently. Thank goodness we ordered food and I now have my flatbread pizza to entertain me.

Once we're finished eating, he realizes his mistake. "Oh, shit! I just spent our entire meal talking about my ex. You must think I am such a loser."

"Nah, it's no problem. We all have our stuff."

I guess that is one great thing about Mick. He may have lots of no name one-night stands, but there are no exes to speak of. Nobody he's loved and who has broken his heart. Why didn't I ever see it that way?

But yes, Keegan, I think you are a bit of a loser.

"Well, thanks, but let's order dessert and you can tell me about yourself."

I don't want to be rude, but there is nothing here. I don't want to waste any more time. I know what it feels like when there is a connection and it's not here at this table.

"You know, I am stuffed and don't think I have room for dessert. Thank you for the offer, though."

"No problem. Let me pay the bill and we can get out of here."

He heads to the bar to get our bill from our bartender/server. He must be on the same page as me because he didn't seem too upset that I wanted to cut things short.

What a relief. I would love to just bail and run out the

door while he's not looking, but that would be rude, so I wait. A few quick minutes later and he's back.

He stands next to the table and extends his hand to help me out of the booth. After I'm out, though, he doesn't let go of my hand. Instead, he re-adjusts his hold and holds my hand as he heads to the exit.

Once outside in the frigid January air, he smiles and with a flirty lift of his brow, he says, "So, your place or mine?"

What the hell? What did I miss?

Trying to get out of this without causing a scene, I reply. "Thanks for dinner, Keegan. It was great to meet you. My car is over two blocks, so I'm just gonna head that way."

Clearly not getting it, he says, "Cool, my car is that way too. I'll walk you to yours and I can follow you to your place." He grabs my hand and my mind is racing. I am not big for causing a scene, but I really need to make myself clear. My mind is scrambling to find the right words to let him down easily. Oh God, I hate dating!

We're all ready to my car when I finally say, "Thanks again, Keegan, but I think I'm gonna call it a night."

"It's only 9:30, Alex. The night is young and I'm sure we can find a way to pass the time." He pushes my hair behind my ear and I flinch. Where is this coming from? I haven't given him any indication that I wanted to go there. I mean, seriously? Didn't he just talk about his ex the entire meal? What is wrong with this guy?

"Keegan, I really need to call it a night. I had a good time, though, and it was really nice to meet you."

Just as I reach for my car's door handle, he pushes me against the car and leans in to kiss me. I try to push back on him, but he just keeps pressing into me. "Keegan, no! I'm not interested."

"Oh, come on, Alex. We could both use some fun. Don't tell me you don't hook up. A girl as hot as you? I have a hard time believing that." Now's he leaning in and I have both of my hands on his chest, trying to push him away.

"Believe it! Now, get the fuck off of me, asshole!"

He lifts his hands and takes a step back. "Wow, what a prick tease! I guess that's an hour and a half of my life. I'll never get back."

I ignore him and get in the car as he turns to walk away. I can't help it when I yell after him. "I guess we know why your girlfriend left you for somebody else! You're a dick! Please lose my number!"

I don't wait for his reply. I start the car, lock the doors and pull my car away from the curb so fast that the tires squeal.

Whoa... did I just do that?

Did I just tell him off?

Since when did I have it in me to tell somebody off? Especially, a man!

I am so proud of myself!

I feel like celebrating!

Of course, the person who I want to call to brag about my sudden growth of lady balls isn't speaking to me. During dinner, all I thought about was Mick. I know it's only one date, but this one crappy date makes me realize what I'm missing. Or rather, *who* I'm missing.

I have a man in my life that makes me happy. He makes me feel safe. He makes me feel sexy and smart, and he wants to be with me. What is wrong with me? I know he wanted space and I've given him a week. It's time for me to put it all out there, just like he has. It's time to put my new lady balls to work. Time to stop being scared of being hurt and give Mick a chance. By giving him a chance, I might just be giving myself a chance. A chance at happiness.

I turn my car toward Happy Valley and am beside myself with excitement. I'm doing it! I'm gonna take a risk and go for it! I blast my music and sing along to every song that comes on during my thirty-minute drive to Mick's house. I should be planning my *please give me another chance* speech, but I'm too happy and excited to think straight right now.

When I turn down his street, I lower the music and prep myself for what I'll say when he answers the door. I pull into the driveway and check myself in the mirror. I add some gloss and fluff my hair, and then me and my lady balls open the car door and try our damnedest not to skip up to his front door.

I take the first two steps up his front porch and see the light coming out of the front window. I look in the window as I take the third step and I can't move. I feel cold. I feel sick. I feel like every feeling I had on the way here was a lie. My world slowly crumbles around me. But brick by brick, the wall around my heart rebuilds itself right here on the spot.

When I feel the first tear fall, I quietly turn back down the steps and I race to my car. I can't get out of here fast enough. How could I have been so stupid? All this time, I knew what I was doing when I said that I wanted to just be friends. I should always go with my gut.

After my confrontation with Keegan, and then the poor decision that lead me to Mick's front steps, I feel dirty. I need a shower. I crash through the front door, slam it shut, and lock it behind me. I rip my clothes off and leave a trail behind me as I sprint to the bathroom and throw the shower on. I spend the next thirty minutes under the scalding hot water trying to erase the vision that is now burned into my eyes.

In a haze, I put on a t-shirt and throw myself in bed. I will not shed anymore tears. My mask is back in place and I think I agree with Mick about needing space. I need a lot of space. Like years of space.

I finally fall asleep with visions of a couch. A couch that has a shirtless Mick on top of an equally topless blond. I fall asleep feeling empty and alone.

Again.

* * *

Mick

"I'm sorry, Melissa. I'm just not feeling it tonight."

"It's Jessica! What do you mean you're not feeling it?" she says, sitting up, grabbing her bra and shirt off of the floor and covering herself.

Fuck! What was I thinking?

Pulling my shirt over my head and getting dressed, I say, "Sorry, Jessica. I really shouldn't have brought you here tonight."

"Really, well that would have been nice to know before you had me on your couch with your hands all over me and my boob in your mouth."

"To be honest, I was using you to get over somebody else, but I'm just not ready. Sorry to be so harsh, but it's the truth."

"Wow, my first impression was right. You really are a dick, Mickey Jacobs!"

She's right. I am a dick. I used her and it's not cool.

"I'm really sorry. I know this was messed up. You have every right to be pissed."

"Whatever. Just drive me back to my car."

After a silent drive back to the bar, she jumps out of the truck, calls me a dick again, and slams the truck door. Normally, I would freak out on anybody that treated my truck like that, but I barely register it. My mind is on Alex and the fact that she had a date tonight. That's the only reason Jessica was at my house. I was pissed and thought if Alex could do it, so could I.

When Emily told me that Alex had a date tonight, I lost it. I know I said that I wanted some space, but what the fuck? I tried to act like I didn't care, but Emily saw right through me. She told me she thought she was trying to get over me and trying to move on.

"Em, I didn't want her to get over me. I just needed some space so that I could be around her without wanting more. God, Em. I know she's your friend, and I'm sure you hate this, but she's the one, sis."

Emily pulls me into a hug. "Mick, do you really think you can be with just her? Can you commit to a relationship? Alex has been through too much, and I can't let her knowingly get hurt. She's a good girl, Mick. If you aren't 100% sure that you can be faithful, then you need to let her move on."

"Damn, Em. You must really think I'm a piece of shit."

I pace the room. I feel like a two-year-old about to throw a God damned tantrum. Pacing helps bring me down a notch. Right now, I need to be brought way the hell down.

"Not at all, big brother. You've just always said that you could never commit to one woman. That's always been your 'thing'."

"I know, you're right. It's my fault, but I'm done with that life. I want the real thing and I want it with Alex. Why is that so hard for everybody to believe?"

"Well, talk to her. It's been a week since your party. Don't call her tonight because she'll know I told you about her date, but talk to her. It's just a first date tonight. You know Alex, she's not the type of girl who's gonna go sleep with some random guy on the first date."

I'm done wearing the carpet down. I can't stay here. I think I might just go crazy if I spend another second in this house. Hearing her name in the same sentence that even refers to her sleeping with somebody else makes me sick.

"Sorry, Em, but I gotta get out of here. Thanks for the talk. I'll see you later."

I hear her shout after me. "Call her tomorrow, Mick!"

I don't reply. I jump in my truck, and as though she's on autopilot, she drives me right to my beloved Kells.

Once my ass is on the bar stool in front of Riley, I have one goal in mind.

Get laid!

It's been months and the one woman I want is out on a fucking date with somebody else. Besides, we're just friends so I guess I could have done this weeks or months ago. How could I have been so stupid to think that I wanted more?

That's not me.

This is me.

After a couple of hours, my ass is going numb from sitting on this damn stool. The night hasn't gone quite how I *expected, but just as I think, maybe I'll head home; I feel a pair of breasts on my back and feel somebody breathing into my ear.*

"Hey Mick, how's it going?"

Shit, it's that blond that called me a dick last time I saw her.

"Hey, how's it going..."

"Jessica, my name's Jessica."

"Nice to see you again, Jessica."

And just like that, she was practically in my lap the rest of the night. We made out in the bathroom and then she was ready and willing to take off to my place. She's a real class act. It may be wrong on many levels, but if this is what it takes to get over Alex, then so be it. Classless blondes never stopped me in the past. Why should they now?

Now, here I am pulling into my driveway alone and it's only 11:00.

I wonder if Alex is home yet.

I wonder if she had a good time on her date.

I wonder what the hell I'm going to do.

I want to drive over there right now, but the thought of seeing her with somebody else makes me sick to my stomach.

Chapter 18

Alex

February

Standing here in the drizzle of Portland rain, I feel nothing.

I am void of emotion.

I know I should be feeling something. Pain. Sadness. Relief. Grief. At the very least, cold from this wet, frigid weather. But I have felt nothing all day. Instead, I've been playing the role of the doting daughter to my grief-stricken mother. I've got my black dress on and my mask is firmly in place. I know I should be feeling something... but I don't.

From the moment my mother called me frantic and sobbing to tell me that my father had passed away, I've been on autopilot. It turns out my father had a stroke in his sleep, and he never woke up. I don't really feel much about that fact.

When she told me what had happened, I could tell that it bothered her that I was simply matter of fact about the news. She kept asking me if I was okay, and I almost thought about turning on the waterworks to make her feel better, but I couldn't. I couldn't fake the emotions this time. I know she wishes that I loved my dad just a little more, but in the end... in the end, I think she gets it. To be honest, I can't understand how she can feel so much loss for a man that treated her like his personal punching bag for decades, and who hasn't *really* been around for years now.

Maybe it's me. Maybe I'm a horrible person. Should I forget the past and mourn the father I wish he had been? Am I supposed to forgive him for the years of abuse? I know everybody expects me to be devastated, like my mother, but I can't bring myself to pretend anymore. I still have the need to make everybody around me happy, but since I shared my truth with those closest to me on Christmas, I don't feel the need quite so strongly. Even though my mask is on, so that pretenses are kept, I can't bring myself to conjure up tears or to feel distressed over his loss.

I was so relieved when my Aunt Lena arrived. I couldn't get out of my mom's fast enough. I needed to distract myself from the underlying guilt that was brewing deep down inside. I needed to stay busy. I took over the arrangements for the memorial, wrote his obituary, and went that afternoon to clean out his room at the care facility.

When I checked in at the front desk, all the women told me how sorry they were for my loss and asked if I needed help with anything. I accepted their condolences and politely refused their offers of assistance, and made my way to the elevator that took me to what was left of my father.

He was my father. Never my dad.

He was not the dad who would sing you a song or read you a story before bed. He didn't attend any school performances and he didn't do all of those things that daddies that are wrapped around their little girls' fingers would do. He didn't tell me he loved me and he never bounced me on his knee or tickled me until I couldn't breathe. He didn't really talk to me much or acknowledge me in anything but a formal manner. I learned at a very young age to stay out of his way and to follow his orders precisely. Do what he said, when he said it, and to his liking and everything would be okay. Make a mistake, and the world came to a crashing halt. At least my mom's world did.

I will always have guilt for the times he took his anger out on her because I had done something to disappoint him. I will never forget the weight on my chest as I would cower in bed and listen to him tell her what a horrible mother she was and that she hadn't taught me a thing. That I wasn't going to amount to anything in this world, and it would be her fault. He provided for me and it was her job to teach me how to grow up to be a respectable woman. I was a kid. Kids make mistakes. There will always be a part of me that hates him for putting all of that on my mom *and* for not letting me be a kid.

His emotional abuse was just as bad as the physical abuse at times. When my father was around, my Mom lacked confidence. She was a quiet and meek woman. When it was just she and I, she was a different person. We would sing and dance and we would always find something to laugh at. When I got older, we loved to watch all the formulaic romantic comedies we could. We would laugh, we would cry, and most importantly, we got to be ourselves. I got to see that strong, proud side of my mother. The woman who knew her own mind and had her own opinions. The woman that would sit and talk with me for hours on end about her childhood, her life before meeting my dad and her first love in high school. She gave me pieces of wisdom and taught me how to have respect for myself. God, she was an amazing woman in those moments!

Only once, during one of our all-night conversations, did she talk about the abuse that my father inflicted on her? That night, she confided that her example of marriage wasn't what she wanted for me. That she hoped I would never fall in love with a man that treated me with anything less than the utmost respect and with love and tenderness. She followed that up by saying we can't always control who we fall in love with, and that even though my father wasn't always all of those things, she knew the man deep down inside and she couldn't help but love him. She told me how sorry she was but that she simply could not, and would not, leave him.

I lived for my father's business trips, hunting trips, fishing trips... any trip that would take him out of the house and as far away as humanly possible. Luckily for us, this happened at least once a month. It was all about him and we went nowhere with him.

Now that I'm older, I wonder if there was somebody else? Or maybe many somebody else's? Did he not only abuse his wife, but did he cheat on her as well?

The thing that I appreciated most about my father's trips was our time together. That she and I got to breathe. There weren't any masks. It was just us. I got to see the real Miriam Stotts. It was a glorious sight to see, but it never lasted long. It was always so deflating to watch my mom's metamorphosis right before my eyes. I could see her transform into the docile housewife the day my father would be expected home. The moment the door would open, the transformation was complete and the quiet, scared, self-conscience woman was back.

It really is quite shocking that I haven't become jaded. That I still believe in love.

Maybe it's the fact that I had examples of true love all around me. Love that didn't hurt. Love that lifted you up and made you better. I was surrounded by those people and those couples. Whether it was aunts and uncles or family friends, I was always surrounded by loving couples. I never doubted that love could be good and strong and that there was such a thing as *the one*.

Or maybe it was all the romantic comedies I grew up on.

Or...it could be because of Mick.

I love that man with everything I am, but is that enough? I watched my mom love my father fiercely, but he still broke her heart every day. That was one thing my mother taught me, and I guess it sunk in. It hurts more when love is involved.

I felt nothing when I flipped on the light and looked around my father's room. And still didn't feel anything when I picked up his things to pack them away. I could have been in any stranger's room. I filled the plastic storage bin that I had brought with me, with his clothes and few personal items. There aren't any keepsakes that really mean anything, but I still gathered it all for my mom. I knew she would want it all.

That was days ago, and my emotions still haven't surfaced. I can feel my heels sinking into the soggy grass as we stand at my father's graveside. I just want the day to be over. I want my mom to finish grieving and finally move on with her life. We're standing under a white tent and the preacher is speaking, but I don't really hear the words. All I can think is that if he knew the real Randall Stotts, he may not be saying the same things. There may not be so many tears shed today.

I hold on to my mom's arm as I help her approach my father's grave so that she can say her final goodbye and place a rose on top of his casket. I'm holding an umbrella over us with one hand and holding on to her tightly with the other. I'm waiting for her to fall apart after giving her last farewell, but what she does next takes me by surprise and wakes me up and out of the fog I've been walking through all day. With her back to the crowd, she takes a deep breath in, releases it and stands up tall with pride and strength. Wiping her eyes, she simply says, "Goodbye, Randall."

She turns to me and smiles. "Thank you, Alexandra. Thank you for being the kind of daughter I could have only dreamed of when I was a little girl romanticizing about being a mom. Your strength astounds me, and I am so proud to be your mother." She reaches up, touches my cheek and whispers for only me to hear. "Be happy, my sweet girl."

She takes my hand in hers and turns us around to take our seats under the big white tent. She takes her place and as I work on closing the umbrella, something draws my attention. I look up through the crowd and my heart stops. All those feelings that were buried deep within me come bubbling to the surface as my eyes take in the breathtaking man in the black suit standing in the rain behind the other funeral attendees.

He's too far away for either of us to say anything, but by the look on his face, I can tell that he doesn't care whether I'm speaking to him or if I want him here. He looks determined. Seeing this beautiful man getting soaked to the bone in a downpour of rain so that he could be here to support me, if even from afar, is a sight that I will never forget.

He's here.

My happy.

I haven't answered his calls, his texts, his emails or his knocking on my front door and he's still here.

All I want is to push my way through the crowd of mourners and throw myself into his embrace and let him nestle into his favorite spot. But I can't. I need to take my place next to my mom and watch them lower my father into the ground. I know that I have to tear my gaze from his, and for the first time since receiving the news about my father, the tears begin to fall. The mix of the stress of the week, the moment I just shared with my mom and knowing Mick is here, is the combination that it takes for my feelings to take shape and finally release themselves.

I take my seat, and my mother's hand and wait as the casket slowly disappears six feet underground. That's it. He's gone. My mom is finally free.

I make a point not to look back to see if he's still here when we stand. My mom and I take our leave and carefully make our way through the wet cemetery to the car that will drive us back to Aunt Lena's, where everyone will gather. All I want to do is find his eyes again. His eyes that tell me he's got me and that everything is going to be okay, but I don't let myself. He makes me feel too much.

Simply put... he makes me feel.

When we reach the car, the driver hands me an envelope and opens the door. I get my mom and aunt settled into the seats of the limo and I move over to the side seat and see he addressed the envelope to Sweet Thing.

With shaky fingers, I somehow get the paper out of the envelope. I can barely read the words he's written on the page because of my trembling hands and my tear-filled eyes.

Alex,

I was so sorry to hear about your dad. If you need anything at all, I'm here. Please give my best to your mom.

I hope you got the flowers that I sent to the church?

I miss you every day.

I know now isn't the time, but if you ever want to talk about that night... I'm here. Day or night.

I can't help but wonder what chapter you're on or if you've put us back on the shelf?

Either way, I'm still here if you need me. Just call.

Please call, Alex.

Know that I am thinking about you and your mom. I am so sorry that you may be hurting right now, but I also hope that your dad's passing brings you some peace. You deserve to be happy, Alex.

Love,
Mick

. . .

I bring the letter to my chest and press it against my heart with both hands. I am just barely holding on, finding it hard to breathe and to not break apart into ugly sobs. I want to read it again and scour it for hidden meanings, but I can't see a thing through the pools of loss, pain, confusion, relief, exhaustion and love that have taken residence in my eyes.

Why did I have to get this note just as all of my feelings have come crashing down on me? Why is he still waiting for me? Why did he sign it, Love, Mick?

I can feel my mom and my aunt watching me and I tell myself that this isn't the time or the place to be thinking about Mick. I need to be strong for the woman sitting across from me. The woman who just buried her husband. The love of her life.

More importantly, I need to be strong for me.

Holding the closest thing to a love letter I have ever received to my heart while looking into the tired eyes of my mom, I realize that it's time to take control of my life. To find my happy.

If I want my happy, I have to be ready to accept it. I need to figure out who I am. Who I want to be. I need to find the me that can *let* herself be happy. The me that doesn't hold everything inside and shares her burdens with those that love her. The me that would be strong enough to have an adult conversation with Mick about what happened. The me that wouldn't be scared to take that leap and give love a chance. The me that could bring herself to call. The me I want to be. The me I deserve to be. The me that could finally be happy.

I feel almost euphoric.

It's strange how on a day like today, I would find that piece of me that is finally ready to try. To live fully. To have no regrets. To love myself so that I can truly love another as they deserve to be loved.

I'm not foolish enough to think that Mick will wait for me to figure myself out, and if he doesn't, I'll be okay. He's already been so patient. He's given me so much just by being here today. Sharing his words and love on paper. He is my superhero in my time of need, and he doesn't even know it.

I can only hope that once I'm ready, he'll still be willing to give us a chance. To let me catch up. To finally be on the same page.

* * *

"So, how are you doing, sweetie?"

It's been a week since my dad's funeral. Since I saw Mick. Since I decided to do what I need to do to find my happy.

"I'm good, Olivia. Happy Hour tonight is just what I needed! Cheers!"

We lift our glasses, clink them together and have the first sips of our drinks. She with her Moscow Mule and me with my Grey Goose and cranberry.

"Okay, now that we got that superficial answer out of the way, talk to me. You've been through a lot, Alex. It's okay to not be great."

Since my epiphany at the funeral, I decided that to be happy; I have to live honestly, and that meant sharing everything with Olivia. I knew that if anybody would understand, it would be her. She knows everything and has even gone to a couple of meetings with me here and there. I'm pretty lucky to have her in my life. I love Cami and Emily, and they couldn't be more supportive, but Olivia has been through some of what I've been through, only much worse. When she says she understands how I feel, she really does. It's refreshing to have a friend like her. She's such a great example of how you can turn lemons into lemonade. She inspires me every day to keep pushing forward.

"It really is true. Olivia, you know how things were with my dad. Yes, it's sad that he died and the last years of his life were what they were, but I don't miss him. I know it makes me sound horrible, but it's a bit of relief, and I can only hope that my mom might start to live her life for the first time since she was a kid."

I take a sip of my vodka-cran and wait for her to tell me what a shitty person I am. But Olivia is my girl, and she does just the opposite.

"Good, I'm glad. I'm not glad that he's dead, of course, but I am glad that it's brought you a bit of peace. I hope your mom's able to find that same peace and she lets herself enjoy life a little. Not to sound crass, but your dad was a piece of shit and didn't deserve you two. Now, the other part of my question has to do with Mick. Have you talked to him?"

"Nope, I'm not ready. Seeing him last week at the cemetery, standing there in the pouring rain even though I haven't even returned a text in over a month, was everything. It meant so much to me, but that's exactly why I'm not ready. I need to be strong enough on my own to give him everything that he gives me. He's always there for me and it's so easy for me to run away. He deserves more than that. I need to keep working on me for a while."

"I get that. I really do, Alex. But how will you know when you're ready? How do you quantify something like that? It's not like there's a test you take that tells you that you're ready to be in a relationship."

"I know that, Olivia. I also don't think he's going to sit around waiting for me. But I just know that I'm not there yet. I have to figure out why I was willing to push Mick away, but I let Kevin in. I'm gonna keep going to therapy, going to group and doing my best to take care of myself. I'm still so ashamed of letting Kevin in and what that says about me. Sometimes it's hard to look myself in the mirror. I know that I act like I'm fine, but I'm not. I've had moments where I was fine since Kevin, but I've come to realize that all of those moments were with Mick. I have to learn to be fine on my own."

"I'm so proud of you, sweetie."

"Thanks, but I'm just a work in progress. Baby steps, I guess."

"We're all just a work in progress, but I'm still proud of you. I know you love Mick and the fact that you're willing to risk losing him to do what's right, to take care of you, to be your own happy... well, that's pretty awesome, and whether you like it or not I'm proud of you."

"Thank you, now enough about me! I'm tired of talking about me. What's going on in your world? How's Tom?"

After about an hour of constant chit chat and much needed girl time, I'm waiting at the bar for our next round of drinks when I notice a guy at our tall bistro table in the center of the bar. I don't know what they're talking about, but Olivia is shaking her head back and forth, and as he leans closer to her, she's leaning back in her chair, trying to increase her distance from him. The hairs on the back of my neck stand up and my need to get back to our table is next level. I grab our drinks, throw money on the bar and haul ass back to our table.

When I reach the table, I hear Olivia say, "Like I said, I have a boyfriend and I'm really not interested."

"Oh, come on, sweetie. I won't tell your boyfriend, scout's honor."

He hasn't even noticed me, so I give him a little tap on his shoulder. He barely looks over his shoulder and when he does, he dismisses me quickly and turns his attention back to Olivia.

Oh really...

"I believe she said she wasn't interested."

He stops leaning on the table and stands up to his full height. With my heels on, I'm a couple inches taller than him and he has to look up at me just a bit. "I don't recall asking for your help."

"Oh, you didn't, but I am asking you to walk away. She's not interested, has a boyfriend and she's here with me. You're wasting your time and ours."

"Bitch, who do you think you are?"

He steps closer to me, and puffing out his chest, and I can feel Olivia panic behind him. He doesn't scare me. I'm done being afraid. Especially of assholes like him.

I don't know where I get the nerve, but I step a couple of inches closer to him and quietly say, "This time, I'm not asking. Walk. The. Fuck. Away." I use my index finger to push his shoulder gently. Just to make my point.

"You fucking bitches are crazy." He turns, walks away and scurries back to the bar where his friends are waiting for him laughing their asses off after watching him not only get shot down but also get his balls handed to him in a snack size zip-lock baggie by a *girl*.

I sit down and take a sip of my drink, and Olivia just stares at me with her mouth hanging open.

"What?"

"What do you mean, what? That was freaking amazing!"

I feel the smile break across my face. "It was, wasn't it?!" I throw my head back, laughing. She holds her glass up to mine and we bring them together once again! "Man, that felt good!"

"I bet it did. I'd say those baby steps just took a giant leap! You go, girl!"

At this moment, I feel strong. I feel confident. I feel good and it's because of me. I did it all on my own. I may be taking baby steps, but I'm on my way!

Chapter 19

Mick

April

I'm lost.

I no longer know who I am.

I know who I *want* to be.

I know who I want to be with.

But she won't talk to me.

She won't return my texts.

I stopped trying weeks ago.

I haven't seen her in months.

I know that *I* said I needed space.

But it only took one lonely week.

One lonely week, and one night of trying to be with somebody else.

That was all it took, and I knew I couldn't be without her.

I know she wanted me too.

New Year's Eve was proof.

She had caught up.

She had finally caught up!

Just as she had always feared, my old ways came back to haunt us.

It ruined us.

One ghost from the past and she was gone.

After Emily explained what Alex had seen, I did everything that I could.

I texted.

I called.

I banged on her door.

I sent flowers.

I even emailed. I mean, who emails anymore?

Emily says that if she's this upset that it must mean that she cares.

I know that it's self-preservation on her part.

The thing is...she was the one that was going on a date.

I only did what I did because she broke my heart.

She decided to move on.

I didn't cheat on her.

Cheating would mean we were *more*.

She wouldn't give me *more*.

She didn't even call me when her dad died.

Now *I* need *her*.

Last night at work has really fucked with my mind.

I need her.

I know it's early on a Saturday morning, but I feel like I can't get through this on my own.

SEXY BEAST

Hey, it's me.

No reply.

I know you don't want to talk to me, but I need you, Alex. Last night at work was a shit show and I feel like I'm drowning. I know it's early but could you come over?

I don't know why I'm asking when you haven't talked to me for months. I had to try, though. We can talk about what happened back in January or we don't have to. I really don't care if we say a word. I just need you, Alex. Please...

I don't know what I expect. She hasn't talked to me in months, so why would she talk to me now?

Thirty minutes go by and she hasn't replied. I can see that she received the messages just seconds after I sent them. I think that's what hurts the most. She knows I need her and she hates me so deeply that she can't even text me back. How did we go from where we were to here? Since when is Alex the type to not return a call or message, even if it's to say that she doesn't want my friendship any longer? I know that it would have been hard on me, too. If I had seen her with another guy... well, I don't even know what I would have done. But we weren't together! She didn't want me!

I know she saw me at the funeral and I know she saw me

at the courthouse for the sentencing of that douche of an ex of hers. She can't return my text? This is not the Alex I know.

Just as my shitty day is getting significantly shittier, I hear a soft knock at my door. Or did I? Maybe I've actually lost my damn mind this time. It was bound to happen at some point. Maybe today is that day?

I hear the knock again, but this time, I sprint across the room and throw the door open.

She's here.

I can't breathe.

I can't speak.

She's here.

Stepping out onto the porch, I pull her into my arms and hold her like I never thought I would again. Because I honestly didn't think that I would.

"You came." I can't help but inhale her scent. I have missed her so much.

She wraps her arms around me and snuggles into my chest. It's almost as if she needed this just as much as I did.

"I came."

I can't believe she's in my arms. I needed her and she came. Thank Christ!

"Thank you." I can barely get the words out. I am so thankful that she's here.

She's so embedded in me I can feel the heat from her muffled voice on my chest when she asks, "Should we go inside?"

"Oh shit, yeah. Come on in."

I step aside and let her cross the threshold where she's greeted by Frank. He looks pretty grateful to see a sane person enter the house. The poor guy hasn't known what to do with me for months, and I know he can tell something is wrong with me this morning.

She squats down and gives Frank scratches behind his ears and says, "Good to see you, buddy. You taking good care of your daddy?" She looks up at me with concern on her face. There's something more in her eyes, though I'm not sure what.

"Ah, he takes good care of me. He's a good boy."

She stands up, puts her purse down on the floor next to the couch and slides her flip flops off. She sits down crossed legged in the corner of the couch. She doesn't have a stitch of make up on and her hair is piled on top of her head in a messy bun.

She is perfect.

"You look exquisite, Alex."

"Mick, I do not." She looks down at her oversized hoodie and yoga pants and shakes her head. "Mick, I'm already here. You don't have to sweet talk me."

"Alex, I mean it. You are the most stunning woman I have ever laid eyes on. To have you here in front of me again means everything. Thanks for coming over."

Not letting me do anymore *sweet talking,* she says, "Do you wanna talk? What happened, Mick?" she's not being rude but it's clear she isn't here for pleasantries.

I join her on the couch, but I give her space and keep a couple of feet between us. "I need to explain what happened the night you saw what you saw, Alex."

"No. I'm not here to discuss the past. I'm here because my *friend* needed me. I don't want to talk about that night. I have to push it out of my mind on a daily basis. I don't want to talk about it."

There it is. She said she's my *friend*. I don't know what I expected, but she's here. It's better than nothing, I think as I sit with my hands clasped in my lap and my head hanging low, just staring at my hands. I don't know how to start this conversation.

We sit for what feels like hours, but I'm sure it's only minutes. She scoots over so that she's close enough to take one of my hands in hers. "I'm here when you're ready, Mick. I'm not going anywhere. Take all the time you need." She rests her head on my shoulder and holds my hand until I'm ready. The room is silent. Frank isn't even snoring. It's so quiet that when I do speak, I feel the need to whisper.

"Alex, I don't even know how to start. There are just some calls that affect me and I have a hard time letting them go. My last call this morning was hard." I stop and try to take some cleansing breaths to gather myself, but I can feel myself shaking. I can't look at her. This isn't my manliest of moments and she probably thinks I'm a total puss. "Sometimes a call can take you from one emotion to another. My body just can't seem to let go of all the adrenaline once it's over. When I got home a couple of hours ago, I was still dealing with the panic that I felt on the call. I just can't seem to calm down. The only thing I could think of was you. I just felt like if I could hold you in my arms, it might calm me. Everything might be alright. I know that's not a line you want to cross and I get it. I just appreciate you being here."

She squeezes my hand to let me know she heard me, and then she waits again. She's letting me do this at my pace. She knows me. She knows that there are times I need a moment to gather myself. This is one of those times. I keep replaying the morning over and over in my head. I just want to make it stop, but I don't know how.

I let go of her hand and rub my hands over my face and through my hair and say the only thing that I can seem to get out right now. "Fuck!"

She says nothing.

In place of words, she repeats what she did at Riley's months ago. She crawls into my lap, wraps her arms around my neck, and lets me nuzzle myself into my spot. My *favorite* spot. My arms wrap around her and I hold on for dear life. Before I know what's happening, there are silent tears slowly falling down my face and onto her collarbone. I don't know where this is coming from. I don't do this. Ever. I think it's the emotions still brewing from the call and having her in my arms on top of it all.

I'm not able to look at her when she pulls back from me and I can feel her looking at me. With one of her petite hands on either side of my face, she gently places a kiss on each of my closed eyes and then her thumbs wipe the tears from my face. I open my eyes and I see something different shining back at me. It's not pity. It's compassion. Or maybe it's passion. I'm not really sure, but something has changed.

She rises from my lap and takes my hand to help me up. Wordlessly, she continues to hold my hand as she walks in front of me. We make our way across the living room, down the hallway, and take the stairs that lead to my room. Once we enter the bedroom, she shuts the door and leaves the light off.

I am so confused.

She lets go of my hands and unzips her hoodie, shrugs it off and lets it fall to the floor. She reaches for the hem of her shirt and pulls her shirt over her head. My heart is beating out of my chest. Why is she doing this? Does she think this is why I asked her to come over?

"Alex, you don't have to do this. It's not why I asked you to come over."

Her soft hands are on my face again. "Shhh... let me take care of you, Mick," she whispers as she leaves a delicate kiss on my lips and takes a step back. She pulls her hair out of the bun on top of her head and her long, dark hair falls all around her. The word I used earlier comes back to mind. Exquisite.

She's standing in front of me in only her black bra and black yoga pants. Yes, she looks unbelievably hot, but that's not what's going through my mind. All I can think is that she is the most beautiful person I know. Inside and out. The part that is making it hard to breathe is the look of reverence and love that is pouring out of those stunning eyes of hers.

She takes off her bra next and then her pants. To see that she is going commando under those tight as fuck yoga pants is fucking hot, but it still isn't what's on the top of my mind. It's there, but it's not the most important thing happening right now. The important thing is that the woman I have been in love with my entire life is giving herself to me.

She wants to take care of me.

It's more than I could have ever dreamed or deserved.

She closes the distance between us to take my shirt off and she is so close that the moment my shirt is off, her breasts are pressed against my chest. She presses her warm lips to my heart and then brings her face up to mine. Her eyes never leave mine as she pulls my shorts off of me and lets them fall to the ground. She rises up on her tiptoes once again and kisses me. Her tongue seeks permission to enter, and soon our kiss grows deeper. Her hands are in my hair and mine are roaming up and down her back.

Still not saying a word, she takes my hand and leads me to my bed. She pulls the blankets back and lies down on the sheets below. Her hair is fanned out underneath her and she looks like the sweetest thing I have ever seen.

She pulls on my hand so that I join her on the bed. I'm following her lead, so I just lay on my side and prop my head up on my hand and lightly trace the curves of her body with my forefinger. I'm not going to assume anything. I am just going to follow her lead.

She brings her hand back up to my face and says, "Mick, make love to me."

"Alex, are you sure? I don't want you to do something you aren't ready for because you think it will make me feel better. That has never been what I've wanted. I want you, Alex. All of you."

She rolls to her side so she can look me in the eye. "That's what I want too. I want you to have all of me, Mick."

"Baby, why now?"

"Mick, make love to me. Give me everything you're feeling. Let me take it from you and we'll talk later."

I don't think she has any idea what her words do to me. It's like I can feel my heart filling with her every word. Until this moment, I didn't know how empty I was. She is giving me the most precious gift that anybody has ever given me. I take a beat to look at her. All of her. I know this isn't our first time, but it's been years since we've been together. What's happening between the two of us right now is different. I don't want to miss a single detail.

I methodically crawl over her body and rest my weight on

my forearms. I kiss her forehead, each cheek, the tip of her nose, her chin and finally drop my lips to hers. I could kiss her forever, but I don't. I make my way to her neck and up to her ear. There are a million things I want to whisper to her, but I also don't want to ruin this perfect moment. I explore her neck all the way down to her collarbone. There is no greater place on this earth than right here. I could kiss, lick and nibble on her neck all night, but there is so much to explore.

I take my hand, and glide it down her sternum and in between the two most perfect breasts I have ever had the pleasure to lay my eyes on. I bring my left hand to her breast and gently drag my fingers over her hardened nipple, while I take her other unoccupied nipple into my mouth. Her back instantly arches and forces her breast even deeper into my mouth. Her reaction to my touch makes my already hard erection throb. I want nothing more than to be inside her, but I need to savor this. I will not rush this moment.

Alex is a woman who should be cherished. I know how fortunate I am that she is giving herself to me in this way. I know about her past. Her most recent experiences with sex were not pleasant or consensual. For her to give herself to me means so many things, on so many levels. The most important thing to me is to make her feel good. And that is just what I intend to do.

Taking her other nipple in my mouth, my hand makes its journey over her flat stomach and over her hip. I can feel her jump when I hit that spot just above her hipbone, and she quivers in anticipation. When my hand finds her warmth, she is more than ready for me. She opens her legs to grant me more access. I slowly rub my thumb over her bundle of nerves and she moans. It's a sound that I will never forget as long as I live. I will dream about this sound for the rest of my days. When I fill her with first one finger and then two, she makes another sound that will be stored away in the recesses of my mind. I find her mouth, and as I increase the speed of my fingers, I kiss her like I have never kissed anybody. I feel her tighten around me and feel her come around my hand as her moans fill my mouth.

I make my way down her body to give her even more pleasure when she grabs my shoulders and says, "Mick, I need you inside me. Please."

"Alex, I wasn't planning this. I don't have protection."

"I'm clean and I'm on the pill."

Tucking her hair behind her ear, I confess. "Sweet Thing, I've never been with anybody without protection. It's been months since I was with anybody." I can tell by the look on her face that both of my statements surprise her. "Alex, since the night you crawled into my lap at Riley's, that was it. I haven't wanted anybody else since. I know you may not believe me, and we'll talk about that later, but I swear there has been nobody, baby." She gives me a slight nod of her head as a sign of her acceptance of my statement.

I can't help but slide my hand over her breast and down to her hip bone again. I know I will never tire of touching her body. I use my hand to spread her leg a little further and I center myself so that I am right where I need to be. I hover over her and look into her beautiful face and can't believe that this is actually happening.

My Sweet Thing is here.

In my bed.

Asking me to make love to her.

I think she takes my pause as doubt on my end and she

tries to reassure me. "Baby, this is what I want. *You* are what I want. I'm sorry it took me so long, but the moment you opened that door this morning, I knew. If you still want *more,* then I'm yours, Mick. Please let me take your burdens away. Give me everything. I can take it."

My heart is soaring. I don't know how to contain my emotions. What her words have done for me is so much more than what she is doing to my body. I can feel the tears filling my eyes, but I don't let them fall. I will not cry twice. Not gonna happen.

Slowly, I sink into her warmth, and the sensation is more than I could have ever imagined. I know it was great when we were together before, but having the emotions behind the actions is like nothing I've ever experienced, and it's more than just because we're skin to skin. As I slowly move in and out of her, I lower to my elbows and place them near her head and interlace my fingers within hers as we hold on to each other. It's then that I realize why this is so different. It's the first time I've ever made love. That's what this is. We're making love and for the first time, I feel like a man worthy of her love.

There's a connection between the two of us that is palpable. Our eyes never leave each other, and I can feel a change in the atmosphere. Our connection is so powerful that it's almost overwhelming. I can feel her running through my veins. This woman soothes me and makes me feel like I have a purpose. Nobody has ever eased my pain the way she does. The way she is. Right now. I'm never letting her go.

More.

Our pace has been slow and gentle. Perfect. But when her moans get louder and her feet that are now wrapped around me push on my ass to tell me to give her more, I can't help but pick up the pace. When I bring my mouth to hers, I can feel her tighten around me, and that's all it takes as we both reach our climax together. I drop my head to my spot on her neck. Her fingers are gently leaving a trail up and down my back, and I feel more content than any other moment in my life. She kisses my shoulder and continues her soothing over my back.

I lift my head and see that I am not the only person feeling content right now. When she feels me gazing at her, she seductively opens her eyes and silently mouths, "Hi." That's all it takes and the tears start to fall again. I do not know what the hell is happening to me. This woman has shaken me to my bones. I'm sure she thinks I'm crazy, but she affects me in a way that I have never known.

She pulls me as close to her as she can get me and holds me while rubbing my head.

"Shhh... It's okay, baby. I'm here."

I finally understand why people who fall in love lose themselves in their relationships. It's all consuming. Nothing else matters.

She is my world.

Please God, don't let this be all there is. Please say that this means what I hope it means. I cannot lose her again.

Alex

I use my body weight to push him so that we roll over together. He settles on his pillow and I bring the blankets over us and lie on his chest. My leg is thrown over his waist, and I pull myself into him as tightly as I can.

"Thank you, Alex."

My reply is a kiss to his chest.

"I'm really sorry about the waterworks. I don't know what is happening with me, but I can assure you that isn't the norm for me."

"Honey, never feel bad for having emotions. It means the world to me that you trust me enough to share them with me. Did you want to talk about it?"

He kisses the top of my head and says, "Not yet. I feel too good right now."

"Whenever you're ready. Why don't you try to get some sleep?"

"What about you? You don't want to sleep your day away; you just woke up."

"Mick, I haven't really slept in months. Not since the last time I was in your arms, here in this bed. Let's sleep you Sexy Beast, you."

I look up to see him smiling from ear to ear. My heart warms. I know I'm where I'm meant to be.

"Sleep tight, Sweet Thing."

Not long after those words leave his lips, I can hear and feel his breathing level off.

When I woke up to the sound of my phone notifying me, I had a text. This is not where I thought my day would take me. Seeing his name on my phone had the same reaction it always has. Butterflies start their assault on my stomach. But then my mind reminds my body that I can't risk my heart again, and the flight of butterflies turns to twisting knots of anxiety and remorse.

When his second text message came through and I saw he needed me—that something was wrong and he wasn't just trying to get me back into his life—my heart took over. I couldn't hear my brain over the emotions that were flying through my body. For Mickey Jacobs to reach out and say that he needs somebody is a big deal. There was no way I wasn't going to leave immediately.

I threw on clothes, brushed my teeth and was out the door. In my rush, I didn't even realize that I hadn't texted him back. Thank goodness it was early on a Saturday morning and there wasn't any traffic. I got to him just as fast as I could, but once I pulled into his driveway, I was filled with anxiety again. Anxiety and doubt. What was I risking to be here? Was it worth it? The real question was... was he worth it? There was only one answer. He was.

These past few months, I have selfishly been putting myself first and not considering how badly he may have been hurting. I know it was important to find myself and figure out my own life, but I didn't even let him explain. Emily tried, but I didn't really want to hear it. It was easier to just not talk about it. As I sat in his driveway, I remembered that in the end he was still my friend and he needed me. Mickey Jacobs doesn't need anybody, but he needs me.

Cautiously, I tiptoed my way to his front door. I don't know if it's because it was so early, but the neighborhood seemed really quiet. The only thing that I could hear was the pounding of my heart. I lightly knocked on the door and waited. Nothing. I instantly started to panic and think that *something must be wrong. I knocked again, a little louder this time, but still only heard my pulsating heart.*

The door flew open and there he stood. The man of my dreams. The man that in that very moment I knew I loved. I've always known, but today, standing in his doorway, it was solidified. My heart broke for him. He looked tired and lost. He's been through something, although I don't know what, and my heart was breaking for him. When his door opened, I was filled with so much relief to see his gorgeous face staring back at me I felt like I could breathe again... for the first time in months. He looked tired, but he was alive and breathing. I knew right then that the best decision I had ever made; I made today. Today, when I finally listened to my heart and not my mind. When he put his arms around me, I couldn't help but melt into him.

Enough shutting him out. I'm not sure why I thought I had to shut him out to work on myself. I'm better when I'm with him.

Now, I lie here knowing that I could finally rescue my superhero. Maybe not to the extreme that he keeps rescuing me, but I know I helped him. That terrified look that was on his face earlier is gone. Seeing the smile that I put on that same face after telling him I hadn't been able to sleep without him... that was everything. Just when I think *I've* saved *him*, he saves me again. My heart soars. I feel strong. Making this man happy makes me feel like I can do anything. This is a high I hope I never get used to.

With these blissful thoughts, I close my eyes and drift off into a peaceful slumber.

I feel soft, warm lips on my shoulder. I can smell him all around me. It feels like a dream. We're spooning, and I can feel every inch of him pressing against me. I'm afraid to open my eyes. If this is a dream, I don't want it to end. I feel him move my hair off of my neck and his lips are now on his favorite spot.

"Morning, Sweet Thing. Well, good afternoon."

"Morning, baby," I say as I snuggle deeper into him.

"Hmmm," he moans in my ear. "Say it again."

"Say what again, Mick?"

"Call me baby again, baby."

I giggle, but of course I do as he asks. "Morning, baby."

"God, I love the sound of that."

I turn in his arms so that I can see his handsome face. "Morning, baby. How you feeling?"

"I'm better. Thanks to you." He smiles that smile of his and the butterflies are back. The difference is this time... this time there is no little voice in the back of my head telling me to ignore them. This time, I embrace every single one of those flutters. Right here, at this moment, I have never been happier.

"I'm glad I could help." I softly leave a trail down his chest and to his abdomen.

"Whatcha doin', Alex?"

"Just thought I would wake you up with a proper good morning, *baby*."

Just as my hand reaches his golden, happy trail, he grabs my hand and brings my progress to a halt. "Is that so?" He rolls me on to my back and it's clear that he's just as ready to welcome the new day as I am. "Well, if that's what you want, that's what you'll get, Sweet Thing."

He settles on top of me, as if we were made for each other, and he slides inside me with no effort at all. Looking down at me, he says, "You feel so good." He takes one of my breasts into his mouth and, as he releases it, he gives it a gentle tug with his teeth.

"Yes, Mick!" I gasp and my back arches instinctively.

He flattens his tongue over my nipple to take some of the pain away while keeping up his slow and steady pace. "What I wouldn't give to wake up like this every day."

He lifts up so that his torso is no longer touching me. He looks at me as though I am his most cherished possession, and then his gaze drifts down my body and to where our bodies are joined. Watching him watch us turns me on even more and I'm already close. He looks back up at me and with all sincerity he says, "I'm never letting you go, Alex." As if to show how serious he is, his pace quickens and his hips thrusts harder. He's covered in a sheen of sweat and in time with his thrusts, he growls. "Never. Letting. You. Go!"

His words. His touch. His all-consuming heart. The combination of it all has me bursting with emotions. As he claims me, I can't help but come with him as we both shout each other's names in passion and ecstasy. Behind my closed eyes, all I see is a galaxy of stars.

"Was that proper enough for you or did you have something else in mind?" he purrs, bringing me back to earth.

"I think it'll do," I quip, teasingly.

"Well, I guess I'll have to work on my skills if that's all it did for you."

I roll us over so that I'm on top of him. "Honey, you don't need to work on your skills, but I'll let you practice on me all you want." I hop off him and head to his bathroom. "Be right back." On my way, I bend down and pick up the t-shirt that I took off of him earlier this morning and give him a little wink over my shoulder.

I clean up, but realize I don't have a toothbrush. I see his sitting in its little holder and figure, *what the hell*. I brush my teeth and look at my reflection in the mirror. I don't have any makeup on and my hair is a hot mess, but I'm glowing. I look happy.

I am happy.

When I head back to the bedroom, it's empty. I steal a pair of his boxers from his top dresser drawer and slip them on. I don't think he'll mind and I love wearing his clothes. I lazily saunter down the stairs and float to the kitchen. The perma-grin that lights up my face is instant.

Busily bustling about the kitchen, he doesn't see me sitting at the table watching and listening to him. He's just finished starting the coffee and is getting out all the fixings for cereal. Under his breath, I can hear him singing, but I'm not sure what the song is? I can hear the occasional *baby,* in what I think are made up lyrics, but that's really it. I think this may be the cutest thing I have ever seen. He bounces his way to the refrigerator as he bends over to grab the milk. He shakes his ass and then when he shuts the door he does a little spin, a 'la Jason Derulo. I'm smiling from ear to ear when he stops mid-spin. He's spotted me and his already there smile gets even bigger as he struts his way over to my perch at the table.

He gives me another little spin and then, with the happiest face I have ever seen, he coos. "You like my moves, baby?" He plants a big sloppy kiss on my face, takes a step back, and does his best to twerk for me.

His dance moves throw me into a wave of hysterics, and I'm laughing so hard there are tears streaming down my face.

I can barely get enough air to reply. "Love your moves, baby." He turns around and shakes his moneymaker in my face again. In just his gym shorts and nothing else, his show is not only hilarious but pretty sexy too. I slap his ass. "Shake it you, Sexy Beast! Sorry, but I don't have any cash to pay for the lap dance, but you can work it off of me later. If that seems fair to you?"

"Damn, Alex! You're gonna make me take you on this table if you don't stop."

"Promise?"

"Sweet Thing, I need to feed you. I'm not much of a chef, but I can make a mean bowl of cereal. Now stop distracting me."

I don't know what's come over me, but I want this man. I can't get enough of him. I have never felt as uninhibited as I do with him. He makes me feel sexy and seductive. I feel a new side coming out of me that even I wasn't aware I had. That is the only reasoning I can come up with for what I do next.

"That means that the stove isn't on, right?"

"That would be correct, Alex. What are you getting at, sexy?"

"Nothing will burn then." I stand up, pull his t-shirt over my head and step into his personal space. I drag my fingernail down his chest and to his golden happy trail. I reach into his shorts and it's clear that his precious cereal has long been forgotten. "What do ya say? Was all that table talk a promise or a threat, big boy?"

"Fuck, Alex. You have got to be the sexiest woman on the God damned planet. If you want it on the table, then the table it is. You just tell me how you want it and it's yours, Sweet Thing."

With the confidence of a high-class stripper, I sway my hips as I approach the head of the table. I purposely bend over much farther than is necessary to move the chair that's tucked under the table. I stand up and face him. Seductively, I move all of my hair over one shoulder, bite my same finger that found its way down his torso and lift my eyes to his. What I find is the playboy of Portland standing frozen to the spot; in shock and with his mouth hanging open. I beckon him with a crook of my finger and when he takes his first steps my way; I bend over once again while I hook my thumbs into his boxers, shimmy them down my legs, and kick them to the side. I turn and lay my chest over the table and I am completely exposed. I am naked and vulnerable and I have never felt so safe. I grab the edge of the table with each hand and with white knuckles. I wait for him to make the next move.

I feel the heat of his presence behind me. Just knowing he is close enough to touch sends shivers down my spine, and I can feel myself quivering. One of his powerful hands grabs me by the hip as the other torturously glides down my spine and to my exposed back-side. He feels me tense and pauses. "Don't worry, baby. We'll save this for another time, but please know that I cannot wait for that day," he practically growls as his finger gently slides over the center of my ass. Even though I should feel nervous that he wants to explore this forbidden territory, all it does is make me hotter.

By the time his fingers reach my entrance, I am internally begging for him to reach. He finds me slick and ready for him to take me. "Oh baby, you are so fucking ready for me.

Knowing that it's me that makes you this hot is the biggest high I have ever felt." I feel him tease my entrance with the tip of his glorious cock and I moan. "To think all I wanted to do was hold you in my arms when I asked you to come over. After today..." He leans over me so his front is resting on my back. Skin to skin. "I don't think I will ever get enough of you. You're mine, baby. And I'm yours." He whispers in my ear as he plunges deep inside me with a new intensity. I have never felt so full, and I have never been so fulfilled. This man is the stuff that dreams are made of. And apparently... he's mine.

His pace quickens, but I find his rhythm and push back to meet every one of his thrusts. He's no longer draped across my back. He is standing behind me, guiding my hips with his powerful hands. From this position, I can fully appreciate just how big Mick is. He feels like he is deeper than ever before. He is filling me to the brink. It's almost painful, but in the best kind of way.

"God, Alex. I wish you could see this. Watching us like this is the hottest fucking thing I have ever seen. God, your ass! Just watching you take my cock over and over is enough to make me come, baby." He reaches around and finds my clit and works me to the point of frenzy. I can feel my orgasm building. It's so intense that I'm afraid that if I come right now, I may disintegrate into a million little pieces.

"Yes! Oh, God! Please don't stop, Mick," I scream into the room.

I feel like all five of my senses are being overwhelmed. The sound of both of us gasping for air and our bodies slamming together in the throes of passion fills my ears. The smell of his musk all over my body is intoxicating. The taste of his kiss on my lips leaves me breathless. Looking over my shoulder, I see his face watching our bodies move together as he slides in and out of me. And it is magnificent. His face. His body. He is pure perfection. His touch brands me. The way he makes my body come alive and hum with electricity is overwhelming.

I am irrevocably his.

"I can feel you getting closer. You're so tight. So perfect. I don't think I can hold on any longer. You ready, baby?"

"Yes!" I shout, arching my back and lifting my chest off of the table. I'm so close that I can find no other words of coherency at the moment.

He thrusts even harder and faster than before, and an instant later, when he yells my name on a growl, my world goes dark. Once again I see stars, and I lay my chest back down on the table.

We both stay where we are and catch our breaths in the afterglow of yet another passion filled experience. There isn't a space in this house that I wouldn't love to experience, not a single one.

In a sexy, husky voice, he finally speaks. "Babe, I am so sorry. Did I hurt you? I got carried away and didn't even think about how uncomfortable that may have been for you." He releases me and helps me up from the table. He pulls me into his arms, cups my head and pulls me into a skin on skin hug. Every part of us is touching, including our hearts and souls.

"I'm good, Mick. You felt so amazing. I didn't notice anything else."

"Now, that is what I like to hear." He kisses me on the top of my head and finds his t-shirt that I had been wearing. As he brings the shirt over my head, he says, "Covering you up is the last thing I want to do, but you are way too distracting and I need to feed you." He gives my ass a little slap, hands me his boxers and turns me in the direction of the hallway. "Why don't you go get cleaned up and stop distracting me? This cereal and toast aren't going to make themselves, woman."

He sends me on my way, and I float back up to the primary bathroom. I get cleaned up, throw my hair up into a ponytail, and put his boxers back on. I can't help but notice the smile on my face when I look at myself in the mirror. It's the same smile that I see on Mick's face. Why the hell have I been pushing him away? Why would I ever want to deny either of us from feeling like we do today? Although, this thought brings to mind the way he looked when I got here this morning. We didn't really talk about what prompted his call to me. I hope my actions didn't make him think that I didn't want to talk. He just didn't seem ready, and I wanted to take his pain away. I hope I didn't handle this situation wrong, and that we didn't simply put a band-aid on things.

Wondering how to bring it up without ruining our current state of bliss, I pad my barefoot feet down the stairs and find him at the table with all the fixings for a breakfast of cereal and toast.

His smile is still covering his glorious face, and if it's possible, it lights up even more when he catches me enter the room.

"Hey, good looking. I like that shirt on you." He says, referring to the shirt I'm wearing that says, "That's What She Said."

That's Mick. Always the center of attention, and always making people shake their head or laugh their ass off.

Secretly, I love his stupid, immature side. I can be a bit too serious. I think we balance each other out.

"As you can see, I went all out. You have your choice of sugary sweet cereal or the healthy shit that Emily got me used to eating. We also have wheat toast with butter. You can choose between strawberry jam, honey or my favorite... cinnamon sugar. I know, it's pretty fancy, but I only bring out the best for my Sweet Thing." He winks and then sprinkles his cinnamon sugar over his toast.

"What exactly is that?"

"What is this? Only the *best* way to eat toast! Open up."

I open my mouth, and he brings his precious toast to my lips, and I take a bite. At first I don't really notice anything, but then the sweet, sugary goodness kicks in. "Ah, Mick. That is the bomb!"

Laughing at me, he says, "The bomb. I love it. I feel like we're back in school again. You are so freaking cute."

I stick my tongue out at him and do some sprinkling of my own.

After breakfast, we clean up the dishes and cereal boxes and find ourselves each on different sides of the kitchen, leaning against counters and staring at each other.

Mick is the first to speak. "Do you have plans for tonight?"

"Nope, you?"

"I don't, but I'm hoping that you and I can just stay in our little bubble and not leave this house today. Does that work for you?"

"I would love that, but I need to go home and take a shower. I don't have any other clothes to wear or my toothbrush. Hope you don't mind, but I used yours early?"

"Baby, what's mine is yours. That means my shower, my toothbrush and my clothes. How about you and I take that shower together, order a pizza later, and stay in tonight? If you want girlie shampoos and lotions, Emily left some in the other bathroom that you can use."

"You sure, Mick?"

He strides across the kitchen and places himself in front of me. His dark eyes canvas my face and land on my lips. He places the gentlest of kisses on my mouth and, as he pulls away, he bites on my lower lip. When he lets go, his eyes lift to mine and he says, "I have never been more sure of anything in my life. Now, let's go see about that shower."

* * *

If I thought the day had been perfect before our shower, I was wrong.

Oh, that shower.

We stayed under the steaming hot cascade of water until it went cold. It was the most intimate moment of my life. We washed every inch of each other with slow, gentle caresses. There were soft kisses that followed the cleansing caresses. It was sweet, passionate, and romantic. It was more than just a hot make-out session. It was sensual and all-consuming.

Mick is all-consuming.

An hour later, I'm clad in a pair of soft grey sweats and a dark blue Under Armour henley. I had to roll the sweats up at the top, and the sleeves of the shirt up as well, but all in all I'm pretty comfortable and I'm wearing his clothes. There's nothing wrong with that. We've settled into his bed, popped some kettle corn popcorn and are watching Mick's all-time favorite movie, *Old School*.

It's times like this that I am reminded of the Mick that I grew up with. The popular jock who was always the life of the party. Always the loudest and always with the smartest mouth. The one that was always ready for a fight. Always driving just a little too fast and living his life the same way. That's not my Mick. My Mick is sweet, kind, protective and gentle.

Mick knows every word of this movie and it's no wonder he named his dog after it. I'm snuggled up under his arm and Will Ferrell is running down the street naked when I realize I'm the only one laughing. I sit up and turn around to look at him and see that he's watching me and not the movie.

"What?"

"Nothing, I'm just happy."

"Yeah? And why are you so happy?"

"You're here. I just can't believe you're actually here."

"Me too, Mick. I can't believe it either, but I'm glad I'm here."

He picks up the remote and turns off the TV. The room darkens and it's just us. He pulls me back to into his arms and we sink down so that we're lying down again. I'm lying on his chest and he's stroking my hair. "This is the best Saturday night I've had in a long time."

"Not your usual style, though."

He kisses the top of my head and sighs into my hair. "Baby, *you* are my style and there isn't anywhere else I would rather be. I can't thank you enough for dropping everything and coming over this morning. You don't know how much it means to me."

"Of course. Speaking of this morning... wanna talk about it?"

"Thank you, baby, but I don't want to bring all of my darkness into your light. I love my job, but sometimes it just gets to me. There are great days and then there are some not so great days."

I put my hand over his heart, and with my chin on his chest, look up at him. "Earlier today, you said that I was yours and you were mine. Maybe it was just in the moment, but for me... for me, Mick... I'm yours. I may not take your burdens away, but I'm here to listen."

He sits us back up and turns us so that we're facing each other. So that he can look me in the eye.

"Alex, I meant every word of what I said. It wasn't just an *in the moment* thing. I hope you know that this is the real deal to me. No more just friends. No more excuses. I'm yours and to hear you say you're mine... baby, that is all I've ever wanted to hear come out of that sweet mouth of yours. "

Inside, I am squealing like a little girl because the love of my life says that he's mine, but I know that now isn't the time. We need to talk about what happened at work last night.

"Then talk to me. Tell me what had you so rattled."

"I don't really know how to explain it or make it make sense."

"Try me." I can tell he's anxious and he's not speaking. I can only think of one thing to do. I pat the headboard, signaling him to sit against it. Once he's in place, I crawl into his lap and give him access to his favorite spot.

"You know me so well," he says with a squeeze. "I could live out my days right here."

272

"Just let me know if I get too heavy. Now, tell me about your night."

On a heavy exhale, he recounts his last call of the night...

"It was around 4:00 am and I was driving back to the station at the end of my shift. I had been assigned to the boonies where not a lot happens and it had been a pretty quiet night. There were lots of hills and land, but not a lot of lights. I was driving up a long road that turned into a steep hill. The road was flanked by steep embankments on either side. At the top of the hill was a three-way stop. The only option was to turn right or left. When you look at the road directly in front of you, it looks like a space with trees, but it's really a cliff. There was a Subaru Outback a few blocks ahead of me and as it neared the three-way stop, I didn't see brake lights. I kept thinking, why aren't they braking? I was in my car yelling, BRAKE! BRAKE! But, Alex, they didn't brake. The car was there one-second and gone the next. They drove straight through the stop sign and disappeared. I could hear the tree limbs breaking as the car made its descent down the cliff.

I instantly called dispatch and gave them my location, and turned on my overhead lights. I asked for them to send medical because I knew that drop off had to have been a hundred to a hundred and fifty feet, and the driver must have been going forty-five miles an hour. There was a stop sign and a utility pole, and she somehow drove right in-between them. I have no idea how she managed it, but she drove right through the middle of the sign and the pole. I know hitting the pole would have been bad too, but Jesus, Alex. The car just disappeared before my eyes."

I don't know what to say and I don't want to interrupt him, so I just hold him and let him get it all out. I can't see his face because it's buried in my neck, but I think it helps him. I rub his head to try and soothe him and just listen.

"I parked my car as close to the drop-off as I could and got out and went to the edge of the cliff. When I looked down, I could see that the car nosed right into a large tree and then slid down the tree and the front end came to rest in the creek below. The branches on that tree were what I heard breaking. I was shining my flashlight but couldn't see much at all.

I turned my flashlight off and was just about to turn back to my car to see where help was when I heard moaning. I could hear a person making noise, so I called out and asked if they were okay. I didn't get a response. I knew there was some-body alive, and I had to get to them. We were out in the middle of nowhere, and I knew it would still be at least ten minutes before help arrived. Then I remembered I had my 'go' bag in the trunk of my car. I ran back to my trunk and grabbed the bag I always keep ready for SWAT calls. I take my 100-foot rope out of the bag and decide that I can static line down to the car. I tied it to the push bumper on the front of my car and wrapped it around my waist above my duty belt. I slowly let out the line and lowered myself to the car below. The rope was about ten feet too short, so I had to untie myself and drop the ten feet. In reality, it probably took me about two minutes to reach the bottom, but it felt like hours.

When I finally reached the car, I could see that there was a female in the driver's seat. She was pinned in her seat by the engine block that had come through the cabin of the car. I couldn't see her legs and the steering wheel had crushed her chest. The windshield was completely gone and laying on the hood of the car. I could smell coolant and oil and burning chemicals. Standing next to her door, I could hear that she was still breathing. After pushing as much of the glass away from the windshield that I could, I got on the hood of the car to try to get into the front passenger seat. I needed to get close enough to give her CPR. I could feel the heat from the engine under me as I climbed my way into the car. It was so hot it felt like I was going to burn my legs. But all I could really think about was getting to her. When I did finally get close enough to approach the woman, I could smell the alcohol on her breath.

Her breathing suddenly became labored, and then she took one last heavy breath. As I was sitting there trying to figure out a way to help her, she passed. I got to her just as she took her last breath. I was too late, Alex. The problem was the way her body was pinned in and with the damage to the car, there wasn't any way that I could really get to her. I couldn't save her. "

I start to say something, but he shakes his head as if to say there's more.

"That was when I saw the car seat in the back. It had been completely pushed forward. The safety harness was bowed. It was bent somehow and it looked like a baby could have been ejected. I was instantly filled with panic. There was a baby there and I didn't see it or hear it. I got on the radio and let dispatch know that the driver was code 55—which means deceased—and that there was an infant missing.

It's dark and I can't see anything. All at once, everything hit me, watching her go off the cliff. Going down the cliff to get to her. Watching her die, the baby seat. I felt an acidy bile building in the back of my throat. I've already lost the driver, but all I could hope was that I wasn't too late to save the baby."

The only lights were the headlights from the car, but they were facing down into the creek and the lights from my car up on the top of the cliff. The area was full of blackberry thickets and I was running through them trying to find the baby. Finally, the fire department and my back up show and the first thing they do is start yelling at me for going down the way I did and alone. Really? Is that what they want to talk about when there is a missing baby? I tell them to fuck off and to bring their asses down the cliff and to bring a FLIR. A FLIR is an infrared heat register that should help us find the baby in the shroud of darkness we're covered in.

My concern was trying to figure out which way the baby may have been thrown. The way the seat was pushed forward, it made me think that the baby could have gone through the windshield since the car was facing straight down when it hit the tree. There were baby blankets and car parts scattered everywhere. Then I wondered if the baby could have fallen out further up the hill and I missed it on my way down. I ran into the water to make sure the baby didn't get thrown into the creek. I was thinking of every possible scenario that I could. I have never felt so panicked. Watching her die sucked Alex. It really did. But knowing there was a baby out there that needed our help and I couldn't find it was making me feel out of control with panic, and I never feel out of control. Especially at work.

The fire guys were now down at the crash site with me. They cut the woman out of the car and tried to do CPR on her while others help me work the hill to find the baby. I was so desperate that I was ripping full blackberry bushes out by their roots to find that baby. By this time, I get word that they've sent a car to the driver's address and they were there notifying the family. I yell up to make sure they ask them if there was a baby *in the car! It feels like days go by without word and because I was losing my mind by this point I yell up to the officers above. WAS THERE A BABY IN THE CAR?! I keep asking over and over. Nobody will answer the damn question."*

I try to rub his back and head to soothe him, but I can feel his entire body tense around me. He's trembling, yet so tense that every muscle in his body is flexed. There's a light sheen of sweat forming on his head and my heart is breaking for him. I just want to make it all go away.

"I kept thinking the baby was under the car, in the creek, somewhere up the hill. Why couldn't I find the baby? Just when I think I might go ape shit crazy if I don't find this baby, somebody yells down from the top of the cliff. The baby was home safe and sound with dad. There was no baby in the car, Alex. There. Was. No. Baby. In. The. Car."

"Oh, thank God, Mick." I kiss his forehead and let him finish.

"That's what I thought too. Oh, thank God. I'm filled with relief that there isn't a baby dying alone out there on the hillside. But the panic that I felt in my chest didn't go away. I still couldn't save the mom. I know she was drinking and she made a mistake, but I couldn't save her and that baby is motherless now. I keep thinking, what if the baby had been out there? Would I have been able to get to it in time? I felt helpless. The fire guys went back to work and I found a rock to sit on and tried to gather myself. It didn't work, though. I just kept seeing her take her last breath, and then flashes of the baby seat and baby blankets everywhere.

Eventually, we used the ropes that the fire department dropped down to us to climb back up. I gave my statement to another officer and came home.

The panic and desperation that I felt from searching and searching for that baby just wouldn't go away. I swear, Alex. I knew there was a baby out there and I couldn't find it. I couldn't find it, and even though I knew the baby was home safe and sound, I just couldn't get myself to calm down.

When I got home, to this empty house, well... that's when I texted you."

He lays us down so that we're on our sides and facing each other. "Thank you, Alex. You saved me today. I was a wreck when you got here, but just seeing you standing at my front door was what I needed to begin to feel okay again. That's what you do to me, Sweet Thing. You calm me. You make me feel like I don't need anything or anyone else. As long as I have you, everything will be okay."

"You've got me, Mick. You've got me."

Chapter 20

Alex

May

"Wait, why do I have two extra screws? And why are there no words on these stupid instructions?" I yell over the music.

Mick and I spent the morning at IKEA and now we're putting together a new shelving unit for the room that was recently occupied by Emily.

"Baby, this is why IKEA is so affordable. They know you're going to lose just a little bit of your sanity when you put this shit together and they feel somewhat responsible. So, they make it cheap. It's the least they can do."

We're both down on our hands and knees putting pieces of compressed wood together when the next song on my playlists starts.

"Shit. This is gonna be in my head the rest of the day now, babe. You have to change it." He throws himself down on the floor and pretends to cover his ears, but I know he loves this song.

I put my extra screws down and crawl over to him. Straddling him, I say, "Ah, come on baby, you can handle it. The more you hear it, the better chance you have to figure out what the heck she's saying." I can't help but move my hips to the beat of the song, and from what I feel underneath me, he may just be changing his mind about me changing the song.

Bending over him, I find his ear and sing along to the words I do know and tell him I will never neglect him or hold his past against him. He sings along to the chorus with me. "Work, work, work, work, work." Just as the song is about to end, I jump up and do a little twerk for him.

"Baby, if this is what I get when this song is on, you can play it on repeat all day long!"

"I thought I might change your mind. Now come dance with me, Mickey Jacobs!"

When the new Justin Timberlake song starts, we're both on our feet dancing like fools!

"This is my jam!" I yell over the music as he swings me around and serenades me about not being able to stop the feeling and how we need to keep dancing. We're jumping around like kids and it turns out that big, bad Mickey Jacobs is a total goofball. He's singing and dancing like he doesn't have a care in the world. Justin Timberlake has nothing on my man.

Yes, *my* man.

It's only been a few weeks since his early morning text led me back to him, but it feels like we've always been together. We've spent every minute we can together these past weeks, and every second has been amazing.

Well, there was one conversation that wasn't so amazing, but in the end, it was important and something that we needed to talk about. Mick insisted he explain what I saw that night. He wanted to make it clear just exactly what happened, why he did it, and how it ended. I understood and recognized it would never have happened if I could have just gotten over his past and realized that he had changed.

That it was okay to give him more.

This conversation also led to me explaining why I thought I needed to move on. During the conversation, I also told him I see a therapist once a week and that I still went to group from time to time. He said that he thought that was great and asked if I wanted him to come with me. I explained it was something that I needed to do on my own and that it came with lots of support. I also told him that if I had really listened to what they teach us in group, then I would have realized that I should have taken the chance with him. In group we're always taught not to live in the past, but that was what I was doing with Mick. I couldn't let his past go because I was scared and insecure. My fear hurt both of us and kept us apart for months. Months that we could have been together. Months that we could have been dancing like fools together. But in the end, I spent the last couple of months working on myself, and that's helped me get to where I am today. Dancing like a fool with this goofy, handsome man.

We're both out of breath and laughing when Mr. Timberlake stops singing. He grabs my phone and quickly picks the next song. With a heated look on his face as he slowly drags his finger down my neck, he says, "This is *my* jam."

Not a second later, Mary J. Blige sings about her *Sweet Thing* while Mick takes me in his arms. He moves us so that we start gently swaying to the music while he sings along and tells me I'm his everything. Who would have known that he could sing like this? He really can sing and it's really, really hot. I don't tell him this. I just want to enjoy the moment. Besides, he doesn't have to know that he's good at everything. His ego is just fine as it is.

Our sweet swaying turns spicy when Mick stops singing and starts kissing me. There is always so much passion behind his kisses. He lights me on fire every time his lips touch mine. I have never felt this much for another person. It sounds corny, but being with him is like living in my own Romantic Comedy. He is the funniest person I know and also the most romantic. It's like his two missions in life are to make me laugh and to make me feel cherished. He does both. Every day. I have never been happier.

His lips leave mine and he sings the chorus in my ear again. He pulls back and stares at me. I can tell that he wants to say something, but he can't seem to get it out. I lift up on my toes and whisper onto his lips. "You're my everything too, baby." And then I kiss him. I feel what my words mean to him with the intensity of the kiss that he returns to me. He *is* my everything. There has never been a truer statement.

As usual, our kiss leads to much more and twenty minutes later we lay on the floor amidst boxes and pressed wood, naked, sweaty and out of breath. Neither of us can get enough of each other. We have a hunger for one another that we cannot seem to ever fully satisfy. We always want more. It's unbelievable that we both feel equally insatiable. It's not just him or just me. We both want everything from each other.

We're finally on the same page and this chapter is so good that I don't want to turn the page. I just want to read this chapter over and over again.

"Hmmm... that was nice. Hope your rug burns aren't too bad?" I can't help but giggle.

"There's nothing funny about what just happened, Sweet Thing. To watch you on top of me like that, I would endure rug burns every day of the week. You are phenomenal, you know that, right?"

I just hum into his chest as we lay on the floor catching our breath.

"You are, Alex. Not because you are the most beautiful person who I have ever laid eyes on and because what you did to me just now was fucking amazing. Baby, you're phenomenal because of what you to do to me in here," he says, pointing to his chest. "And how you make me feel every second of the day. You make me a better man, Alex. Being with you makes me feel like more of a man than I have ever felt. And let's face it, I'm pretty damned manly."

I just chuckle and shake my head. Leave it to him to make me laugh while reaching deep inside my heart and filling it with love.

"Alex. I mean it... I like the person I am when I'm with you. I know this is all happening fast, and it's new and scary, but I'm ready, baby. I want this. Us. You're it for me, Sweet Thing. If I had my way, you would never sleep another night anywhere but in my bed."

"Mick, I've slept here every night that you weren't at work for weeks. At some point, you are gonna have to come to my place and *you* can live out of a bag."

"No can do, sorry."

"What? You can't be serious. Why should I have to live out of a bag, Mick? Sorry if my place isn't as nice as yours. I didn't take you for a snob, Mickey Jacobs!" I feel myself getting worked up and our blissful moment is coming to an abrupt halt.

"Alex, that's not it at all. Come on. You know me better than that."

"Then what is it?"

He doesn't speak and I can feel his heartbeat quicken underneath me.

"I can't sleep in that bed. I know what he did to you in your place, in that bed. I can't do it, Alex. Nobody but you has been in my bed. The girls moved in right after I did and I haven't had anybody else in that bed upstairs. It's only had you in it, baby. Please don't ask me to sleep in the bed where he forced himself on you. Alex, you're all mine and to think of somebody else touching you and doing what he did to you is more than I can handle."

This man... this man really cares about me. He surprises me more and more with each passing day. "I get it. I'm sorry I hadn't thought about that. I guess I'm just on autopilot at home. I try to push it all away and forget he was ever there." Trying to lighten the mood I say, "I must admit it's nice to hear that I'm the only woman that's been in your bed, so I totally get it." I'm so used to turning my emotions off I didn't even think about what it would feel like for Mick. Knowing I am the only woman that's been in his bed is all I needed to hear. His place it is! "Now, let's finish putting these shelves together so we can go back to my place and I can get my clothes for work tomorrow."

We get dressed, build shelves, and then head to my place for a while. I hate that I'm leaving Blazer so much lately, so we stay for a bit and watch some of my shows off the DVR and I make us dinner. He cleans up and I head to my bedroom to gather my things for the morning.

"Baby, you sure you aren't gonna make it to California next weekend? How can you let Emmers get married without you?"

He catches me off guard and makes me jump when he speaks. I bring my hand up to my chest and say, "Mick, you know I have an event. I've been working on this for a year now and there isn't anybody that I can just hand it over to. It's a two-day, offsite event. This is a rare opportunity for me and one I've worked really hard on. I want to be there more than you know. I hate that it's all a surprise and I can't explain to Em why I'm not there. Mick, we're hosting a former president. This isn't just a company party or a wedding I can hand off. This is big."

"I know. I do. Emily will understand what a big deal this is for you. But I still don't want to go without you." In just a few strides, he's standing in front of me and holding me in his arms. "I know it makes me sound like a sap, but I don't want to be away from you. I don't want you home without me, and I don't want to travel without you. It feels like we have so much lost time to make up for. I know it's fast, but you've already got me whipped and I couldn't be happier."

"I do not have you whipped, Mickey Jacobs. I'm just irresistible, and you can't get enough of me."

Suddenly, he looks serious and he lowers his voice. "I'll *never* get enough of you. You know that, right?"

"It sure is nice to be on the same page. I really like this chapter, Mick." This is the only reply that I can think of, and it seems to be enough, because he places a soft kiss on my lips.

I see his eyes move to my bed and I can feel his body tense. I know he's thinking about Kevin and I don't want him to feel uncomfortable. "You can wait in the living room. I'm almost done in here." He kisses me on the forehead. Watching him leave the room, I can feel myself getting angry. I hate that Kevin is still somehow affecting my life.

Mick's life.

Our life.

I finish gathering my things and as I'm walking down the hall with Kevin on my mind; I stop short. It's just now that I remember I saw Mick before that morning, just a few short weeks ago. He was there, just like he always is.

I find him on the couch with Blazer in his lap and the remote in his hand.

"Mick."

"What's up, babe?"

"I can't believe I forgot to say thank you."

"Thank you for what?"

"I saw you at the courthouse. Even though I wasn't speaking to you, I saw you there, and it meant the world to me. You didn't need to be there for Kevin's sentencing, but you were. I was so scared Mick. I never wanted to see him again and the thought that I would have to testify had really been taking its toll. When plead guilty after all the other women came forward, I was so relieved. I still couldn't eat for days leading up to his sentencing. I knew I would have to be in the same room with him, and the thought made me ill. But when my mom and I were walking to the courtroom and I saw you waiting in the hallway, I knew it would be okay. You didn't have a reason to be there, but you were. Just like all the times before, you were there to save me. You may not have known it, but that's what you did. You saved me from my fears and reminded me that I wasn't alone. Seeing you there also reminded me what you had risked for me, and I knew I had to be strong. I had to do what I could to put Kevin away and that when it was my turn to speak, I had to be steadfast. You putting your job on the line needed to be worth it."

"Alex..."

"No, don't say anything. I just wanted you to know that I knew you were there and it helped. I'm sorry I was so stubborn that I didn't call or text you that day to say thank you. It's the least I could have done." I pick Blazer up from his lap and set myself down in his spot and straddle him. I rub my hands through his short blond hair and his hands have made their way to my butt. "Thank you."

Mick may not have known it, but he really got me through that day, even if we weren't talking. Well, Mick and the other three women that came forward and told their stories as well. It turns out I wasn't the only person who Kevin had used his power to abuse. He had done similar things with women in three other states. He had taken things to a new level with me, though, if what was in his trunk was any indication. After the other women came forward, Kevin plead guilty to avoid trial. That meant that I only had to be in the courtroom for the sentencing. I was so relieved not to have to tell my story up on the stand. Having the support of the other women's testimonies, as well as knowing Mick and the rest of my support system was there, made me strong. I found a strength I never knew I had and I am so grateful to have Kevin and all that he represents behind me. I'm also glad that I was brave enough to stand up in the courtroom that day before he was sentenced and tell Kevin that he may think that he broke me, but he didn't. I let him know he didn't win and that I hoped he would rot in prison for a very long time so that other women didn't have to experience what myself and the other three women had to.

"Of course, Sweet Thing. I couldn't have been more proud of you. You were so strong. You did good, baby." He places a sweet kiss on my lips and then says, "You ready?"

"Yep, I'm ready, Mick."

Chapter 21

Mick

I'm standing at the top of Patriot Hill with my arm around my mom, watching all of my sister's dreams come true. When I heard Jonathan yell that Emily had said yes to marry him, I wasn't surprised at all. The three of them were meant to be together, and I couldn't be happier for them.

What did surprise me was the wave of emotions that hit me square in the chest. Seeing the three of them with their arms around each other with their heads together, and tears streaming down Emily and Jonathan's faces, hit me hard. Hearing Ireland ask Jonathan if he would be her daddy shattered my heart into a million pieces, but seeing how proud he looked to tell her yes put it right back together. I want that. I want a love that strong.

I do have a love that strong. We may not have said it, but we both know it. I have never felt more certain about anything in my life. I just wish she were here. I wish she could see this. I want her to know that I want this too. I want us to be a family. I know it's fast, but we both know we've been in love with each our whole lives. That makes it different, right? There's no law that says we have to date for a specific length of time to move on to the next step. I've never let what people think dictate how I live my personal life. Why should I start now?

I tried to FaceTime her when we heard Emily and Jonathan had made it to the top of the hill, but she didn't pick up. I tried to call, but I just went right to voicemail. Her phone must be off. I'm sure there's specific protocol when hosting a former president for a charitable event that you've been planning for a year. I still think seeing the look on my sister's face when she found out she wasn't only engaged, but she was getting married tonight would be better than hanging out with a president.

It's been a crazy 24 hours. Getting everybody that Emily knows and loves, including her daughter, out-of-town yesterday without her noticing, was no simple thing.

I must admit that Jonathan Kelly is the shit. Not only did he get Emily's family and friends from home here, but he also got her old friends from California here as well as Ireland's old babysitter, Charlotte. It's also pretty cool to have met the Fanuas. It's clear that they care about him just as much as he cares about them. They are the only family that he has left and it's really cool that they made it here. Jonathan's best friend, Liam, was a blast to hang out with last night. He's a riot and reminds me a lot of myself right up until about seven months ago.

We're all taking turns hugging the newly engaged family when it's finally my turn to hug Emily.

"Congratulations, sis! I couldn't be happier for you. You guys are gonna be quite the little family." I step back from our hug and pick Ireland up with one arm and put my other around her mommy. "You are gonna be the prettiest little flower girl ever. Promise to save a dance for me tonight?"

"Pwomise, Uncle Mick."

"You too, Emmers. I'm gonna be rollin' solo at your big shindig tonight, so be sure to save me a dance."

"You aren't gonna try to pick up any California girls while you're here?"

"Very funny, Em. You know those days are over. I've got my girl. No need to look anywhere else. Speaking of my girl, Alex is really sorry that she couldn't make it here today, but you know she's had this date with the President planned for some time now. Shere, ally wishes she could have been here, though, and she made me promise to video the whole thing."

"It's okay, Mick. I wish she was here, but I totally get it! A former president is a pretty hot date. I don't blame her at all. I think it's safe to say that her date has been in the works a lot longer than my wedding." Her eyes practically bulge out of her head while she jumps up and down and screams, "Ah! I'm getting married! Can you believe it? I'm so glad you're here!" She throws her arms around my neck and much quieter she says, "Thank you for coming all this way, Mickey."

"I wouldn't have missed this day for the world, Emmers," I say, placing a kiss on her cheek.

Jonathan calls us all to attention when he lets out an ear-piercing whistle.

"I just want to thank y'all for coming all this way. I know getting up to the top of this hill wasn't easy and we all still have to get off it. There's a lot to do before the ceremony so I'm gonna ask that y'all start back down to the cars so we can get this party started!" Our group all let out whoops and hollers. "Emily and I came up the long way, but she has a spa day ahead of her, so I'm gonna have her go down with all of you, but I'm gonna ask that Devon and Liam go back with me. Robert, Mick, if you'll make sure that all of these lovely ladies get down the hill safely, I would sure appreciate it. I'll see you at the cottage as soon as you have the ladies settled. Thanks again for everything everybody!"

We all gather and I see a still-stunned Emily whispering to Jonathan as he kisses her goodbye and then races down the steep side of the hill. She doesn't move. She just stands there staring after him.

"Come on, girly, you only have so many hours to turn into Bridezilla. We better get a move on." I grab her by the shoulders and turn her toward the trail that leads to the four wheelers that we all took to get here.

"Where are we going?"

"Your fiancé left me a list as long as my arm, with all the instructions of where to take you and errands for me to run. Don't you worry your pretty little head about a thing today. I know where we're going."

* * *

"Dude, I gotta give it to you. You've got good taste, my man," I say while checking myself out in the mirror. "I mean, I know I make everything look good, but you chose well, my friend." I do a little spin in my taupe suit pants and vest, white button-down shirt with the sleeves rolled, and tan flip flops. It's a beach wedding and there are no tuxedos required, which is just fine with me. I shoot the groom the always cocky and *always* annoying double gun fingers. Jonathan just rolls his eyes. I know how annoying I can be. But I can't help it. I can tell Jonathan's getting nervous and the mood needs to stay light until we get him down on that beach to marry my baby sister. Besides, it's what's expected when you're in the presence of Mickey Jacobs.

"Yeah, man, I almost feel bad. Your groomsmen are looking good. I sure hope we don't steal your thunder, brother," Liam says, backing me up.

"See Devon, I told you getting these two together would be bad news," Jonathan says over his shoulder while putting the finishing touches on his suit. He's wearing the same thing we are, only he has a jacket as well.

"That's what I'm here for. Balance. I promise not to steal your thunder, Irish," Devon replies while lining up shot glasses and opening up a bottle of tequila.

"But D, you're the prettiest one here," I exclaim while batting my eyes and placing a peck on his cheek. He just shoos me away and wipes my kiss off of his baby smooth face.

He really is a good-looking dude. I can't even imagine the ass he would have gotten in life if he hadn't been in a relationship since he was in high school. I would say it's a waste, but my view of life and love has changed since Alex became *mine*. I get not wanting anybody else when you have *the one*. It doesn't hurt that Gabby is fine as hell, too. The two of them look like they've walked right off the pages of a fashion magazine, but the truth is... Devon and Gabby are prettier.

"Watcha got there, D?"

"Well, Mick... I thought we'd have a little shot of tequila to kick things off. Gentlemen, here you go," Devon says as he hands each of us our shot glass full of tequila. I'm not a big shot drinker, but one shot won't hurt and it's for a good cause.

We all lift our glasses and Devon raises his voice and exclaims! "To Jonathan and Emily and to getting your girl back!"

"TO JONATHAN AND EMILY!" We all yell and then slam down our shots.

Just as we slam our glasses down on the counter, there's a knock on the suite door.

"I got it." I say, opening the door to a smiling Robert. Seeing him wearing the same thing we are and beaming with pride is a reminder that my father isn't here for his daughter. I know it's what Emily wants, but it still sucks. "Come on in, Mr. F. Our boys are ready!"

He enters the suite, looks us all over and says, "You boys clean up nice."

"You're not looking too bad either. Thanks again for being here."

"Jonathan, I wouldn't miss this for the world. I'm honored to watch you get married to that beautiful girl. Now what's wrong with you? You look like you're gonna be sick." Robert asks him with concern.

Jonathan paces the room. He walks into the bedroom, then back out to the living room area where we all just follow him back and forth. In and out of the bedroom. He's suddenly a mess.

"Son, what is it?"

He stops his pacing and then looks at each of us and then brings his attention to me. "Is it too much? Should I have done all of this without her? What if she felt pressured to say that she wanted to get married tonight because everybody was here? What if she hates her dress? What if she hates it all? What the hell was I thinking?" He's practically hyperventilating and I can see his level of panic elevating with each word that comes out of his mouth.

I give him a little shove to his shoulder. "Dude, she's gonna love it all. She loves your Irish ass and has dreamed of marrying you for years. Cami and Alex know her better than anybody, and they helped you with all the girlie shit. Alex may not be here, but she helped you plan the whole thing and she's damn good at her job. You have nothing to worry about. My little sister loves you and she would have married you up on that dirty hill today. She doesn't care what she's wearing tonight as long as you're waiting for her down there on that beach."

"You sure?"

"I'm sure."

"Thanks, Mick. I hope you know that this isn't a case of cold feet. I would have married your sister a long time ago if I had thought she was ready. I promise you, I will do everything in my power to make Emily and Ireland happy."

"I know you will. You don't want to know what will happen to you if you don't." He gives me a nod, letting me know he hears me.

Robert claps his hand on Jonathan's shoulder and looks him dead in the face. "My dear boy, I just saw your girl and there is nothing about her that is unhappy or scared. You have made both of those little ladies happier than you'll ever know, and she is more than ready to marry you tonight." With a soft reassuring pat to the face, he says, "Today's your day, son. It's all gonna be just fine."

Not trying to break up their emotional moment, but

knowing we need to get this show on the road, I interrupt. "Now, go splash some cold water on that pretty boy face of yours and let's go get you married to my baby sister."

Minutes later, we're all walking down the hall together on our way to the beach. This may be a community center, but it's actually really nice, and once the lights are shining on this place tonight, it's gonna look great. Alex did a banging job helping him plan it all. It's perfect.

The five of us men saunter our way down to the beach like we own the place. There are just a few rows of white chairs and a flower covered archway waiting on the beach.

Because there wasn't time for a rehearsal, Jonathan meets with the minister now, just minutes before the ceremony is about to begin. As Jonathan finishes up with the minister, a double check is done to make sure that Liam has the rings, and then I'm given the cue to go get my mom and escort her to her seat when the music begins playing.

My mom looks beautiful and she's beaming when I extend my arm to her. When we reach her chair, she gives me a hug and then grabs my face and says, "I'm so glad you and Alex have each other, sweet boy. I'm not rushing you, but I hope that one day you'll be having your own special day. She's a special girl, that one."

"She is Mom. I hate that she's not here for this. It's just not the same without her."

"I know, sweet boy, I know." She smiles up at me and pats my cheek like she always does and takes her seat.

I take my place up at the front with the rest of the groomsmen and Jonathan. Then I get my phone out and get ready to video the whole thing for Alex. I know it's not wedding protocol, but my girl gets what she wants. I double-checked with Jonathan, just in case, and he said it was cool.

The music changes and I get my phone ready just in time to see the prettiest little flower girl come walking in our direction. Ireland couldn't look any sweeter in her little white dress, with a pale blue sash around her waist and flowers in her hair. She looks like a real life little princess. She does a perfect job of dropping her rose petals in the sand, then she stops and stands in front of Jonathan and he bends down to give her a hug. It's a good thing I'm distracted and getting this on video for Alex because I would be an emotional mess right now.

Next comes Gabby in a pale blue dress with a dark blue sash and she looks beautiful as always. I'm watching the procession in my phone to make sure I'm getting it all when my screen lights up with the most beautiful woman I have ever seen.

"Sweet Thing," I whisper and she must be able to read my lips, because she gives me a wink and a smile and then blows me a kiss.

She takes her place next to Gabby, looking beautiful as always, and her eyes never leave mine. When I see Cami standing next to her, I realize that I'm still taking a video, but it's just been trained on Alex and I've missed Cami and her walk down the sand. Alex motions with her hand that I can put the phone down now that she's here. She's here! My Sweet Thing is here! All is right in the world. I feel my body relax and my face is beaming with the happiest smile anybody has ever seen.

The music changes yet again and this time I know it's because my sister is about to make her big entrance. This is the only thing that makes me turn my gaze away from my girl. When I turn my head to look up the aisle, Emily isn't moving. She's just standing there and not walking towards us.

Liam turns to me and says, "Now that the surprise of your girl is no longer a surprise, you need to go walk your little sister down the aisle."

Confused that Liam knew Alex was going to be here, but not having time to question him, I take off down the aisle to my sister. My sister, who should have her dad, walking her down the aisle. I'm happy to fill in for him, but it really is a shame. Emily has tried as of late, and I am so proud of her. Not only has she been spending time with me and Sidney, but she even went with me to dinner with Dad the other night. It didn't go as she had hoped. As always, he drank too much, didn't accept responsibility for his actions and behaved just as Emily expected he would.

I think that was about it for me, too. Having Alex in my life has made me see my dad through fresh eyes, and I don't like what I see. Yes, he's still my dad, and I'll always love him, but that's not enough anymore. He doesn't deserve a relationship with Emily and Ireland, or with me, for that matter. I can't believe how stupid I was all of these years. It was so much easier to believe that my dad was right and that men weren't meant to be with one woman their entire life. My dad clearly didn't love my mom because I can't imagine wanting anybody else but Alex. There was no need to argue with him over the matter. I don't think my dad is going to be a huge part of my life in the future, but I will stay in touch enough to keep Sidney in my life. Watching her and Ireland play together is pretty awesome, and I have a feeling they're going to be really close.

"Hey sis, I hear I get the honor of walking you down the aisle."

"You do, if you don't mind? We couldn't have you back here with me because then Alex wouldn't have been a surprise. Good surprise?"

"The best. Now let's get you down to your man. I don't think he can wait much longer."

I offer my sister my arm and we make the journey down the sandy aisle until we're standing in front of Jonathan. He can't take his eyes off of her and he's still holding Ireland's hand. There are tears in his eyes and it's clear to everybody here that this man loves my sister with all of his heart. I have no doubt in my mind that he will take care of my niece and little sister fiercer than any man ever could.

The minister asks who gives this woman away and I tell him that my mother and I do. I look over to see Jonathan isn't alone. Emily and my mom both have tears streaming down their faces, but they're both smiling through their tears.

"I love you, Emmers," I say as I give my sister a kiss on the cheek and then place her hand in Jonathan's.

Taking my place next to Devon, I finally take in just how beautiful Emily looks today. The dress that Jonathan picked out for her is perfect. It's a simple long, white, flowing dress with tiny spaghetti straps. Watching her hair and dress blow in the wind... she looks beautiful. Like an angel.

As the minister speaks, my eyes move back to Alex. I think she can feel me staring at her because her eyes find mine. While the minister talks about loving one another through rich and poor and the good times and bad, I can't help but think that I already love Alex like that.

Her eyes leave mine when she hears Emily say, "I do."

When she looks back at me, there are tears in her eyes, and she dabs them with the tissue that magically appeared in her hand.

"Jonathan, you may kiss your bride," the minister says, and the minute their lips meet, our small gathering goes crazy and starts cheering. "Ladies and gentlemen, I am proud to introduce Mr. and Mrs. Jonathan Kelly!"

There are more yells and whistles and Emily and Jonathan lift their hands in the air. Emily takes her flowers back from Cami and then she, Ireland and Jonathan walk hand in hand through the sand and up the steps to sign their marriage certificate. I was so enthralled watching Alex's hair blow in the breeze that I didn't even notice the ring exchange. I missed most of the ceremony, come to think of it. I can't help it; Alex takes my breath away. I don't think I will ever get used to her beauty. Her chestnut eyes and her long dark hair against her tan skin is pure perfection. She is a walking dream, and I know I am the luckiest man alive.

Devon and I switch spots so that we can each walk back down the aisle with our ladies, and I can't get to Alex fast enough. We both take the last step toward each other up at the altar and I can't help but take her in my arms, pull her tight to my body, and kiss her senseless. She doesn't protest and melts into me and my kiss. I can feel Devon and Gabby walk past us and soon it's just Alex, the minister, and me standing front and center. If only I was marrying this woman! We're standing here, we've got the minister, we've got the altar. Wouldn't that be the shit? But today is Em's day and I'm not sure Alex is as ready for all of that as I am.

I finally release her lips and say, "You're here."

"I'm here."

The sound of the minister clearing his throat brings me back to reality, and to the fact that we should have already walked back down the aisle by now. Instead of simply offering her my arm, I put my arm around her waist, and she follows my lead and does the same, and then we finally walk down the aisle in each other's arms. I can't help but notice the smile on everybody's face when we finally join them up at the little outdoor courtyard where the reception will be held.

We all watch Emily and Jonathan sign their marriage certificate and I can't believe I am actually jealous of a piece of paper. There are a multitude of hugs and congratulations passed around. Soon Jonathan is directing everybody to the tables that are covered in white with strings of lights hanging above. The sun is just dropping below the horizon, and it couldn't get much better than this.

While everybody is taking their seats, I grab Alex by the hand and pull her into a little alcove just off the courtyard. I grab her beautiful face and ask, "What in the world are you doing here?"

Her smile beams across her perfect face, and I can feel my knees weaken. "Well, when Jonathan originally picked the date, I didn't think there would be any way that I could get here. When I figured it out, I knew I could get here for the ceremony, but not the proposal. I figured it would be fun to surprise you, so everybody played along. You aren't mad, are you?"

"Mad? How could I be mad? You're here! That's all that matters!" I kiss her again and she just giggles. "I'm glad you're wearing these flip flops and not heels because you are gonna be dancing your pretty little ass off tonight. I think of our first night on a dance floor often, and I can't wait to recreate some of those memories."

Her tongue darts out and traces my upper lip and then she takes my bottom lip between her teeth and gives it a little tug. "Some moves that I'd like to recreate with you may not be appropriate for *this* dance floor." Good God! I want to take this woman right here and now!

"Is that right? Well, I'll do my best to see what I can remember, but I might have to depend on you to help remind me just exactly what those moves were."

"Oh, that won't be a problem. I've got that night etched into my brain for eternity. I'd be more than happy to help. Now, we should probably go celebrate. Jonathan's worked hard for this night and we don't want to miss any of it." She places a peck on my cheek and then pulls me back to our table.

Jonathan really has thought of everything. I know Alex has been helping him, but he's done a lot for a dude. There's a DJ spinning tunes to go along with the dance floor we'll soon be tearing up. There's a cake, a buffet dinner, flowers, little white lights everywhere and bottles of champagne on every table. The place looks great, but turning to my left to see Alex sitting next to me makes the place truly light up.

Still holding my hand, she gives me a squeeze and whispers, "Hi." It's now that I realize that I'm just sitting here like a grinning fool staring at her. I don't want to speak and ruin the moment, so I bring our hands up so that I can kiss the back of hers.

"I'm so glad you're here, Sweet Thing." I finally say.

"Me too."

We're interrupted by the DJ as he asks us all to stand as

he introduces the bride and groom. My sister and her new husband join the rest of us and look happier than I have ever seen either of them. I know I'm a guy and guys don't say shit like this... but they are both glowing. I couldn't be happier for them, but right now I feel something that I'm not accustomed to. Jealousy. I so badly want what they have. I know I have the right girl. I know I love her madly. Now, I need to grow up and figure out what to do from here.

The next couple of hours are filled with speeches, cake cutting, food, toasts, and dances. The night is filled with the best dances of my life. My sister asked me to dance with her during the father/daughter dance and since this was all a bit unexpected and we don't exactly have a song, we just rolled with my style. I asked the DJ to play a little *California Love* for us. I know it's not a typical sappy song to dance to, but the song title fits why we're here, and anyone who knows me knows that this is one of my all-time favorites. Emily loves my selection and we dance around the floor like nobody's business. She's Tupac and I'm Dr. Dre. As soon as Emily and I finish showing the rest of the gang how we roll, Ireland throws herself at me and hugs my legs. I hold her on my hip with her arms around my neck and we slow dance. She giggles and talks a mile a minute about the day. At the end, she gives me one of her sweet little kisses on the cheek and jumps out of my arms and over to Liam. She really knows how to make all of us men do whatever she wants. I am dreading her teenage years.

As I watch Ireland run away, I feel a tap on my shoulder and hear my Sweet Thing ask if she can have the next dance.

"Of course you can, baby. You know you don't have to ask. I'm all yours."

Her face lights up and she puts her arms around my neck as the next slow song begins. "I like the sound of that."

"Me too, baby. Me too."

Eventually, my mom heads back to the hotel with Ireland, and Robert, Fiona and Charlotte, Ireland's old babysitter, leave with them. We may be a small group, but the rest of us keep the party going. I can't keep my hands off of Alex and even if we're doing a group dance to the classic, *We Are Family* or *YMCA,* I can still find a way to keep my hands on her. When it comes to Alex and that long, lean, sexy ass body of hers, there is no way to keep my hands to myself. I'll always find a way to be connected to her somehow, some way.

The DJ is slowing the music down, and I know the night is about to end. In the middle of a slow dance, I take Alex by the hand and guide us to the beach, where we can be alone. We can still hear the music down here and without words, I take her back in my arms and start our slow dance back up again. No words are spoken as we enjoy the sound of the waves and the distant tunes that we dance to.

I know she knows without me saying it, but I feel like it's time that I make 100% sure that Alex and I are finally on the same page.

Pulling back from our embrace so that I can see her gorgeous face but still keeping her in my arms, I tell her exactly how I feel.

"Alex, your kiss saved me." I can see the shock that crosses her face at the sudden conversation and the serious- ness in my voice. Her eyes light up with love as I continue to speak. "I was faking my way through life, but with you, I can just be me. And the thing is... I like that me. The me that I am with you. Because I'm better with you."

She leans forward and places a soft kiss on my cheek, and then whispers in my ear. "I like that Mick too, but I like all versions of you. Always have."

I take her beautiful face in my hands and search deep into the eyes that make me whole. The eyes that don't judge me and give me clarity when I feel lost. Eyes that see right through me and still want to be with me.

Holding her face in my hands and making sure I have her attention, I make it very clear how I want our story to end. "Alex, I want that." I motion my head in the direction of the reception happening up in the courtyard. "And I want it with you."

She doesn't say a word, but I feel her nod her head every so lightly. She doesn't seem able to form words at the moment, but I have no problem telling her *exactly* how I feel. So, I carry on.

"Every word to every love song says how I feel about you, Alex. Every time I see you walk into the room; my mind is blown. The fact somebody as beautiful as you inside and out actually exist, is simply mind blowing. You have stopped my heart every time my eyes have landed on your breathtaking face, since the first time I saw you hanging out in my little sister's room. You were Em's friend and therefore off limits, so I never even imagined you would be 'the one'. If I really think about it, though, it's always been you. I told myself that I didn't do relationships and didn't want to be tied down, but the truth is, I met the love of my life as a kid and nobody has ever really compared to you. You're my best friend, Alex. The thing is... well, the thing is I am in love with my best friend. I never knew I wanted more but you are my *More* baby, and I want you by my side for the rest of my life. So, what do you say, Sweet Thing? Will you be my more?"

I try to wipe away the tears that are flowing down her face, but there are too many falling and they are falling fast.

"You love me?" She barely whispers on a choked sob.

"With all that I am and I know you love me, too. I mean, what's not to love?"

She needs the giggle and leans forward and puts her head on my shoulder.

"Does this mean you're my *More* too?"

I kiss the top of her head and lean back so that I can lift her gaze back to mine when I answer. "Always have been, baby. It just took me a while to figure that out. I'm yours in this world and the next, if you'll have me? I don't have a ring, and I'm not officially asking you to marry me, because I want to do it right, but I will marry you one day, Alexandra Stotts. One day... very soon. I'm going to marry you and make you the happiest woman alive. I want you to be the mother of my children and I want to grow old with you."

"Well, then I can't wait to say yes when you do ask. I love you, Mickey Jacobs, and I can't wait to make *you* the happiest man alive."

"You already do, baby... you already do. Now kiss me."

* * *

Alex

It's been an amazing day. I'm so glad that I was able to be here for Emily. I hate I couldn't get here soon enough for the proposal, but I got to stand up with her tonight, and that's the important part. She and Jonathan couldn't look happier or more in love, and it warms my heart. They've both been through a lot and I'm so glad they've found each other.

I'm also glad that I'm here with Mick on this special night. To see his face when I started my walk down the aisle was priceless and something that I'll never forget. He was taking video for me, just like I had asked. As always, taking care of me even when I'm not there. Not only was he surprised that I was here, but I had never seen him look so happy before. If he only knew what his heartfelt smile did to me.

Our eyes were glued to each other for most of the ceremony and then we barely made it back down the aisle after. We danced the night away at the reception and witnessed nothing but love and joy all night long. The love around us came in so many different forms. The love of friends, family we were born into, and the family we create as we navigate our way through life. I love my family, but this family... the family that I have chosen and that have chosen me, means just as much to me.

Hearing Mick tell me he loved me and that he wanted to create a family with me made this the absolute best day of my life. Today is better than all my days that have come before it. I know I will never forget the words that he spoke to me tonight on that beach. Mickey Jacobs loves me. He's going to marry me, and apparently, I'm going to give him babies. Nothing has ever sounded so good to me. I can't wait to make all of his predictions come true. If only *we* were having a surprise wedding today, too. He said soon, though. Let's hope that prediction is right because I don't want to spend another day away from him.

It's late and we're all in the limo that's taking us back to our hotel. Jonathan had rented a jeep and hired a driver to take him and Emily back to their cottage. He really did think of everything, and I know the jeep means more to Emily than a limo ever could. We'll meet up with them again tomorrow for lunch at Duke's. Duke's is apparently the home of the best cheeseburger on earth and one bars that Emily and Jonathan spent time at the week they met. After that, it's drink's at Ole's—where it all began for them. Jonathan has reserved the window seat Emily loved so much and the bar knows to expect us. I can't wait to toast our friends and send them on their way to the Irish countryside for their honeymoon. Emily is going to freak out when she finds out where she's going.

As we ride back to the hotel and recap our day, that was full of happy tears and lots of laughter, I notice Mickey is engrossed in his phone and not really engaging in the conversation. He's usually the life of the party, but he seems preoccupied. Liam and Devon are full of wise ass remarks that he would normally one up with one of his own and with Kate, Sam, Steph, Gabby and Cami here to give him all the female attention he usually loves. I'm starting to worry.

Trying not to stress myself out, I just ignore him and continue to join in the conversation that fills the limo. A few minutes later, he whispers in my ear. "Sweet Thing, come here."

I turn to look at him and before I can say a word, his soft, warm lips are on mine and his arm is out in front of us as he takes a selfie of our kiss.

"Here," he says as he puts his arm around me and brings his phone up for another picture. This time we smile for the camera. Then he moves his lips to his spot and takes a picture of him kissing the crook of my neck. This makes me giggle and he brings his kiss to my cheek. "Thanks, baby."

And just like that, he's back to obsessing over his phone. The limo has gone quiet and I turn to see that there are seven grinning faces staring back at me.

"What?"

Cami is the only person to reply. "What have you done to him?"

"What do you mean?" But I know what she means.

"Mickey freaking Jacobs has got it bad. I mean, I know we've talked about it, but witnessing everything tonight and whatever that was, is like looking at a mythical creature. It's like we have a living, breathing unicorn among us. It's a sight to behold."

"Oh stop, Cami. You're just being silly."

"Um, I don't think she is," Gabby says, holding up her phone. "At least not if Facebook has anything to say about it."

"What are you talking about, Gabs?"

"Well, I just got a new friend request. Here, check it out yourself," she replies, handing me her phone.

I gasp when I see what's on her screen. She's on Mick's new page and his first picture posted and his new profile picture is the picture of me giggling into the camera while he kisses *his spot*. Above the picture he has posted 'She. Is. Everything.'

I hear oohs and ah's around the limo and know that everybody else has their phones out, too. I can feel him watching me. I turn to him and he just smiles and says, "Hi."

I don't know why, but the first thing I say is. "But you don't have a Facebook page."

"I didn't, but I wanted the world to know that I'm yours, and I figured this was the easiest way to do that. Besides, Ireland is more advanced than I am at all this technology stuff, so I guess it's time to join the world of social media."

"You are crazy, you know that?"

"No, I'm 'in a relationship'. I mean, if Facebook says it's true, then it must be." He takes his finger and swipes the picture up and there it is for the world to see. Mickey Jacobs is in a relationship with Alexandra Stotts.

"You are such a dork."

"I'm your dork. Now give Gabby back her phone and get over here."

I do as I'm told and hand Gabs her phone. She gives me a little smile and a wink, and I can't help but grin from ear to ear. I scoot back in my seat, but not for long. Mickey grabs me and puts me on his lap and finds his spot on my neck again. His strong arms wrap around my waist and mine go around his neck while my head rests on the top of his. I can feel his voice vibrate against my skin when he hums. "Mine."

The vibration reaches my heart and I feel all the places that were once dark and cold, secluded and closed off, filling up with light and love. Opening up to new possibilities and a new future. A future I never dreamed of because there was no way it could ever be possible. But it is possible. Because here I am in his arms.

This.

Right Here.

Right Now.

Are what dreams are made of?

Epilogue

10 years later...

It's Saturday night and here I sit at the bar alone. It's a nice bar, in a really nice hotel. A classy joint, really, but I'm still alone at a bar on a Saturday. It's not my usual MO, but I was told that if I showed up at 9:00 pm, it would be worth my while. Another thing that's not my MO is the feeling of anxiousness that I can't seem to hide with my bouncing leg.

It's 9:10 and I'm starting to wonder if I'm being stood up. I take a look over each shoulder to make sure that I'm in the right spot and just as I turn back around to my rum and Coke, I see her. She is easily the most beautiful woman in the place. Her long hair floats past her shoulders and she carries herself with a calm confidence, just like I like in my woman. Her simple black dress hugs her perfect curves just right. When she rounds the bar and I get a full view of her she takes my breath away. Those legs... in that dress... with those heels... it sure would be nice to have those legs wrapped around me later tonight... with only those heels on.

She is a thing of beauty, and I can feel my heart stutter as she saunters in my direction. When she walks past me, I can smell her perfume and it's like an instant high. There are several empty stools on each side of me, so it takes me by surprise when she takes the one to my left and perches her fine ass on it.

"Grey Goose and cranberry, please," she says to the bartender.

It takes everything I have in me not to turn my body in her direction and work my charm on her, but this woman sitting next to me... this woman looks like she wants to be in charge of things tonight.

The bartender brings her the vodka cranberry she ordered and when she reaches for her purse to pay, I step in. "Put it on my tab." The bartender nods his understanding and walks away.

"You didn't need to do that, but thank you."

"No problem."

She's quiet after our brief interlude and seems preoccupied. I try my best to leave her alone, but with her sitting this close to me, I'm finding it impossible. She's just so damn beautiful, smells amazing and I sure would love a taste of her. Let's see if I've still got it?

"You having a nice night?"

"We'll see."

"Oh, are you meeting somebody here?"

I anxiously await her reply while she takes a leisurely sip of her drink. I can't help but watch as her tongue slowly cleans up the bit of her drink that was left on her lips. Good god! This woman is lethal! And when she finally answers, her voice is sultry music to my ears.

"I'm supposed to be meeting a date here tonight."

"Oh yeah?"

"Yep."

"Me too."

"You don't say?"

"Scouts honor. What's your date look like? I can help you find him."

"Well, he's ridiculously handsome. Some might even say a bit of a pretty boy."

"Ugh. He sounds awful already. Please continue, though."

"Well, he's got short blond hair and big, beautiful, dark brown eyes. He's a few inches over six feet tall and a pretty fine specimen as far as his build goes. He's pretty hot."

"Really? What more do you know about him?"

"Oh, I don't think you really want to hear more about my date, do you? What about your date? What's she like?"

"Nice way to change the subject, but that's okay. I'll play along." I say with a wink. "Let's see, my date is one of the most beautiful women to walk the planet. Tall, legs for days, dark hair, dark eyes, and flawless skin. She's the whole package."

"Wow, she sounds pretty great. You sure she's meeting *you* here?"

"Ha! I know, right. It makes little sense to me either. I'm a pretty lucky guy. I'm hoping my night's gonna be pretty lucky, too."

"You seem to be pretty sure of yourself."

"Well, there isn't anything I wouldn't do for her, and she knows it. That helps my case just a bit."

"Ah, so you're just a softy deep down. Is that what you're trying to tell me?"

"When it comes to this woman, I am as whipped as they come, and I am not too proud to admit it."

"So, she's got you wrapped her little finger, then?" She says while holding her little finger up to me and giving it a wiggle.

"Yes, ma'am."

"Interesting..." She crosses her legs and turns on her stool so that she's facing me. I turn as well and there's no stopping the smile stretching across my face. She. Is. Exquisite.

Her hand slowly glides up my leg while she looks up at me through her thick lashes. "Just how whipped does she have you?" There is confidence oozing out of her. I like it.

"Oh honey, I'm on my knees, bound, gagged and whipped for her."

I hear a hitch in her breath at my confession and her hand stops on my thigh. She lifts it so that she can take a sip of her drink. I can feel myself getting harder by the second as I watch her tongue come out to wrangle her straw into her luscious mouth.

Releasing the straw that I am more than jealous of, she asks, "So, do you think she'll have you on your knees tonight?"

"If that's what she wants, then that's what she'll get."

"If you'll excuse me, I'll be right back. If you could order me another drink, that would be great." She whispers this in my ear and then drags a finger across my shoulders as she walks away. Watching her walk away is something to behold. That is one fine ass!

I need to rein myself in and cool down before she gets back. I order her drink and keep nursing mine while imagining myself on my knees in one of the hotel rooms above us.

The bartender slides her fresh drink in front of her still empty stool. "She's something else, man. Damn, she is fine."

"Yes, that she is."

I know the minute she's back in the bar. There is a sizzle in the air, and when I look up, she's on her way back with that same sexy walk that she had the first time she walked in. She approaches her stool, but instead of sitting, she stands next to me and whispers in my ear.

"I like your suit, but you're missing something."

"Is that so? And what would that be?"

Without answering, she brings her hand up to the breast pocket of my suit jacket and puts something inside. "That's better." She says once she has arranged it to her liking.

Looking down, I see red lace peeking out of my pocket up at me. I lift my fingers and rub the lace between them. "Is this what I think it is?"

"Hmmm…" She lifts her glass to her mouth and goes to work on that straw again.

"Does this mean what I think it does? You missing something under your dress right now?"

"Wanna find out?"

"Just what do you have in mind?"

"Why don't you get the check and close your tab while I finish my drink?"

"Check please!"

I'm feeling bold tonight. I'm a fairly confident woman, but I wasn't always this way. It took a special man to make me feel this strong and it's stayed with me. Tonight, that confidence is spilling out of me. There is just something about the man in the sexy suit on the stool next to me that has me so full of need that I'm having no problem taking what I want.

He's making it really easy. He seems eager to do just about anything I tell him to. He may not be much of a challenge, but I think I'll enjoy playing with him for a while.

He pays the bill and turns in his seat and I can feel him staring at me while I casually finish my drink, taking my time.

Once I finish, I put the glass down, purposefully lick my lips and then spin around on my stool, grab my clutch and stand up. I don't say anything. I simply start walking toward the elevators. I don't look back to see if he's behind me. I know he is. He's following me like a little puppy.

When I make it to the elevators, I push the up button and wait. When the bell chimes and the doors open, I finally turn around and see him waiting patiently. I grab his tie and turn around, pulling him behind me. I select the nineteenth floor with my free hand and watch the doors close. He doesn't move behind me. He stands still while I keep him in place, still holding him by the tie.

After a long, quiet ride, we finally reach my floor. I gently pull him behind me and down the hall to room 1921. I drop his tie and say, "Stay."

I open my purse, pull out my key card, and open the door. I take his tie in my hand again and pull him into my room. He still hasn't said a word, but he does make sure all the locks on the door are locked before his attention is back on me.

I pull him further into the room and stop us at the foot of the bed.

"Take off your jacket."

His jacket drops to the floor and a sexy smirk lights his eyes.

"Don't get too sassy, pretty boy. The night is still young."

"What exactly did you have planned for me?"

I take the two steps needed to get close enough to untie his tie. "Earlier tonight you mentioned being bound, gagged, and whipped."

He lifts one of his cocky eyebrows just as I pull his tie off of his neck. "Is that so?"

"Only if you behave yourself."

"Oh, I'll behave."

"Good. Now take your off your shoes and socks."

I step away and take my phone out and turn on the portable speaker that I had brought with me. I select my song of choice and turn back to see him waiting for his next command.

When Mary J Blige starts singing, he smiles and gives me a wink. I ignore his smile and get back to business. I reach for his belt and undo it with ease. I pull it out of his belt loops so fast that it makes a loud crack through the air. "We'll save that for later," I say, tossing the belt on to the bed.

"I love the way your mind works, woman."

I step as close to him as I can get but keep my eyes on his as I unbutton his suit pants. I slowly push his pants over his perfectly sculpted ass and drop them to the floor. He's now standing there in just his black boxer briefs and his white button-down shirt. I can't help but look down to see what I felt behind his pants as I pulled his zipper down.

With my hands still on his ass, I lift my eyes back to his as Mary continues singing on a loop in the background. I take his right hand in mine and undo the buttons on his shirt sleeve. Without taking my eyes off of him, I take care of his left sleeve as well. Next, I move to the buttons on the front of his shirt while his eyes penetrate deep inside me. His stare has an effect on me, like I wouldn't imagine I would still have at this age. He makes me feel like a teenager on a date with her high school crush.

Once I have the last button undone, he suddenly pulls me near him and his hand reaches around to the zipper of my dress. But I reach back and stop him. "We'll get to that." I reach my hands up and under his shirt to push it off his shoulders, loving that I'm in total control. Once I feel the shirt fall, I can't help but step back and look at the sexy as hell man before me.

To say that I did not expect to see what I see would be an understatement. I can't help but burst out into a fit of laughter and my confident, sexy moment is out the window.

"What in the world?"

"You don't like it?"

"What did you do to yourself?"

Looking down at his gorgeous chest I see that with a marker he has drawn on a Superman shield only it has an SB instead of a single S. He's also drawn on a little bow tie at his neck and when he brings his hands up to fake adjust his tie, I see he has also drawn on fake little cuffs at his wrists. My mouth falls upon in disbelief. He cannot be serious!

With his smile beaming, it's clear he's proud of himself. "Happy Anniversary, Sweet Thing. I didn't know if you were going to be in the mood for a superhero or your Sexy Beast, so I thought I would give you options. You like the Chippendale look better than the superhero look, don't you? I can tell the bow tie and cuffs are working for ya."

"You are suck a dork, Mickey Jacobs."

Pulling me closer, he replies. "I know and I do kinda feel

bad. You were doing so well at the 'meeting a stranger in a bar' role-playing. I was looking forward to seeing where that was going, but I guess I ruined it. Sorry, baby." He unzips my dress and lets it fall to the floor. Now, I'm just standing in my black heels and red lace bra—since my matching panties are currently in his suit jacket pocket. "Do you forgive me?" He says with lust filled eyes.

"It was going rather well and I was having fun, but this is pretty fun, too." I trace the SB on his chest and can't help but think of what a lucky woman I am. Ten years of marriage and my husband is still up for trying new things and still making sure that he always makes me laugh. When I suggested we take our long-time game of making up stories about the strangers we watch when we're out, and making up one of those little stories for ourselves, I thought he might laugh, but he was all for it. But I should have known better. Mickey Jacobs is never afraid of trying something new. Even after two kids and a decade of marriage, he never lets me down. He really is my superhero and my Sexy Beast all wrapped up into one amazing man.

"Oh baby, the fun is far from over. It's just beginning."

The Hotline

The National Domestic Violence Hotline
1-800-799-SAFE (7233)
TheHotline.org

The Hotline provides lifesaving tools and immediate support to enable victims to find safety and live lives free of abuse. Resources and help can be found by calling 1-800-799-SAFE (7233) or for Deaf callers on video phone 1-855-812-1001 (Monday to Friday, 9 a.m.—5 p.m. PST) or TTY 1-800-787-3224.

If it's not safe for you to call, or if you don't feel comfortable doing so, another option for getting direct help is to use our live chat service on their site, TheHotline.org. You'll receive the same one-on-one, real-time, confidential information from a trained advocate as you would on the phone. You can chat here on our website every day from 7 a.m.—2 a.m. CST.

What To Read Next

Disregarded Heart

A Grumpy / Sunshine, single dad contemporary romance.

The Between the Pines Series

Meet *The Crew* from Eastlyn in this series of standalone contemporary romance novels about found family.

Raised On It

Bottle It Up

Want to read Reece and Rachel's story? Sign-up for my newsletter and get their novella for FREE! Click here for your copy of We Are Tonight!

Blackbird

Standalone second chance contemporary romance.

The Gorgeous Duet

A steamy, suspenseful romance about breaking the rules and following your heart.

Gorgeous: Book One

Gorgeous: Book Two

The You & Me Series

Read this three-book series of sweet and sexy standalone novels filled with love, loss, secrets, and sass.

You & Me: Part One

You & Me: Part Two

More

Something Just Like This

Acknowledgments

I really cannot believe that I am writing the acknowledgements to my second novel. When my writing journey began, I had no idea what would lie ahead. I never would have imagined that I would become an indie author or that readers would actually want to read my words. The fact that I have readers leaves me dumbfounded and humbled. I knew that Emily and Jonathan and the rest of the You & Me crew were special to me, but I didn't know if anybody else would fall as hard as I had. Parents always think their babies are beautiful and well, You & Me was my baby.

Speaking of babies... the one I am the proudest of is my son. He is turning into such a kind and good young man, and I can't help but beam with pride when I look at his handsome face. Love you, buddy.

My son wouldn't be the young man he is if he didn't have my husband for a father. Baby, you are such a genuine soul and I thank you for your years of love and support. You are my best friend and I couldn't do any of this without encouragement and steadfastness. Please don't ever forget that I will *always* love you so much MORE.

To my editor, Laura Allison, thank you for being so much more than my editor. You are my friend and one of the best humans I know. You are strong, smart, kind, loyal, and funny as hell. Girl, you are fierce! #BitchesBeCruel

To Nadia at Kiss & Tell Design Lab, thank you for EVERYTHING. I may be able to write a book, but when it comes to picking the font or color for something, I can't make a decision to save my life. I know I make you crazy and I thank you for not kicking me to the curb just yet! Thank you for your patience, friendship and making everything pretty!

To the endless list of friends and family members who have been nothing but encouraging, I thank you. There are too many of you to list, but know that your support is amazing and the love you have all shown has blown me away. Thank you, thank you, thank you.

To the READERS. I am beyond humble. The fact that I have readers at all is enough to leave me dumbfounded! Just knowing that any of you have taken the time to read my words leaves me truly mystified. I appreciate each and every one of you who took the time to not only read You & Me, but to also review it. Thank you. My heart swells with joy each and every time a reader reaches out to me and shares how much they love Emily and Jonathan. For a brand-new indie author, every review and every kind word means the world to me! Missy M, you are amazing. You have been such a big supporter and have helped to spread the word about You & Me more than any other. You have gone above and beyond and you always bring a smile to my face. Thank you for everything. Readers rock!

To the bloggers that have helped spread the word and have shared their reviews, thank you. I can't imagine where I would be as a self-published author without you all. There is no way that I can list all of you that participated in promoting You & Me in some way, but I sure want to try. I must start with Lisa B. at Southern Vixens Book Obsessions. Lisa, you are the best and I thank you so very much for everything. Thank you to Paige at A Is For Alpha B Is For Books, Shannon and Linda at Once Upon An Alpha, Abby with Not Your Mama's Romance, Sassy Southern Book Blog, Witchey Richey's Bookstastic Reviews, Little Shop of Readers, Twin Spin Book Blog, Fallen for Books, Rochelle's Reviews, 1 Girl Lost In Romance Books, Just One More Page Reviews, Book Boyfriend Blog, Read Review Repeat, Book Bellas, Nerdy Dirty & Flirty, Sassy and Delicious: Books, Authors, Boys, Girlfriends and Our Book Obsessions, Hell-mouth's Book Blog & Reviews, Book Babes Unite, This Mom Loves Alpha, Valley of the Book Doll, Reviews By Red and many, many, more. Thank you, thank you, thank you!

Thank you to our men and women in uniform and all that you do for our country and our communities. I thank you for doing a thankless job that many will never understand.

Love, L

About the Author

Lisa Shelby is a USA Today bestselling contemporary romance author, a self-proclaimed love geek and cake-pop addict. Born and raised in the Pacific Northwest, this is still where Lisa calls home with her husband and their dogs. When she isn't writing her next happily ever after, you can find Lisa with her husband traveling, listening to live music, and impatiently waiting for her next FaceTime call with her son, who is currently deployed with the United States Marine Corps.

www.ingramcontent.com/pod-product-compliance
Lightning Source LLC
Chambersburg PA
CBHW051331250626
47155CB00007B/2554